THE APOSTATE

CHRIS TARDIO

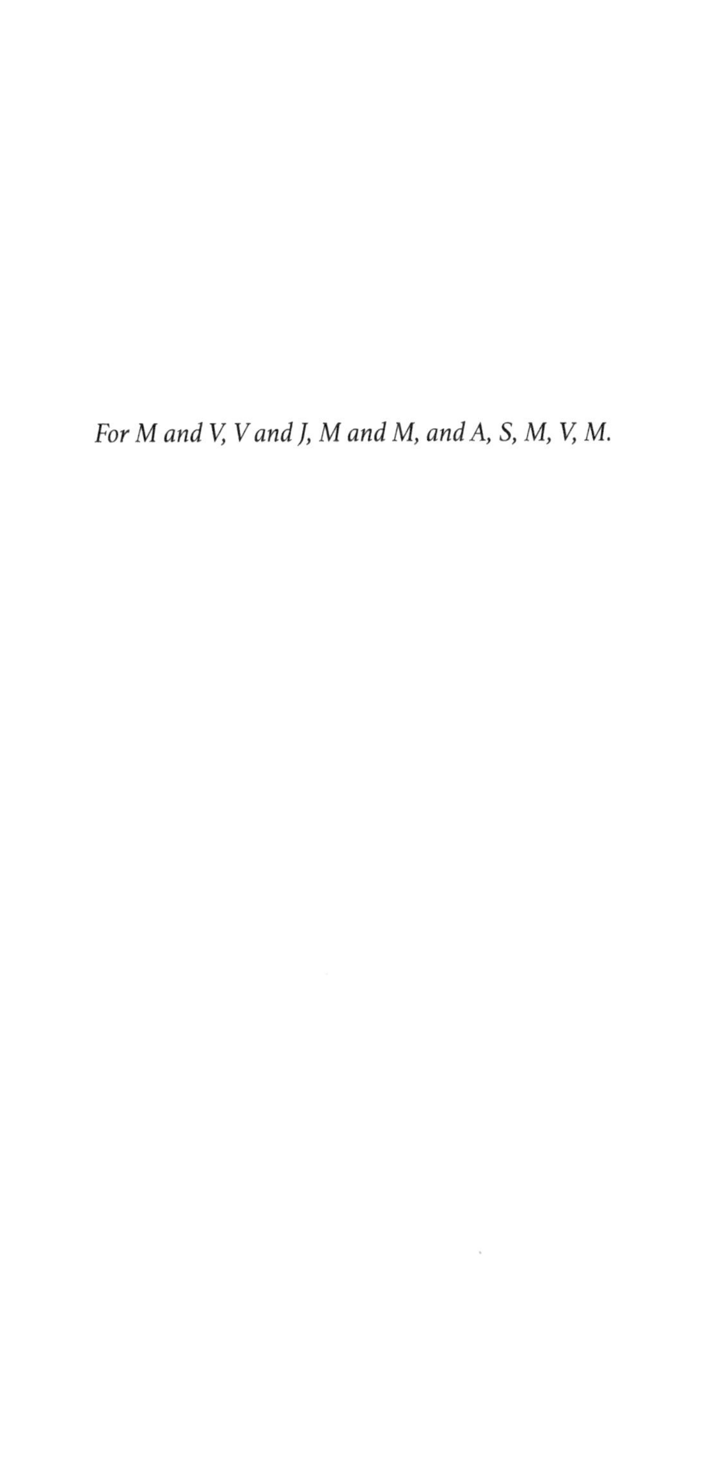

For M and V, V and J, M and M, and A, S, M, V, M.

The spiritual journey is not a career or a success story. It is a series of small humiliations of the false self that become more and more profound.

— CARL JUNG

CONTENTS

BOOK 1

1

I'd believed I straightened it all out, summed it up perfectly: Nadia buried me, Emily resurrected me. But I'm not reborn; I'm in a sort of limbo, haunted by memories that linger like grief, that awaken in a scent, a sound, or an image—memories that seem like things I might have dreamed.

Perhaps, instead of saying Nadia buried me and Emily resurrected me, it's more accurate to say that Nadia prepared me—the Aries, the sacrificial ram—for Emily, such as a priestess prepares a child, bathing it, walking it to the pyre, whispering of glory, knowing all the while its fate. How is it that I was in the fire, yet I'm neither purified nor untouched? I need to know then: who was sacrificed?

My impressions of Nadia and Emily shift like fluids seeking levels. There's the image Nadia put forth, who she believed herself to be, and there's the Nadia I perceived. There's the reality of the events surrounding Emily and my perception of those events. Then there are the facts that have come to light that want to disenchant this chain of events, explain them, and rewrite them as prosaic. Ceremonial magic? Manifestation? The altering of reality by the application of the will? How do facts filter in here? What are facts but antecedents to truth, like the nouns and verbs in a sentence, an arrangement of general things and actions to which we ascribe meaning? Meaning draws lines, says that was this and this was that. Even those who are blindly wrong about this and that are delightfully so in that they have found meaning. No, the facts do not satisfy my experience; therefore, I must include the wide catalog of intangibles. That is why, here in this apartment, I wrote *Apophenia*, the bestseller, to bear witness, to extract significance out of calamity, and to warn others, those whose identities were also laid on unstable foundations, of the dangers in the occult.

I met Nadia when I was twenty-nine, still guided by the belief that success as a writer, making a living doing what I loved, would equal my happiness. What's more, I felt fortunate to have a calling, saved from the pressures of choosing a career. It seemed the work one did, the *chosen* career path, often led most into a life that looked more like death. I also believed a calling was a promulgation of success; happiness must surely be an accompaniment. Well, I'm no longer what can be considered a young man and as it turns out, my life has never been about career or money, even when I believed it was, yet somehow career and money are what's left.

Last week I closed on my first house, a Spanish style, multi-level arrangement of well-lit rooms set on a hillside in Beachwood Canyon. Clusters of eucalyptus and oak trees enclose the modest front of the house. The rear, its views, account for my worldly success; south-facing, wide, high windows look on a pine-mottled ravine that tapers off at the foothills, which blend into the sprawling city of angels below. I should be proud of my accomplishments, but something gnaws at me, something Gabriele once said: "A dwarf on a mountain is still a dwarf."

Los Angeles was never meant to be home; it was a career choice. Friend, I've come so far, so unwittingly far from home, and not only from home, but also from what I was, that there is no comfort in notions of home, in who or what I am anymore. For now, as the last details of the sale are worked out, I'm here in Los Feliz in the one-bedroom apartment adjacent to Barnsdall Park. Spacious and cheap, this characterless box of poorly taped sheetrock and cracked floor tiles is the cocoon I'm shedding.

The sky here is a radiant blue, cloudless on most days. Despite recent downpours, my plants have all wilted. Lusterless leaves on my potted lime tree shiver in the cool breeze that reminds me: *breathe*. These views are enviable. Griffith Observatory. The Hollywood sign. Morning light makes long shadows like tiger stripes across the overlapping hills, hills that stretch west and blend into a scrub of sienna, sap green, then burnt umber at the vanishing point. At sunset, streaks of reds and purples slash the sky, recalling images of fresh wounds, and as the process plays out, the streaks dissipate into orange and pink hues, until at last, just before dark, the wounds heal and that radiant blue returns.

To the east, the olive trees of Barnsdall Park foreground the view, but the eye shoots to the distant, snowcapped peaks beyond Altadena. Or maybe mine do to avoid Barnsdall. Every time I look, I see what was there on that evening two years ago. Yellow police tape was stretched across the wrought iron fence to block the park entrance. Four police cars, a fire engine, and an ambulance crowded the parking lot. Officers had cleared the hillside of the homeless— mostly mentally ill or drug-addicted men and women of varying ages—and lined them up against the park fence for questioning. At the back right corner of the hill beneath an olive tree, crime scene investigators huddled around a body.

With these memories, it hasn't been easy to resume what one might call an ordinary life. The nightmares persist, the unwelcome visits. Every so often a voice in me cries, *wake up!* I suppose then, what gnaws at me is the question of my responsibility. Perhaps I've erroneously concluded that none of us were to blame. We wanted what everyone wants: acceptance, love, admiration, to find a way of living that would insulate us against the harsher realities and our own limitations. Such a discovery would equal success in anyone's book.

This morning, before my eyes even opened, I felt that ball of energy lodged in my gut. I paced the kitchen while the coffee brewed, then poured a cup and wandered onto the dewy balcony, where I sat to examine myself. I'd give it all—the new house, the bank account, the bestseller—for a plateau, a stretch of the manageable that doesn't ask for more than I'm willing to give. But that's death, isn't it? I wanted to dismiss the spell of anxiety, chalk it up to an unfortunate astrological pairing, the squaring or opposition of transitioning planets applying pressure to loosen my grip on a pattern of thinking or behaving that no longer served me, but as I sat there, I felt the past reaching up from inside me. Then, an email notification lit my cell screen. The date was displayed: December 17th. Mid-breath, I froze. Yes, that was the reason I felt anxious—the sublimated pain I'd experienced two years ago on this very day was awakening. Or was it just a coincidence? I'd have liked to leave it there, but I'd gone too far into my psyche to entertain the notion of coincidence. Perhaps I should also believe that Emily randomly chose December 17th, which marks the beginning of the feast of Saturnalia on the ancient Roman calendar, after her repeated insistence that Saturn's alignment would bring destruction. It's as improbable for me as a belief in coincidence.

Still, I tried to force myself to carry on with the day and not dwell in the past. Once I finished my coffee, I went inside to pack away my books for the upcoming move and a second omen cut me. From the shelf fell my dogeared copy of *The Dialogues of Plato*. Just the sight of the cover and the feeling, as though I'd made a grave error, struck. You see, that book binds me to Nadia and her successor, Emily. More specifically, the Androgyne Myth related by Aristophanes in the *Symposium* to explain the origin of the human longing for union and the instinctive drive to find our other half. This paradoxical quest of seeking union—*that* is what my life was always about, only I was ignorant of what being whole truly meant. Ignorance is a chasm, a darkness too thick for epiphany; only courage, that veiled form of grace, can bridge the gap.

No one believed he was more sophisticated or above the view that ours is a world governed by unseen forces than me. And I'm not referring to the law of gravity or any other known scientific law. There exists order and chaos, and mysterious energies wielded in their directions. And here I say "energies" as if I must tiptoe around the matter. *Other* life forms surround us. They inhabit us. Saint Paul said it best: "For we do not wrestle against flesh and blood, but against the rulers, against the authorities, against the cosmic powers over this present darkness, against the spiritual forces of evil in the heavenly places."

Yes, I know. God and His thou-shalt-nots are dead and all that archaic, provincial, superstitious religious blabber about angels and demons and good and evil has been relegated to the fantasy genre. Perhaps it's best to believe that man is alone, unimpeded upon. That the synchronicities that take our breath away are merely coincidences. How I wish I could regain that point of view and along with it, the belief that success as a writer would've equaled my happiness.

Dusk is quiet here. Hollywood Boulevard hums in electric light. Beneath an intensifying three-quarter moon, I cross the length of my spacious balcony and rest my hands on the paint-chipped railing. Now, the park is empty and dark, darker still beneath the olive trees. There's something, though...voices. Yes. Like those of angels. The park? No. There. Shadows dance on the walkway before the garden apartments, those of the little Indian girl and the Polish immigrant's son. They play rock-paper-scissors on a porch by the front gate. Perfect in their innocence, wholly absorbed in their game, nothing else exists. Contagious giggles tumbling through shadows, up the risers, and onto my porch pass through me like an unobstructed echo.

2

———

She called it research. The Brits *are* witty.

My story could easily begin with Emily. From the start, she seemed extraordinary. She took me up like an object of nostalgia she wanted to revivify. The first time we were alone together, that day in Luce's garden beneath the avocado tree, she confided, "Like attracts like by the principle for which a sympathy can exist between them, an energetic pattern."

I believe she saw in me a reflection of her need to heal; she, too, was broken. That's why astrology and all the systems she practiced, those in which I believed she had some esoteric education, appealed to me; they gave me hope. "The planets aren't out there in space. They're energies inside you, swirling in micro-orbit." She drew my birth chart and showed me the pattern in the stars on the day I was born, thereby lifting the fingerprints of the Unseen off the grand scheme of my life to give my struggles purpose and meaning. All that I had gathered around me, she put inside me where it had always been. Emily, the Scorpio who spoke about death and resurrection and gave herself wholly to her art, had literally reached into my tangled psyche and color-coded my villains.

But I couldn't have been open to Emily had Nadia not preceded her. She was the snow on the mountain peak, whereas Emily was the ocean at the river's end. The night we met, Nadia said, "God is something you must experience." If not for her devastating beauty—I was shallow, helplessly prone, disrupted by beauty—it would've seemed idiotic talk. After all, I wasn't seeking God, I was seeking the object of my lust. How could I have known the two were connected? That in all our endeavors we are seeking the sacred transcendence, whether we are aware of it or not?

Nadia had no rival. After nine years I still discovered expressions or angles of her face that I'd not yet known, terrifying discoveries that suddenly made her a stranger, so I'd kiss her to prove that it was her, that this new expression or angle was, as she was, mine. The prophets say, love is of the spirit, lust is of the flesh, and the flesh is stronger. Ah, Nadia—the gem I coveted, stole, then lost in the sea of colored glass.

Steel and glass glinting in sunlight—that was my impression of Manhattan as a boy. I'd only seen the city from afar, through a window from the backseat of my parents' car as we crossed the upper level of the Verrazano Bridge en route to visit relatives in Brooklyn. My eyes would wander the wild crosscurrents of the bay, creep to the Statue of Liberty, then cut a hard right to view the clustered skyline and ponder the place where it seemed all the world was gathered. Then later, day trips with my parents to city museums, parks, or Rockefeller Center at Christmastime brought me into contact with the city, its motion, the chaotic ensemble of congested avenues and streets with over-crowded sidewalks and busy people rushing here and there, which changed that young boy's glossy impression. The sad music of loose change in paper cups preluded the smell of indifference rising off beggars wrapped in layers of filthy, tattered clothes while sharply dressed businessmen and women, who seemed more important than us, the working class, entered and exited taxis and chauffeur-driven sedans in the momentum of self-pursuit. The midtown and down-town buildings, some impossibly tall, crafted in metal and sheets of glass, others of stone with elaborate detailing and mansards, and the neighborhoods above and below of brownstones and townhouses that recalled Dickens' novels and seemed more suited to be of a place called Manhattan than New York, the latter made coarse by the grit of crime rates and racial divides.

The year after I'd attained a bachelor's degree in English Literature from St. John's University and was subsequently denied entry into the master's programs in fiction to which I applied, I left my family home in Staten Island and took a small studio in a pre-war building on East 10th Street in Alphabet City. The studio had stripped wood floors, eroded brick walls, and long, rectangular windows that looked onto the fire escape and water tower of the neighboring building, a sight that defied time: the people living there a hundred years ago and thirty years ago had looked out on the same view. That abiding sense of timelessness somehow made me believe the studio possessed a magical artistic influence that would aid me in my writing. Now I know that's what I believed, but I wasn't so quick to catch the sentiment back then, the belief in things such as magic.

Regarding spirituality, my connection had no bars, so to

speak. Though I'd attended Catholic schools, I'd given up God; that is to say, the religion that had taken the spirit out of the word. Not for that reason though. Once I'd discovered the opposite sex, Catholicism had become too inconvenient. Tell me no, and I must.

To meet my new financial responsibilities, I took a waiter job at Mon Amour, a chic West Village restaurant frequented by celebrities and socialites. The money was good, consistent, but working at Mon Amour had an unforeseen perk: it came with a ready-made social life and entry to the "in" scene. I developed friendships with some of the patrons and the wait staff and from both pools plucked lovers. The nocturnal nature of my job and my burgeoning social activities left little time for a writing routine.

Four years—I call them the blurry years—passed with little to show for my attempts at writing. My lack of productivity was shameful; I'd amassed a catalog of experiences which, in more disciplined hands, would've made for juicy stories. When customers asked what I did, because no one was looking to make a career waiting tables, I felt dishonest saying I was a writer. Then, one day, following the realization that waiting tables had become my career, in a rare bestowal of clarity, I caught a glimpse of the me I'd meant to be when I'd moved to the city; the stark contradiction unsettled me. My innate precociousness had taken on a life of its own. The nature of the will and the forces acting upon it were beyond my understanding at that point, but thankfully, I had an ego that coveted merit. There was so much to learn, and I was late to the table.

From that day on, when I wasn't working at Mon Amour, I was home writing short stories and poems, reading books on writing, or reading the writers that made me want to write. But what did I want to write? I knew I wasn't looking to turn a yarn for shits and giggles, to create warmth, or promote brotherhood across demographics. I had always felt like an outsider, an imposter and I wanted others to experience this sort of self-conscious torture. I wanted to write novels that transformed points of view and disrupted lives by burrowing into the reader's souls so that they were forced to question all they claimed to believe about themselves. Disillusionment has been my curse, a sort of x-ray vision that revealed how contradictions and meaninglessness fractured the bones beneath the skin of life. Call it a tragic worldview, which isn't a choice but how one perceives what life distributes; the choice to deny the tragic is, well, tragic. The full experience of life requires entering all that is. I suppose disillusionment is what resulted in my precocious disposition in the first place; I was seeking heightened experiences, pleasurable experiences to feel something real, something so powerful that it couldn't be reduced by suffering.

Writing had to be a job like any other: wake and work. That Mercury is in my eighth house, the mundanity of routines was always a struggle. I needed to elevate the writing process, excite and connive myself into sitting at the desk. To this end, I developed a writing ritual for drawing the muses that consisted of queuing a classical music playlist, lighting a stick of nag champa incense, and reciting a short prayer, an invocation I'd glommed from Chaucer. Then, I'd prepare the coffee press with my concoction of loose teas and lay out my cigarettes and ashtray on the Ikea desk positioned before the window with the magic view. The ritual was effective, but it didn't take long before the habits I was denying presented me with a struggle. After all, I was twenty-eight, a fire sign full of curiosity in a city that catered to whatever one desired. The pressure would build, then I'd throw open the valve, go for a night out in search of a little trouble, possibly a one-night stand, which occasionally boiled into a long weekend. Such is the force of the subconscious needs and their ability to interrupt the conscious desire.

This was my life before I met Nadia. I still don't know how it was that we frequented the same places, ran in parallel social scenes, yet I remained unaware of her. I later learned that before we'd met, we'd slept with the same couple. The girl, a waitress at Mon Amour, cheated with me and the boyfriend, an investment banker, with Nadia.

3

———

I t was late August, minutes from dawn, and we were at The Coffee Shop in Union Square. The focus of my dead-eyed stare bypassed the dried spit on the window through which I watched the last shades of night lift off the park. My fingers felt fat—they were slightly bloated—and I imagined my face must have looked pale, a sickly green. I'd had one too many Obans at the hotspot we'd hit and was waiting for my breakfast burrito to soak up the scotch in my belly.

Julius removed the unripe tomato from his veggie burger (he'd sent back the first because they'd put cheese on it and he's lactose intolerant). I'd just reminded him that I'm from Staten Island and he did what most people do, roll his eyes.

"Staten Italy," he said and suddenly pulled himself upright. "Do you know Nadia? She's from the island." I must've looked as if I was straining to place her. "No, honey," he said, "you wouldn't have to remember." His hand shot up as though he was about to swear an oath. "She makes *me* want va-j-j." The hyperbole failed to amuse me. His teeth, picket fence-white, chomped into his burger bun. Dreading the imminent sunrise, drifting into a food coma, I could think of nothing but my bed. Abruptly, I stood. "Wait for me to finish, bitch," he whined. I tossed money on the table and as I emerged on the sidewalk, found myself annoyed by his unflagging energy and that I'd broken my writing routine for an uneventful night.

The next day, as we folded napkins before our shift, Miles, an actor and fellow waiter at Mon Amour, told me that he'd met a beautiful girl from Staten Island at a party. She'd spent the night at his apartment.

"Nadia's her name. She's a smoke-show." I sat back in my chair, smirked. "What? You know her?"

"No," I said.

Miles and I were in a sort of competition when it came to women. We had similar tastes so we were always eyeing the same customers at the restaurant or chasing down the same female co-workers. Maybe it isn't fair to say that we were in competition. You see, I was never satisfied with myself. As far back as I can remember, it seemed there was always something I needed that I didn't have, always some vague benchmark I was missing that, if reached, would make me complete. Just being good at certain things didn't suffice; I wanted to be the best. The best at Atari video games, pulling wheelies on BMX bikes, the best at my high school football position, best dressed, best hairstyle, date the best-looking girl, and it goes on and on. In my mind, visions of greatness accompanied the voices narrating the legend of Victor Cerrone. But this germ infecting my thoughts, it isn't hard to gather, made me somewhat tyranni-cal. When playing football, if teammates weren't performing up to my expectations, I'd berate them in front of others like an enraged father. And when I didn't perform up to my expectations, I did the same thing to myself. That's the whole point—I was hard on myself. I've often thought had I admitted my mediocrity sooner, perhaps things would've been easier, at least on everyone else, but accepting mediocrity was not part of the design. Not yet.

Still grinning with the memory of his previous night, Miles flattened a napkin on the tabletop and began the fold. I wanted details. "So, tell me." He sent a glance, flourished his eyebrows, then placed the folded napkin atop the stack as if it was a winning poker hand. As dishonest as Miles was, when it came to women, he never lied. I continued folding my napkin, aware of the burn in my gut over a girl I'd never seen, completely unaware that I'd soon learn when something is destined, the forces of nature suggest it in uncanny succession.

A week or so later, while walking West 10th Street, something in a bookshop window display caught my eye: Breton's *Nadja*. For an instant I braced against the sensation of freefalling. The feeling that followed was strange, auspicious, like an unvalidated certainty. I smirked, turned to go on my way, when Julius came strutting around the corner. He was ripe over an argument he'd had with another booker at the modeling agency where he worked and went directly into a diatribe that sustained a six-block walk and didn't end until we were seated in a café and a waitress delivered my coffee and his café latte. I saw my chance. "That girl Nadia? She get around?"

Julius looked hurt, as if I'd not paid attention to a word he'd said. He shrugged, brushed a hand over his perfectly round head; his flawless, dark skin was gleaming in the cascade of natural light coming through the window. "She always with some pretty boy. But a girl looks like that in a city like this got the pick of the litter. I was a bitch, that's the bitch I'd be. Mmn, brother!" He curled up in exaggerated laughter, which finally petered out in a series of huck-hucks. I waved off his theatrics as he leaned toward me, whispered, "Why you asking?" Those soft brown eyes glared up through lined lashes. My smile told him exactly why I was asking. "Baby, I'm gonna make it happen. When she get back. She traveling or something."

Months passed. I wrote and read in a self-prescribed isolation that I only broke for shifts at the restaurant. I didn't see Julius, and Miles never mentioned the girl from Staten Island again. The mysterious Nadia slipped my mind.

ON A NOVEMBER NIGHT after a particularly promising day of writing, I was preparing for one of my pressure-release rendezvous. While fingering my hair before the mirror and imagining the crowd at De Sade, the new hotspot, a voice in my head rose into awareness, said *Nadia*. I paused, caught the glint in my eye. Yes, what had happened to Nadia?

One could not just freely enter De Sade; there was the whole New York nightlife pageantry of having to be picked by a doorman. In this case, the doorman was Rolphe, an ornery transvestite who stood behind the velvet rope between two musclebound security guards. If you were an unfamiliar face, Rolphe indignantly said, "Guest list only." If you were a familiar face among the in-crowd and not of celebrity status, Rolphe, in a commiserating tone, said, "Give me a minute." A minute was closer to ten minutes in which nothing seemed to happen, then the rope was opened, and entrance was granted. As I've said, by default the job at Mon Amour made me a familiar face.

De Sade was, as the name suggests, decadent. Swaths of texture: velvet curtains, nail-studded suede banquettes, patterned silk and velvet pillows, dimmed crystal chandeliers, gothic candelabras dripping red candle wax. The specialty cocktails had names like Justine Juice and Bugger's Milk. Julius was holding court in a corner banquette. He waved me over and without losing dedication to his boisterous monologue, kept his eyes fixed on me as I crossed the length of the crowded bar and plopped down next to him. When he finished his story, something about Francis Bacon, whom he'd once met, he leaned toward me.

"Where you been, mister?"

"Working. Writing."

He feigned excitement, clapped his hands, but he cared nothing about my writing, nor did he care about Bacon's art. His abacus was set to the calculations of purely social things. And to that point, he was grinning ear to ear. "Guess who's coming tonight? She turned thirty yesterday. We're celebrating. Wish I had a bow to tie around you."

I sipped a scotch, scanned the crowd of beautiful faces, and found myself glancing at the curtains before the doorway each time they parted and someone new entered the milieu. Two acquaintances drew me into their debate, assuming, because I was a waiter, that I knew the characteristics that differentiate a cabernet franc and a cabernet sauvignon. As I spouted the same sort of crap I did to customers in Mon Amour, I noticed Julius rise from the banquette, clasp his hands, and press them under his chin. I followed his eye-line.

Moving across the dimly lit space, she seemed weightless, like a firefly brightening the air around her, what I perceived as an emanation of grace. In black high heels, black jeans, and a black cashmere sweater, she exuded style, the kind other women took pains to achieve. It was impossible not to stare as the sudden, intense desire to know her skin, the color of orange blossom honey, and the nuances of her mineral-rich brown eyes, overcame me. She sank into Julius' embrace as though he were a pillow and once he'd sufficiently absorbed her, he spun her toward me. "And here's your gift, baby," he said. "Nadia, Victor." My hands were trembling, I felt warm and cold at the same time. I offered a plastic smile. Julius kissed her cheek and said, "Wear him in good health." He winked, ceremoniously bowed, then slunk off.

Nadia was blushing. So was I. "He's something, huh?" she said.

I nodded, spurted, "Happy belated," a bit too eagerly.

"Thank you," she said. "He adores you, you know?"

She wore no makeup, only black eyeliner, which eroticized her dark features, took them from the European to the African side of the Mediterranean. She seemed to be waiting for me to say something, but I was outside myself, floating away in an anxious escape; it was the first time I had met a woman who conjured a desire so intense that it left my mind barren, as if my ability for cheeky banter or sly, well-placed double entendres belonged to another.

"So, you're from the island," she said, ending the awkward silence. "Feel like we had to have crossed paths at some point."

"I would've remembered," I said, which, to my relief, she took as a compliment. A passing couple jostled us, and I realized we were blocking the lane carved by the mass of bodies before the bar. I sprang into action, took Nadia's hand, guided her toward the banquette, and helped her squeeze by the wide table as the hookah's apple-scented smoke wafted between us. The beat of Morcheba's *The Sea* drew me out, helped me recover my composure.

Nadia settled in, made a timid survey of the fashionistas, actors, artists, and socialites packed into that tight venue. She was drawing glances from men and women alike, seemed painfully aware of the attention, and averted her gaze to her lap, inhaled long and slow, exhaled the same.

"You okay?" I asked.

"Experiencing a little culture shock," she said. "I just got back."

"From?"

"India. Well, that was the last stop."

Throughout the next two hours, she drank several glasses of champagne while I ignored all the busy eyes seeking to steal her gaze. I had her undivided attention and by now I was wild with the sense that Julius had played matchmaker behind the scenes. She told of her three-month spiritual journey that began in Africa, segued to Israel, and ended in India. At points, she grew animated, and to emphasize what she was saying, to stress particularly impressive locations or the details of ancient temples, she touched my shoulder, then ran her hand down my arm and held me at the elbow. I can honestly say I was never as interested in what a woman was saying even though I lost much of her story thinking things like, *I want to eat you alive*, or *I wonder what it looks like*. I even remember doubting the possibility of consummating my desire; when she described the Ganga Dussehra festival at the sacred Ganges River, she used words like "cleansed" and "devout." Could this be the woman I'd heard about? It just didn't make sense. Give herself, this noble gift, to that fool Miles, with his lousy hygiene? As she continued talking, a strange insecurity came over me, had me measuring myself against her, and left me aching to be more than the sum I'd calculated.

Julius burst out of the crowd, began voguing before us, then planted his hands on the table and jutted his face forward. "Um, we're supposed to be celebrating!"

"We are," Nadia said. She lifted her champagne glass as if to toast him, then smiled at me.

Julius sent an impish glance my way, then took Nadia's hand and said, "Glad you're enjoying your gift, baby." He went off, bopping to the music. She sipped her champagne. My eyes traced the soft jawline that seamlessly blended into the elegant slopes of her throat.

"I feel foolish," she said. I shrugged. "I've talked about myself all night." She seemed to chastise herself for her lapse in awareness and said something along these lines, "I talk a lot when I'm nervous." Yes, it was that, I remember, because I felt my loins bristle. *I* was making *her* nervous? "Do you have a practice?" she asked. "Spiritual, I mean."

"Writing." She stared at me for a moment as though everything had changed, then placed her glass on the table. She inhaled and, as if to realign with life, looked around the club. "I'm kidding," I said. "No. I don't have a practice."

"You grew up Catholic, right? Sure, Italian boy from Staten Island."

"Italian, Scottish, and Greek, but I got convinced otherwise," I said.

"You're an atheist?" she said as if atheism was cancer.

"Let's just say, whatever seems divinely bestowed in my limited view can be logically explained by someone, somewhere."

She smirked, which, I later learned, was her way when she disagreed with someone, and said, "God is something you must experience." But the way she said it, and the look in her eyes? What certainty! What had she experienced? I suddenly lamented my ignorance of spiritual things; nothing seemed more important. Then and there, my curiosity was born.

The rest of the conversation blurs in memory but for the closing remarks, which bore a significance nothing short of prophecy. She asked, "When's your birthday?"

"March," I said.

She nodded as if her suspicion was confirmed. "Aries. A fire sign. I'm Virgo. The earth."

"That means I'll burn you up," I teased.

"Or I'll smother you," she rebuked.

WE EMERGED in the blue-hued dawn. A cool breeze cleared the city stink, added a freshness to the air as we strolled across 7th Avenue and through the quiet cobblestone streets of the West Village. I had no qualms about meeting the dawn, no worries about my writing routine; I was full of energy, inspired by the mystery that guides us and how sudden circumstances arise with a promise that life will never be the same. This very sensation and the ability to comprehend it originates in the spiritual faculties, only I didn't know it then. Spirituality for me was strictly bound in a naïve idea of a punishing God, of angels and demons, the reality of which seemed absurd.

By now I'd learned she'd been married and divorced. "He was older. Had money." They were only dating six months before he proposed and the velocity that turned her into a housewife managed to blur the dreams she'd longed to fulfill, those that taunted her when she found herself laboring over a washing machine or an ironing board. The husband, also a fire sign, was a successful corporate lawyer, not the kind of man who likes to be challenged, especially by his woman. "I thought it was what I was supposed to do, you know. A girl gets married, right?" Her constant restlessness prompted by daydreams of fabled Paris cafes and the other fantastic places her husband had no interest in visiting, haunted her like misdeeds. "He's a terrible person, my ex. I didn't love him. I'm not proud of leaving. I tried, I did, but."

"I'm glad you left," I said. She sighed, but not in response to what I'd said. Now that she was back from her travels she needed to find a job. "What do you want to do?" I asked. She shrugged and grunted as though work was a source of frustration to consider. "What about the dreams you left your marriage to pursue?"

She was on the verge of an answer but stopped herself, then asked: "How did you know you wanted to be a writer?"

As a boy, I didn't harbor ideas about a dream career, never imagined myself as a firefighter, police officer, astronaut, not even a writer. My first, conscious longing was for my Staten Island neighbor, Rosemary, who was two years older than me. One humid summer afternoon when I was just eight or nine years old, our mothers caught us kissing in the downstairs coat closet of our house. The sensations of arousal quickly transformed into embarrassment. Moments later, we were standing side by side at the threshold of my family's garage in the elongated shadows of our mothers, who shielded us from the midday sun at their backs. Near tears, Rosemary, my little princess, hid her face beneath her knotted blonde hair while our mothers explained in careful, stern tones that the natural thing we were exploring was wrong. Shifting my weight from foot to foot, I became distinctly aware of the grease smell from my father's plumbing tools mingled with the clean scent of laundry wafting from the exhaust vent on the side of the house. To prevent a bout of nervous laughter, I averted my eyes and traced the cracks in the gray cement floor, seeing in them the lightning bolts from Metallica's "Ride the Lightning" album cover. When the lecture ended, Rosemary's mother took her hand and walked her back to their house, and my mother went inside to resume her housework, but I ran off into the woods possessed by a supreme sensation—I had kissed Rosemary's plump, sour lips.

Nadia waited on my answer. I spoke what came to mind. "I lied a lot as a kid. Not to get out of trouble or anything. I liked to make up stories and see if people bought them. Then in high school and college, I wrote term papers for money."

"Really?"

"Yeah. I didn't mind sitting there and typing. Plus, I was learning, you know, about whatever I was being paid to write about." I paused as another piece of information that seemed relevant came to mind. "I used to write the corniest love letters and poems to girls I was infatuated with." This was all true, and at that moment, though I'd never joined these pieces of information as telltales for my future career as a writer, it felt right. Everything felt right.

"So, you're a romantic?"

I laughed. "Should've been born in 1800."

"Why?"

"Period of Romanticism in English Literature." She nodded, looked as if she was recalling the content of some high school lesson, but the silence that followed compelled me to help her along. "Romanticism wasn't about romance between men and women. The Romantics championed emotion over rationalism, nature over industrialization."

Again, she nodded, but I saw she was clueless. "Blake? Shelley? Keats?" She shrugged. "You'd know their poetry," I said.

"Maybe you'll read me some." And with that, she slipped her arm through the hook of my elbow and drew herself closer for the remainder of our walk. I remember the sun was coming up and the sudden joy I felt at being in the city, the place where all the world was gathered, which was prompted by the forethought of how perfectly she fit to me; the stride of her gait was designed to complement mine.

We arrived at her sparsely decorated duplex apartment; she'd taken it a month before her trip and hadn't had time to decorate. Her luggage was spread on the floor amongst tissue paper-wrapped trinkets she'd purchased in India and Africa, such as wood-carved icons of goddesses and gods, elephants and giraffes. Richly colored silk pillow covers and curtains with intricate designs and patterns spilled from two cardboard boxes. "Pretty, right?" She held up a pillow cover and traced its design with her finger.

Narrow stairs led to the loft where her bed sat beneath the slanted ceiling's skylight. On the wall beside the bed, three frames held illustrations of fairies perched in trees with swirling limbs. "Those are cool," I said.

"I made them," she said, then lit a series of aromatic candles positioned around the bed. Just before she dipped into the bathroom, she cued low-playing classic rock. It occurred to me: earlier that evening while I was dressing, I thought of her and now I was lying on her bed marveling at the softness of her faux sheepskin blanket.

The sound of the bathroom door as it opened. I inhaled as her head pressed to the pillow. The scent of gardenia infused the breeze of her motion. We were eye to eye. The kiss was remarkably familiar; our mouths had no trouble finding rhythm. I kept my eyes open; I wanted to see her.

And minutes later, as I stood above her viewing her body, a stern look occupied her face; not in rejection of what was happening but to convey the solemn awareness that she was giving herself to me. Her understanding of what we were doing seemed greater than mine.

A slow-building intimacy paled the routine dash toward the orgasm I'd been accustomed to. We relished deep kisses that seemed their own acts of consummation. My hands elicited sighs. She dizzily swayed, tossing her head, locking her ankles across my lower back. With my thumbs, I swept the hair from her face, our eyes connected, remain fixed in a wholly new sort of communication that reduced all my previous sexual encounters to aggrandized forms of masturbation.

It must have been two in the afternoon when I awoke from a nightmare. Moments before, I'd been strapped to some sort of wooden torture device, watching my spirit leave my body and float toward the ceiling of what appeared to be a medieval dungeon. Now awake, the audible thump of my heart disturbed the strange quiet of a new room. My skin felt tight, as if my insides had expanded somehow. There she was, sleeping beside me. Flashes of the night before, the sex, were all coming back, the silent vows I'd made behind our kisses. I needed to be away, to leave, collect myself.

Careful not to disturb her, I slipped from the bed, hurriedly dressed, and just as I was moving toward the stairs, "Hey." She peeled herself up onto an elbow, gathered the sheet to cover the oxblood areolae of her nipples. Her puffy eyes widened to aid focus. "You're leaving?" I couldn't articulate why I needed to leave; I felt drained, weakened, like a disjointed puppet.

"I have to," I said.

She gave a suspicious examination of me. "Thought we'd at least have coffee," she said, now sitting lotus position, stretching her arms above her head, bending side to side. Merciless Beauty. "You have to leave? I mean, it's cool if you want to."

"It isn't that I want to, I just—" Before I could say another word, I was bounding toward the bed in surrender.

4

———

A week later, in her candlelit apartment, incense cones burning in an urn like our newfound bliss, she suggested we collaborate on an oil painting. The idea was to hang it on her wall once it dried. I'd never painted with oils, only watercolors and acrylics in a college art class. She'd gone to The New School for illustration and was hoping to major in fashion design, but due to the strain of her ongoing divorce, she'd dropped out in her second year and relegated her artistic pursuit to hobby status. To pass time, she made illustrations and painted 8x10 abstracts, which she used to decorate her apartment or give as gifts to friends.

She laid the canvas across our laps and taped a piece of cardboard down the center to create a vertical divider so we couldn't see what the other was painting. "Paint without thinking, whatever comes to mind," she said. After a brief tutorial on how to use the oil paint, we began. Of course, I wanted to paint something good, to impress her. Maybe fifteen minutes in, she caught me peering over the cardboard divider. "Hey! Don't look." We painted for a stretch, then it came time to remove the cardboard. Her side was a burst of yellows, reds, and white. Mine was an abyss of burnt umber, midnight blue, and black. She'd painted a radiant angel in the heavens; I'd painted a demon rising from black smoke. Hers showed ability, mine ambition. She examined my demon. "Wow. Is that you?" Her look turned quizzical. "Or is it me?" Wondering myself, I shrugged. She held up the painting. "Light and dark. You don't think it's strange?" I thought it was funny.

As a boy I was overly conscious of the existence of something other, tormented by some unseen presence. At times, I'd wake in the middle of the night as if gently shaken from sleep, wake into a silence like that which follows some terrible accident or argument so that the energy of the event still electrifies the air. I'd scan the darkness, and though it's true that I never did see anything lurking in my room, I could feel something hovering, watching. Or I'd be in the basement, completely absorbed, playing with my action figures when the cold sensation would ice the back of my neck and disturb my play, send a chill throughout my body. I'd stop, look over my shoulder. Again, I saw nothing, but I knew I was no longer alone. The hum of the fluorescent lights and the tick of the boiler would suddenly become supernaturally infused horrors, the characteristics that came to represent the appearance of this unseen presence.

My parents told me I was imagining things. It's worth mentioning that this presence I sensed was automatically presumed to be something to fear, something malevolent rather than benevolent. Of course, when the idea of God came into the picture, I'd pray, hoping to be saved from this unseen intruder that occasionally made itself known. Then, and it's hard to determine exactly when, these experiences just stopped. My indoctrination had won, closed off my awareness of such things. Soon after, my education and pleasure pursuits delivered me into a state of rational materialism and carnality which obfuscated my spiritual senses and therefore the ability to believe in God. I willingly embraced what was considered dark; there seemed a fount of energy and power to be drawn from taboo.

I often wonder if what I sensed in my boyhood had resulted from the macabre lyrics of the heavy metal I listened to and my pondering the album covers, such as Bruegel's infernal *Triumph of Death* on Sabbath's *Greatest Hits*, or if the interest in the dark side was what created the impulse toward heavy metal in the first place. Maybe it was the surge of horror films in the early '80s, those my older brother and I secretly watched without our parents' consent, that left me peeking over my sheets at the dark corners of my bedroom. Perhaps it was because I had the melancholy soul, prone to a vague discomfort that cloudy, rainy days intensified like arthritis, when suddenly, in the grayish light, even the most mundane objects seemed numinous, somehow alive. Was I ever alone in a room? Whatever, our joint painting never made it to her wall. Nadia seemed afraid of it, as if it were an omen. She hid it in the back of the closet behind all the boxed stuff she'd retained from her marriage.

A couple of months into our relationship, she'd gotten a part-time job at her friend's design studio. It consisted primarily of clerical work, but she took initiative, involved herself in creative discussions, and was soon casting models for photography shoots. She would sometimes ask my opinion. "Him? Or...him?" I'd be looking at two photos, both with devilishly handsome men, eyebrows seductively arched.

"You're around these guys at the studio?" She looked at

me, then swiped the pictures out of my hands, impatient with my concerns. You see, that was what started it, my concern, my need to guard my treasure. I was suddenly more attuned to the goings-on at her job. We'd never discussed what was happening between us, never declared ourselves monogamous. It was assumed.

"No one's ever looked at me like that," she'd say, and I took it to mean that she understood what I did, that we had found our other half. Arm-in-arm, we hit the town—parties, events, dinners—and I was the envy of every man. Intense feelings began consuming me, pleasurable and dreadful feelings that robbed my peace of mind; in one moment I felt as alive as a lion cub, in the next, as fragile as a maimed gazelle in the Serengeti.

As for writing, I fit it in when I could, but between Mon Amour and Nadia, there wasn't much getting done. The truth is, I was deterred. Only days after we'd met, I received several rejection letters for stories I'd submitted to literary publications. Rather than fight through the resistance and continue submitting, I used the letters as an excuse to allow my distraction. Another truth, with her in my life, my need to write had eased; I felt I had already achieved something beyond my expectations. That is love, isn't it?

I remember the day I surrendered, the moment. I was reading Durrell on the daybed when she arrived at my apartment straight from work. By then, she had a set of keys. The door opened, she entered, hair beaded from the misty rain outside. I watched her remove her herringbone overcoat and slip off her Chelsea boots. The scent of gardenia came to me like a love song and with it a feeling so familiar and comforting that I imagined we must have known each other in a previous life—no doubt a result of hearing her speak of reincarnation and such. "Have a chill," she said.

Nearly giddy that my long search was over, I took her in my arms and kissed her damp hair. She shivered against me as she glanced up. "What?"

"Live with me."

And I remember that moment precisely because of what happened that evening. I'd randomly stumbled upon the explanation of what I'd been feeling. Had I been a bit more aware at that point in my life, I would've caught the unseen agents at their game, possibly avoided identifying with the ideas they'd suggested; suggestion is how the Unseen work in the mind, but in me, they also seemed to orchestrate my emotions, stoke them beyond reason.

Scanning my bookshelf, seeking inspiration, I came across the *Dialogues of Plato*. I happened to open it on *The Symposium*, the setting of which is a banquet where those present are challenged to give a speech in praise of Eros. I was half invested until Aristophanes relates the Androgyne Myth. The androgyne was created whole, masculine and feminine united in a round body with four arms and four legs and a head with two faces; the circular body represented the heavenly bodies, sun and moon, a creation in the divine image and likeness of the gods. But the powerful androgynes, who were dissatisfied with being created in the image of the gods, rebelled. Fearing their power, Zeus split them into two, separate beings, condemning them to spend their lives in search of their other half. Here was the explanation that specified what was previously a vague desire in me, and as such, had resulted in a scattered sort of promiscuity. Ignorant as I was and prone to literal interpretations, I surmised: *Nadia is my other half, that which I'd been seeking in all my previous affairs.* I cast her as my ideal, the goddess image I'd unconsciously created since my youth out of an amalgam of women—friend's sisters and mothers, celebrities, heavy metal video vixens, my own mother perhaps. I wrote terrible poems declaring her:

Archaeologist of my heart
who exhumed
my most tender relic
my earth sign
my New World.

5

———

Beneath the spring soil lurks the blight. There is much to be said about unconscious needs formed in the early years and how they create emotional and behavioral patterns, especially when it comes to relationships. That thing in me longing to be the best, the unsatisfied I'm-not-enough tyrant, came screaming to the surface. As I've said, I was the envy of every man; with the sight of her, young and old alike were helpless to hide the desire she conjured in them. My need to keep my other half and guard my happiness made me fiercely vigilant, keen to the covetous eyes of the thieves.

This burgeoning fear had enhanced my contempt for Miles. During shifts at Mon Amour, whenever he was near me in the side station, so close that I smelled his rotten breath from the persistent nasal drip caused by his daily cocaine use, I had to restrain myself. I'd imagine attacking him, could feel the sensations of my fists beating him to a pulp. I'd return home from shifts to find Nadia waiting in my bed and have to unwind before I could go over to her unaffected by what I can only describe as disappointment in her for giving herself to a man without one redeeming quality.

Come spring, she'd given up her apartment and was now living with me in my 10th Street studio. With shimmering Indian silks everywhere—pillows, curtains, shams —she'd transformed that tiny, poorly lit space into a world of color that visitors likened to a dollhouse or a Klimt painting. Evenings, I read her the poems of Wordsworth and Byron, and even though she preferred Rumi and Hafiz, she listened attentively. In turn, I made Herculean efforts to concentrate when she tried teaching me the meditation technique she practiced or when she'd usher me to her friend Kim's yoga studio, eager for me to embrace the "spiritual practice." Having her close relaxed me some, created the illusion that I had control over the situation. But my possessiveness, which she attributed to my ego, made her anxious. Her sincerity was unrivaled the morning she offered me her cherished books, *The Tibetan Book of the Dead* and *Autobiography of a Yogi*, holding them close to her heart before handing them over. She believed they would soften me. I matched her sincerity by devouring them straightaway, never imagining they'd play into my destiny.

Yes, I'd been intellectualized out of believing in the existence of a God who intervenes in the affairs of humankind, and I've said I was far from any spiritual practice, nonetheless, Nadia's beauty, in the sense of Beauty as a godly virtue, threw open the doors of my soul. I wanted to be spiritual because she was. Her interest in Eastern philosophies, yoga, and the mystical Vedas intrigued me. The familiar icons found in churches and in my childhood home were replaced by the images of exotic nagas and the blue-skinned god and many-armed goddess, of sultry gurus and wild ascetics with painted faces immersed in sacred rituals. She and they seemed mystical, aesthetically mystical. And since I'd discovered the magic yaki nestled between her slender thighs, I'd been spellbound, helplessly heathen. I tell you now, to mingle with the spirits of other cultures was my fall from grace.

As I read her books, I found myself pondering strange tales about Buddhist monks who used magical mantras, sages who lived for hundreds of years, and yogis with powers akin to Jesus, who healed with his hands, even raised the dead because, as Yogananda said, Jesus was a self-realized master. These books led to other books that made extraordinary claims regarding the human potential to obtain extrasensory powers, siddhis they were called, by harnessing unseen energies. It made me think of an episode of *Ripley's Believe It or Not* I'd seen as a boy, in which a swami, hands tied behind his back, used telekinesis to turn the pages of a book. It was just a trick, wasn't it?

So began my secret meditation sessions. For instance, I'd practice trying to move a sewing needle by focusing my concentration but could hardly assume the posture for more than a few minutes, let alone develop anything close to concentration. This newfound interest had also bent my mind to what was happening in the world around us. I began making connections, discerning patterns in the recurrence of numbers and words, synchronicities I now saw as signs that were telling me I was on the right path. But this was no brush with apophenia. There were unexplainable occurrences, proofs that ours was a cosmic love. On a weekend trip to Massachusetts, we were photographed sitting on a jetty. When the film was later developed, we were stupefied to see the dedication crudely graffitied on the rocks behind us, *VC luvs NS*. Our initials. Of course, we hadn't graffitied our initials on the rocks, nor did we notice them when we were there. Other lovers with the same initials from another time had memorialized their love. The sheer fact that we found this place and were photographed as though staged between our initials seemed beyond chance. Then there was the night we were watching Bergman's *The Seventh Seal* in the 10th Street studio and something like a beam of light shot from the television screen and entered me, causing me to shudder and shed a single tear, and when I turned, I saw that Nadia was also touched and there was a single tear glistening on her cheek. If I were the only one who noticed these things, or if I had to dig to find significance in them, perhaps they wouldn't have seemed profound.

One thing was for sure: despite my desire to acquire extrasensory powers, the spiritual side of life I had completely denied was calling me to acknowledge its existence, and it seemed Nadia was its gateway.

THEN IT HAPPENED. Miles withheld cash tips from the tip pool. I only knew because I'd taken the closed check with the cash from the table and handed it to him just as he'd emerged, wiping his nose from one of many bathroom excursions. Forty dollars was all he'd pocketed, of which maybe three would have ended up in my pile, but three dollars is three dollars. I despised him, his cocaine use, his grayish skin, and the unwarranted confidence he exuded.

My accusation caused a bit of a scene. My face was hot and a rage much too great for the issue at hand swelled in my center. Because Miles was a friend of the owners and the manager, they of course were reluctant to accept that he stole. The wait staff, gathered in a furor by the bar, wasn't as surprised. A simmering, defiant Miles was sitting on a chair, arms folded across his chest. In the instant we made eye contact, he ejected from the chair, came at me, finger thrusting, "Go fuck yourself!" It happened quickly, him moving toward me, the rush of aggressive energy, and the punch I threw to defend myself that sent him careening over a table piled with stacks of folded napkins that went to the floor with him. Then it was happening slowly. We seemed to have entered a completely different reality—there wasn't even a sensation in my knuckles from the blow. While the staff remained suspended in various reactions, the manager hurried to a dazed Miles, lifted him onto a chair, then looked up at me in bewilderment. Now I was the defiant one, bubbling with a sense of power, and before he could condemn me, I tore off my apron, threw it at him, swiped my portion of the tips from the bar top and sauntered out of the restaurant.

In my mind, that act had vindicated Nadia for her mistake with Miles. I'm sure she must've seen it that way herself, as a mistake, and not only Miles but her many trysts. She now had a clean slate in my eyes. If only she knew how I'd defended her honor. Of course, I couldn't tell her what I'd done. The sullen guise I presented upon entering the apartment belied the ecstatic hum that sustained my walk home; I was piqued as if suddenly conscious of every atom vibrating in my body.

"What's wrong?" she asked.

"They let me go," I said. "Business has been slow, and well..."

"What are you going to do?" She asked.

"I know a place where I could get a bartending gig." And I did. Julius made a phone call to the bar manager at De Sade, and a week later, I was training.

"Oh," Nadia said. "Now you're going to have all the young model girls throwing themselves at you." She said it with a smirk, but she wasn't joking. She had a possessive streak also; it excited me.

"Cleopatra couldn't steal me away," I said, then chased her down, my fingers snapping at her ass until she reached the bed and I sacked her.

THERE WERE weeds in her garden, but I kept telling myself, *How often do weeds turn out to be elixirs?* For instance, Nadia showed no interest in my writing. Reading was a chore for her—unless it was a book written by a guru. Even the poems I wrote about her went unread. How could she love me and have no interest in my art, nor the wherewithal to summon interest, even feign it to mollify me?

Money had never been an issue. We had what we needed and wanted for nothing, or so I'd thought. I recall a summer afternoon; the temperature was in the 90s as we strolled north on Broadway, sipping Thai iced teas, hugging buildings for meager relief in the shade they offered. The suffocating heat rising from the sidewalks was only intensified by droves of sweaty tourists looking for pirated DVDs or Louis Vuitton knockoffs, and the racket of horns blaring from Broadway's congested lanes. Nadia released my hand and approached a jewelry table set outside a Chinese import store. I waited at the curb to avoid the jostle of the crowded sidewalk and watched her like a wolf watches a doe; she resembled a doe with her sleek, brown skin, elegant neck and limbs, and soft, feminine eyes. Something on the table grabbed her attention. She waved me over. In the seat of her palm was a turquoise ring made of glass. On the table was a bowl with hundreds of the same turquoise rings. "Put it on me," she said. I slid the weightless ring onto her ring finger. She spread her hand wide to view it and said, "That's all I'll ever need."

Shortly after, one night as we were eating dinner in the apartment, Nadia looked at me as if with contempt and said, "I'm tired of being poor." She'd been quiet that day, somewhat distant. "I want to do things and I'm tired of working for pennies." I glanced at the turquoise ring on her finger.

"Well, if I get going as a writer, we'll be fine." She scoffed. "What?"

"We live in one room." Her words unsettled me, made me feel deceived; this uncharacteristic display made her seem a stranger. Suddenly, it occurred to me that if I wanted to keep her, I needed to start selling my stories. The pressure interfered with my ability to write as I began questioning whether the story ideas I'd been working on were sellable. This kind of concern had never been filtered into my process.

Still, other behaviors of hers came into focus. Whenever anyone complimented her hair or clothes—she received endless compliments in both areas from friends and strangers—or some achievement of hers, she'd toss it off in a sort of restless denial. What I'd first perceived as an exemplum of humility was really a concession, as if she were seeking atonement for some sin I wasn't sure she had committed. And her mood swings? One day she was an empath, the very next, apathetic and outright cruel. I wondered if this had anything to do with losing her father. He'd died when she was only three years old. "Imagine? To be a girl and not have a father's love? How do you know your worth?" She had only one memory of him from a park outing, in which he tickled her nose with a daisy. Whenever she spoke about it, she grew emotional, bitter, as though his dying was an act of spite against her. It didn't help that her mother later married a man Nadia despised; she was a teenager, weathering that rough time of life, and the smarmy stranger suddenly living in their space had further complicated things. "My stepfather," she said. She was sitting on the daybed finishing her third glass of wine. "I didn't like the way he looked at me. I was a kid. And I told my mother. She didn't listen." I read between the lines. That I had never inquired further was a failure on my part.

It had been years since she'd spoken to her mother and her siblings. She claimed they'd sided with her ex-husband during the divorce. They felt she was making a mistake and didn't support her decision to leave. The pain this might have caused her is understandable. Still, I imagined a spiritual person such as herself would be open to reconciliation at this point, especially since I'd witnessed their attempts to contact her and how she'd ignore their calls as though they were telemarketers.

One evening after dinner, while I was reading a Carver story on the daybed, a telling thing happened. Suddenly, I felt her above me. She was weeping, trembling. I sat upright, surprised and alert as if I'd missed something. "What?"

"Hold me," she said. I took her onto my lap and stroked her hair, tucking the wayward strands behind her ears as she cried. "I hate myself," she said.

"What are you talking about?"

"I'm selfish. I'm..."

"No," I said, not knowing what to say.

"I cheated," she said. A freeze cut through my gut and just as I was about to rip into her, she said, "That's why my marriage ended. I hurt him. He didn't deserve it."

That she hadn't cheated on me, relief came. "But you said he was terrible."

"Maybe *I* was," she said. "He wanted a family, and I didn't." She settled some, stared blankly at the wall. "In India, I had no past. Everything I saw was new. I felt free. I really believed I wasn't going to come back."

Her confession had changed my impression of her. This new, unsettling information not only made me believe she was untrustworthy, it also connected the dots. Since we'd been cohabitating, I'd noticed a pattern. Every couple of weeks she'd plunge into spells of depression, of which the duration varied. My efforts to liven her up only annoyed her. I began to feel helpless, estranged. You see, there was this other thing I started to pick up on, this sense that as much as we were connected, her deeper dimensions were inaccessible.

6

———

It wasn't until a year in that I'd learned about Charlie, an interior designer Nadia dated before me. One spring afternoon as I was planning to go read in Washington Square Park, my eye caught an unfamiliar book jacket tucked atop a row of my books. *Enchanted Poems*, the title, was laid over a colorful mandala. It was Nadia's book of mystical poems from which she'd read Hafiz and Rumi. As I opened the cover, several pages followed its momentum, but I'd gleaned writing on the title page and flipped back. A handwritten dedication: *Moon, you are the reflection of this Sun's love. Charlie.*

"We dated on and off," she said, the right corner of her lip cinching toward her nostril. She kept her eyes on the plate as she cut her chicken breast, carefully choosing words to explain their "unique relationship." She confessed, "Charlie came with me."

"Came with you where?"

"On my trip." She was referring to the trip she'd taken just before we'd met, the trip she'd spent that entire first night describing. Charlie had accompanied her on half the journey, from Africa to Goa, then they went separate ways. She recalled his parting words, "Go expand your circle."

"What the hell does that mean?"

"I don't know," she said. "He's one of those rich trust fund guys. Can't commit to anything." The logical conclusion was that she wanted more from Charlie, but her love was unrequited.

Fears rushed my mind; I felt disoriented, duped by her and myself. Uncomfortable feelings, hot and cold sensations arose in my center. I breathed, talked myself down, tried to hold fast to my ideal of Nadia. *That was all before you. She's here now.* I didn't want to know any more about her past than I already knew, lest I color it by putting my own experiences and meanings on her.

After a long silence, she admitted, "He recently called but I didn't answer."

"How recent?"

"Last week." *She has secrets?* I was dizzy; the food in my belly felt like freshly poured concrete.

"Do you still love him?"

I regretted asking, even before she said, "I do. But it isn't like that anymore."

I stood from the chair and paced; I had to move, distance myself from her for a moment while I surveyed the new territory we'd entered. She watched as I gulped down my wine, my hand trembling so badly that I nearly dropped the glass. "How could you love him and love me at the same time?"

"It's different," she said. "He's a good person. I love what he's about." She came to me and wrapped her arms around my neck. "Stop," she said. "He never looked at me that way."

Charlie was rich and I was barely making ends meet. He was a "trust fund guy" and I was hardly a writer. I recalled the comment she'd made months earlier, "I'm tired of being poor." Just like I wanted to be spiritual because she was, I now wanted to be rich because Charlie was. And knowing that he had recently called? For days, I was beset by anxiety over my financial situation, but in the end, I committed to remaining the kind of writer I wanted to be. I wouldn't pander to a market, not for a woman, even if she *was* my other half. I would write what came to me and in the way I was meant to write. So how to bridge the gap?

The idea of gaining those extrasensory powers the monks and yogis had, became a tantalizing proposition. If I could harness my concentration, perhaps I could manifest the career I needed to keep my goddess. Again, I returned to the meditations, the visualization practices that I believed were sending my intentions into the infinite sea of atomic energy to attract what I desired. But as it goes, my dedication to this practice was short-lived.

A couple of weeks passed. We were seated on the sidewalk patio of an Italian restaurant in the West Village when this guy walked by with his hands tucked into his pockets and his shoulders pinched in that way reminiscent of James Dean. Because he was stylish and handsome, I thought he must be famous or on the cusp of fame. His glance brushed mine, landed on Nadia. At once, his brooding visage morphed into a smile. He was standing fifteen paces from us, waiting for her to see him as though he was some long-awaited gift.

She caught sight of him, seemed unsure if he was really there or if she was imagining him. Then, all expression fled her face. As he made his approach, her hesitant eyes shot to me.

"Nadia," he said.

"You're back," she said.

"I am." He opened his arms wide to match his smile, then tucked them across his chest and rocked on his heels.

"Charlie," she said, motioning toward me. "This is Victor." His eyes stayed on her.

He said, "You look amazing. I called. Several times." She squirmed, glanced from me to him, to the table, to me, to him, as if trying to figure where her loyalty laid. I clenched my fists beneath the table. "Was that the meatballs?" Nadia had gone on and on about the meatballs, how we had to order them, they were the best. He pointed at the plate with the remnants of spicy gravy and flakes of chopped parsley on its rim. She nodded. Her unease was making me itchy. *For the love of God, spare the girl.* I peered up at Charlie to hint that he was disturbing us, but he continued to ignore me. My toes were curled so tight, I could feel the seams of my sneakers giving. "We should meet for coffee or something," he said. "I'll call you this week," he added, placing a hand on her shoulder, keeping it there until she looked up at him with a crooked grin. "I'll come by the studio." With that, he walked off and didn't even extend me the common decency of a nod. Nadia saw the state I was in.

"I'm sorry," she said. "—Victor!" She made a move to stop me, but I was too swift.

I caught Charlie at the corner of 6th and Bleecker. "Charlie," I barked, waving him over. He came steadily, chin cocked. The arrogance struck me. I stepped toward him, grasped his arm, yanked him so we'd come face to face; I wanted him to see it in my eyes. "You're cute, you, huh?" I said. I could hardly speak. He scoffed, looked down at my hand clenched around his bicep as though I was doing something I'd regret.

"You had your chance," I hissed. "Kick rocks." With a shove, I dismissed him. Manful pride snagged, he lingered, couldn't just walk away. "What? You got something you wanna say?" But as I bounded toward him and it became apparent his hands were about to be full, he desisted and crossed Bleeker. "You fucking fuck," I muttered as I watched him go, fighting the impulse to chase him and unleash what he had summoned.

I returned to Nadia. "What happened?" she asked, fidgeting through the moments it took me to speak.

"You don't have coffee with him. That fucking punk."

"What did you say to him?"

"I told him he had his chance. To stay away."

She seemed disturbed by my anger, but I misread her because a moment later, she was smirking, sucking her cheeks, assessing the claim I'd made on her. "That Aries fire." She took my hand, kissed my knuckles. "I didn't answer his calls, right? Let it go."

When we returned home, I went at her like a man sprung from a twenty-year prison bid; I had something to prove. But once she'd fallen asleep, my mind went into overdrive. *How did Charlie know she was working at the studio?* I kept imagining her and Charlie in sexual scenarios doing the things we did. Then Miles.

The following night I'd been unexpectedly cut from my bartending shift at De Sade. When I entered the apartment, I found Nadia curled up on our bed, sobbing. Lying next to her was the book, *Enchanted Poems*. I don't know why, but I just backed out of the apartment, shut the door, and sat in the stairwell beneath the window. Here was the hallway I'd been traversing for years and only now did I notice the scuffs on the wall, the crack in the stairwell window. *She'd said she still loved him.* I shuddered. I was afraid. Twenty minutes must have passed when finally, the door creaked open and her head popped out. She tip-toed down to where

I sat, wrapped my arm around her, and leaned her head on my shoulder. "Thank you for understanding," she said. But I didn't understand anything.

Not long after, Nadia went into one of her spells. For four days straight, she called in sick to work at the design studio, and on the fifth day, she quit. As I sat by and watched her numbly relinquish her responsibilities, I couldn't help but feel Charlie's reemergence was responsible. Even if she hadn't answered his calls, he was still inhabiting her heart. Regretfully, I understood the control I thought I'd gained when she moved in with me was an illusion. Not only was her interior world a threat to my happiness, the city itself was. Yes, the city that never sleeps, with its Darwinian ethics and its maddening, dizzying pace that sucks one out from within and disquiets the heart with insatiable confusion one mistakes for her own.

BY THAT TIME, discussions about the future had turned the pronouns "I" and "me" into "us" and "we." Nadia began hinting that she wanted us to marry. My hesitation was wrongly received. I had no doubts about my feelings for her; I'd been envisioning the country house with the porch, the flower and herb gardens, and our dark-haired beauty Ines— the name she chose if we had a daughter—running around on the lawn. I've failed to mention that we never used contraception, which for me was more irresponsible than it was uncommon, but she had assured me pregnancy was not a concern. She was convinced that undiagnosed endometriosis was the cause of her painful periods. "No!" she'd declare if I tried to extract myself and cling to me like a marsupial until my body went limp.

"Outside of writing," I said, "I give you my undivided attention, but there are times when you're not fully here." I let that settle, then spoke what I'd been thinking for some time. "Maybe you should see someone."

She dropped the kimono she was folding and spun to face me with wrathful eyes. "What? Like a psychiatrist?"

"Or a therapist," I said. "Just to talk—"

"So they could put me on anti-depressants?"

"No. To gain perspective."

"It's too heavy," she said. "And don't put this on me. What about you? How are we going to have a future if you refuse to get a real job? You need a career. How do you expect to support a family?"

"I don't have a family," I said.

"Don't we want one?"

Now she was challenging my career choice, calling it unsuitable for its ability to support a family? Was it that or was she tired of being poor? Did she expect me to shrug off my calling to support the lifestyle she wanted? True, it was difficult to claim writing as a career at that point. If a story I wrote was accepted and published by chance, as infrequently as it happened, the compensation was like gift money—welcomed but never enough. But the hypothetical family? I thought to use her endometriosis as a rebuttal, say something like, *What family are we going to have if you can't conceive?* Good thing I didn't.

7
———

A rainy, autumn day. She was sitting on the daybed weathering my silence, obsessing over a wrinkle in her jeans, trying to run it smooth with her fingers. I stood across from her, again in unfamiliar territory. Finally, she said, "I don't need a big wedding. I already had that."

"I haven't," I said. It wasn't that I wanted a big wedding, it was what she had just revealed and what it meant for me that had me questioning things. I sat beside her, took her hand. "Are you absolutely certain?"

She nodded. "We could just go to city hall." Two things were being presented and discussed, a baby and marriage, though I wasn't sure one required the other.

I exhaled and crossed to the window, which screeched as I threw it up. The racket of the downpour outside spilled into the room. I lit a cigarette and became aware of it for the first time: the idea of what I believed I wanted, and the reality of what it required from me, were meeting. Since she had come along, I'd wanted nothing more than to have her, yet now that circumstances were forcing me to commit, I wasn't sure I was prepared to make the necessary sacrifice to support a family by settling into a career in something I had no interest in. But who was I kidding? There on the desk, my computer screen displayed a fresh rejection email for a story I'd submitted to a half-rate literary magazine. And there, she sat, wiping her eyes, two months pregnant, turning the turquoise ring round her finger.

I stamped out my cigarette and returned to the daybed. "Are you ready for this?" I asked. "I mean, in your heart?" She touched her belly, looked at me, nodded. "All right," I said. She searched my eyes to gauge my concession, see if it contradicted what I felt inside. When she'd concluded I was sincere, her chest heaved as with a swell of relief, and she threw her arms around me.

All that month I was tense, preoccupied, unable to concentrate enough to write. *Had she deceived me?* She'd said she couldn't get pregnant. But each time she'd enter the apartment after we'd been apart for a while, say after work or when she'd return from some random errand and I'd see her face, knowing my child was growing inside her, I'd soften. I'd defer to the photographs on the jetty, the time we watched *The Seventh Seal*, the proofs of our cosmic love. I suppose, when having a child becomes a reality, fear strikes men and women alike, forces them to reassess their values and goals. To do it right means sacrifice. The self must be surmounted.

Nadia had been ponderous, also. I imagined she was going through what I was going through. I didn't know the pregnancy had become troublesome, that she was hiding the stabbing pains for which she secretly visited the doctor until the night I awoke and found her on the toilet, keeled over, white in the face. Through the space between her legs, the water in the bowl was a muted pink then crimson and nearly black around a sunken, gelatinous glob with streaming tentacles. The veins in her temples swelled as she moaned, "I told you." At the hospital, the doctor confirmed endometriosis had caused the miscarriage. She glared at me, said, "You're off the hook, huh?"

IT WAS THE FIFTH YEAR, and we were still living in the 10th Street studio. Nadia called to say that she was coming home with company. Making her way east from a job interview at a chic hotel in Soho, she had come across her friend Kim, the one with the yoga studio, who happened to be in the company of Navid, a famed spiritual healer. At five foot eleven inches, with platinum blonde hair and sapphire blue eyes, Kim amassed a small fortune modeling, a career she'd given up once she got serious about her yoga practice. She used the modeling money to open the yoga studio and whenever Navid came to town, she hosted his seminars.

They arrived. Nadia radiated excitement such as I had not seen in a long time. She grasped my hand and held it tightly as she presented Navid, who piously nodded as he crossed the threshold, Kim in tow. He appeared to be in his mid-sixties, Arabic, not fit nor out of shape, with medium-length hair, curly and black as freshly paved asphalt. He was wearing a plain, yellow t-shirt like one finds at dollar stores, acid-washed denim jeans, and old Nike running shoes. What was remarkable in his appearance were his penetrating, cobalt eyes garlanded by long, black lashes that intensified their color.

I offered Navid a chair, and once he sat, he said, "Will you please fill a bowl with water?" He held out his hands to estimate the proportions of the bowl he required. He added,

"Not clear glass. Something other." I pulled our glazed ceramic salad bowl and showed it to him. He smiled, said, "A plate and a dishtowel, please." While I filled the bowl with tap water, he surveyed the pictures on the walls, the books on the shelves, the patterns on the Indian silk pillows. I placed bowl on the table, along with the plate and the dishtowel he requested.

He motioned for Nadia, who was sitting on the sofa fidgeting with Kim's hand, to sit in the chair across from him at the table. I joined Kim on the sofa as Navid removed an ordinary deck of playing cards from his knapsack and adroitly shuffled them; the economy of his movements, or his stillness rather, was captivating. When satisfied with his shuffle, his seer's eyes found an anxious Nadia. He began by asking her questions about why she wanted the healing, and suddenly my opinionated girlfriend was lost for words. He relieved her attempt to explain with a gesture that made it seem he understood, not to worry. I don't remember how he used the deck of playing cards—what happened after the cards overshadows all that came before—but they served some purpose, something with numbers that had spiritual significance in her life.

"I am going to ask my spiritual adviser to assist me," he said and waited for her to nod. He closed his eyes, raised his hand in the air without any pretense and mumbled in a language I couldn't quite make. Nadia watched closely, we all did, as he repeated the strange words, eyes sealed, torso rocking. After a few moments, he grew still. "The scar on your hip," he said, "from the concrete."

Nadia's face reddened, she drew back in the chair. Apprehension gave way to a stiff nod as if she was suddenly questioning what she'd gotten herself into. "I fell off my bicycle," she said. "I had to get stitches." I noticed her hand caressing her hip; I knew of the scar there beneath her jeans.

"Yes," Navid said, "but there is more. Stay with the concrete." Nadia looked at me. Not even her ex-husband knew the story, but I did. I felt Kim's stare begging for an explanation, but I ignored her and gave the slightest nod to urge Nadia along.

Her voice came low, tremulous, "My father planted fig trees, a flower garden, and grass. After he died and my mother remarried, my stepfather tore it all up. He put concrete everywhere."

Navid's eyes opened. He smiled. That was what he wanted. "It's okay," he said. "We will take that pain now."

He instructed Nadia to sit on the floor, placed the bowl of water before her, and covered the bowl with the plate, then wrapped the dishtowel over both. He sat across from her, the bowl between them, and told her to lay her hands atop the covered plate. He spread the thin, dark fingers of one hand, laid it atop hers and raised his other hand into the air, again calling to his spiritual adviser. Now as he chanted incantations that echoed off the brick walls, his voice quavered like a Native American medicine man invoking spirits and his raised hand rattled and shook in the air. Nadia, eyes closed, looked uncomfortable; her breathing was labored, she was vibrating with emotion, rocking as if entranced. Navid's chanting persisted, and then he was motioning, throwing his hand down from the air as if to douse her with some invisible liquid. "Shake the bowl," he commanded, and she did, gently at first, but as his voice pitched higher, her body twitched and she shook it more vigorously. Suddenly, Navid's voice completely changed; he seemed to be channeling some entity—his spiritual adviser? The authenticity of what I was witnessing had me riveted; I felt the intense excitement of being privy to this foreign ritual, recognizing how when I woke that morning, I had no inkling as to what lay in the day ahead.

Eyelids squished and sealed by wet lashes, Nadia released sighs, groaned as she shook the bowl. Now water spilled over the sides of the bowl—dirty water. I'd filled that bowl from the tap. Kim clenched my wrist as I leaned closer to be sure of what I was seeing. Indeed, the water was brown, murky; as the spillage seeped into the dishtowel, it left a residue of silt on the fabric.

Abruptly, Navid's voice cut. Only Nadia's whimpering was heard. Slowly, she came back; it was like she was waking from a deep sleep. Navid's cobalt eyes opened, and it was as if he was also returning from some lapse of presence. He regained himself, said, "Take away the plate." She used the back of her hands to wipe tears and perspiration from her cheeks, then noticed the dirt stains on the towel. Our equally astonished eyes met. She removed the towel, the plate, and there in the bowl, floating in murky water, were leaves, twigs, and flower petals. Navid sunk his hand to the bottom of the bowl, lifted his wet fist out of the water, and unraveled his fingers to show Nadia the dirt and pebbles sifting through his whitish palm. "Now you are free." Everything I believed I knew about life stood in contradiction; I had witnessed actual magic.

That night, Nadia and I laid awake in bed, trying to figure out how leaves, twigs, and flower petals appeared in the bowl. Navid had explained that the twigs, leaves, and dirt were the manifested thought-forms connecting her to her past traumas. That during the healing, with the help of his spiritual adviser, the thought-forms had been reawakened by her emotions and purged from her subconscious mind, so that they no longer had power over her.

She turned to me, eyes bright with understanding. "I'd always felt betrayed, you know. By my father dying. By my mother, who said we needed my stepfather. When she sided with my ex during the divorce." She exhaled, looked into my eyes as with pity. "I'm sorry I've been, I don't know. Difficult," she said. "It will be better with us now. I feel it."

For a week straight, she had an ethereal glow, was present, more engaged, and her laughter was genuine, full. I'd swear, all that week I saw traces of her movements in the air, fine lines and soft angles, as if she were making movement a Cubist medium. The healing ritual, the plausibility of what I'd witnessed, left me dedicated to figuring out how Navid did what he did. I spent all my free time researching and pondering what I'd read about unseen energies and siddhis, only to concede that I had truly witnessed something supernatural—at least in the efficacy of the healing. It *was* magic. But who was this spiritual adviser he'd invoked? Invocable spirits?

Before Navid left town, Nadia arranged a healing for Virginie, her wealthy French friend who had recently lost a daughter to opioid addiction. Since the funeral, Virginie had been tearing through Reiki practitioners and bioenergy healers, desperate to release the pain. She visited medium after medium, bent on finding one who could contact her daughter's spirit.

On the day, Nadia accompanied Virginie to Kim's studio, where the healing took place. I was home writing, fruitlessly trying to flush out an idea that didn't want to fit the short story or novel form. All I had was the monologue of a woman railing about mendacity in a sort of chiaroscuro lighting. When Nadia returned, she entered quietly, walked right to the sofa, sat, clasped her hands, and stared at them.

"What?" I asked.

She looked up, her lips tensed and turned under. "He puts something in the bowl. Slips it in when he covers it with the plate and the towel." Her face looked severe. "He saw me see him do it. A little pouch. It must be stuffed with the dirt and leaves. It dissolves in the water." I sat beside her, and soon the weight of her head on my shoulder, as if the thought-forms she believed were purged had jumped back into her skull, felt enormous and somehow transmitted the totality of her defeat. "But how did he know about my stepfather?"

Navid had specified, "Not clear glass. Something other." And I gave him the glazed ceramic salad bowl. He was the one who placed the plate over the bowl, then wrapped both in the dish towel, which would have been the moment he slipped the pouch into the water. A sleight of hand, a simple magic trick? What about the chants? His spiritual adviser? How he knew things about Nadia he couldn't possibly have known?

Later that evening, after navigating my disappointment —I wanted to believe in Navid's magic and was reluctant to accept it as mere trickery—something occurred to me: the healing was successful nonetheless, wasn't it? By granting Navid the power to heal, Nadia believed she had finally released childhood traumas; that is until she saw him slip the pouch into the bowl during Virginie's healing. The playing cards, the bowl, the ritualistic antics, the chanting— just tools of the trade meant to establish his authority. I suspected he knew the power of the healing was in Nadia's willingness to believe. The placebo effect. Belief is the key. Sustained belief. Suddenly, what I'd only vaguely under- stood in the propagations of the gurus matured: all is mind.

I sometimes wonder if Nadia would've completely over- come her sorrows had she not attempted to help Virginie with hers. The experience with Navid left her altogether dismayed, and just like that, she dropped her yoga practice and with it, any inclination toward serenity. Dust settled on the covers of her spiritual books. God forbid I were to mention them or try to find the light in it all; she'd lash out and remind me that I was a hypocrite because she turned me on to it all and if I believed in any of it, I wouldn't still be jealous and crazy, especially when old men looked at her. "Don't kid yourself. They want to fuck you, too."

As for me, the Navid experience turned my sights to the study of mind mastery, but not for spiritual purposes. I was seeking self-dominance; if I could control my mind and thereby my emotions, jealousy, rage, and my other flaws would no longer disrupt me. Perhaps I could summon belief in myself as a successful writer and thereby earn the kind of money that would set Nadia at ease about our future. The only problem was that in all I'd read, the emphasis of a spiritual director, a guide, was essential to progress. Where does one find such a spiritual director? Well, it is also said that when the pupil is ready, the teacher appears.

LATER THAT YEAR, a bedbug infestation forced us to abandon my cherished 10th Street studio. I wasn't aware bedbugs were such a nuisance. Not only do these pesky bloodsuckers reproduce at an insane rate, a process known as traumatic insemination because the horny male will penetrate the female's shell to inject her with sperm, but they can also survive nearly one year without feeding. When they bite you, they inject an anticoagulant and an anesthetic; the first keeps you bleeding for the feed, the second prevents you from feeling their bite and knowing you're being preyed upon. As I understood it, once a building is infested, it's quite difficult, nearly impossible, to get rid of them. I wasn't prepared to move from my studio, but Nadia seized the opportunity and quickly set up viewings for new apartments. On the first day, she fell in love with a one-bedroom on Hester Street. It had its charms: original mahogany shutters and high ceilings that made the living space seem larger than it was. Despite the five hundred dollar rent increase, we took the apartment.

Change never came easy to me. The gurus talked about change, or impermanence rather, as the one certainty in life; everything changes for better or worse, and there is nothing that can be done about it. We have but two choices, accept or reject. This supposition antagonized me, and while I recognized its truth, I was unwilling to accept it. My resistance hovered in the vague understanding that impermanence is the threat to the illusion of happiness, which relies upon stasis. My half-understood notions about man and his relation to what is seen and unseen had me using generalized terms like "the universe" and "karma" to explain the undesired shifts in life, such as having to move because of a bedbug infestation. As I said goodbye to my magic writing studio, I tried to reconcile my resistance, repeating over and over, "Change is good," bent on believing. Belief is the key. What I failed to even consider was that perhaps the unwanted change was a result of the intentioned meditations I had been practicing.

8

———

It is true when they say with loss something new is gained. In this instance, it was a friend, Frankie Galante, proprietor of Frankie Yaki, the sushi restaurant on the ground floor of our new building on Hester Street. Could I ever forget the wrinkled smile on Frankie's lean face, how it curled that dyed mustache, or the strange comportment of his thin, recessed hair that somehow seemed suited to the timbre of his wild laughter? The night we met, he'd invited us to join him for "teatime." The conversation, induced by the familiar experience and cultural bindings of New York Italians, went on for hours and cost Frankie a bottle of top-shelf scotch. Thereafter, invites for teatime at Frankie Yaki had us mingling with all sorts of interesting neighborhood characters—artists, gallery owners, knockaround guys—as they wandered in for evening cocktails with Frankie, a true bon vivant. When spring arrived and the sidewalks became a fanfare, Frankie pulled tables together and seated us by the retractable windows that made Frankie Yaki feel like an open-air café on the Mediterranean. We were so engaged in our new reality, belonging to a neighborhood, I could never have seen what was coming.

Halvor Grimstad was a theater director I met one evening at a Frankie Yaki teatime. The handsome Norwegian had searing blue eyes and striking Scandinavian features. Tufts of whitish-blond hair poked from the sides of his navy sailor's hat, which was embroidered with gold piping. His outfits never failed to include some eccentricity, such as an ascot or pearly redshank buttons on a black corduroy coat. The night we met, Halvor and I discussed the classical plays and why he had no interest in directing them. "If I were to place a perfectly preserved phonograph in front of a millennial, or one of the Z Generation," he said, "the appreciation for it could never match that of one who grew up on vinyl, getting lost in the record jackets, the imagery of the covers. But to my point, and this is perhaps the greatest tragedy of all, the language of the classical plays creates a psychological distance between playwright and audience. Today we're aware of the flaws in language, in communication. We've given up on words. We have emojis."

"What about Shepherd?" I asked. "Shanley?"

"I'm looking for something original," he said, "about life now. Besides, doesn't all that seem sort of archaic? The world has drastically changed in the past twenty years—technology, politics, democracy. Of course, survival, love, fear, pride, and so on are at the root of everything. This will never change. But the means to those things change. For instance, love is not found in the same way it was thirty years ago. Nor is it even thought of in the same way." He shrugged, looked over the thigh of his crossed leg, pulled a piece of lint from his wool trousers. "Who even knows how to love?" He smirked, sipped his scotch. "I had a woman in Bergen. Katarina. I believed I loved her. I thought we'd marry. Then one day, I became aware of a trait of hers—she held her chin whenever she was making a decision. It's wrong to say I'd only become aware of it then, but it struck me that day like a revelation. I hated that she did that. It somehow made her seem manly. Such a small, irrelevant thing, yet my attraction to her beauty and intelligence suffered greatly and I was forced to admit that what I called love was not love. True love has no conditions. If I truly loved her, perhaps that trait would have been endearing."

This was after I'd surprised him. Earlier in the conversation, when he'd asked what I write, not hiding his assumption that I was genre chasing because I was an American, I expressed my desire to master the craft of fiction. I made it clear I was not writing to sell pieces or pander to market trends. He asked what writers I revered. "Hamsun is my favorite," I said.

He narrowed his brows and a smile slowly formed as though I was pulling his leg; Knut Hamsun was Norway's most renown, albeit controversial writer. "Knut? Really? What have you read?"

"All of it," I said, and from that moment on, it was as though we were equals.

Halvor explained that he saw human existence as a struggle between order and chaos, the Apollonian versus the Dionysian, both of which served the cause. Both were necessary to bring about individual fulfilment and societal advancement. The problem was that society in general seemed polarized, choosing one camp while denying the other its rights. The changes that were happening in the world, the motivations behind them and the direction they'd taken, made him wary.

"Mankind in its breadth is in a mid-life crisis." He lambasted modern technology, which he said posed great challenges for the coming generations, such as the need to maintain suitable employment in the face of increasing technological automation. "We have god power now but it's being wielded by beasts. We're an anxious species whose actions most always further our own causes. Growing up in Norway, it was different. We had an understanding of collective power. Of fairness. We took pride in our heritage. But that's changed. Oil has made us rich. We've been invaded by the internet, and I hate to say it, the mindless consumerism of a capitalist society. Everything is about money. More and more, importance is being placed on the wrong things. And look what technology has done—enhanced our narcissism. Robbed us of autonomy." He swiped his cell phone and held it up to make his point, to accuse it of the charges he'd just inveighed. "Right now in Norway, there's this trend among the women, this thickened eyebrow craze—it's really quite absurd. It came from some esthetician's Instagram feed. What's funny, we worry about artificial intelligence taking over humanity." He waved his phone again. "We're already part machine. Hostage to an advanced calculator. And it's because we are told what to believe. Who has an original thought anymore?"

But it wasn't all doom and gloom; Halvor believed art had the potential to redeem humanity, theater especially, which grew out of the ritual honoring of Dionysus, god of fertility and religious ecstasy. In one form or another, the Greek tragedies represent the suffering god, who is sacrificed and reincarnated so that mankind may come into existence. Due to some inborn flaw, the tragic character fails to submit to the will of the gods, goes against nature, and pays the price. "Suffering is necessary. Death is for resurrection. And isn't that what good theater does? Metaphorically. It's a beautiful idea, but who thinks of theater in such a transformative way besides those dedicated to the theater?

"There is no cohesive metaphysical reality today. Classical mythology, that model of the universe, seems archaic to us. Religions have failed—well, Catholicism. At least in the Western world." He exhaled, at a loss for words, vanquished by all he understood and what now seemed pointless to try and communicate. Nevertheless, he was determined. "The radicalization of Islam, the crimes against the innocent women and children, are abhorrent. I can understand their rejection of the material values of the West, but the violence annuls any claim to righteousness. So where do we turn for spiritual nurturing?" His question wasn't rhetorical. Now I was at a loss. I shrugged. "India. Tibet. The East has become the place of pilgrimage. In the East, spirit is inseparable from life. But for us, a Norwegian and an American, to go there searching is useless. We must find our teacher in the life we live. No need to go into seclusion or travel across the world. The greatest distance one must travel is from his mind to his heart." He paused to drink his scotch. His thin fingers walked the table to his pack of Nat Sherman's, flicked the top back, and withdrew a cigarette.

"Halvor, I'm not challenging you, but isn't everything you just said a perfect reason to direct the classic plays?"

"Vic, we must recreate the myth in our art. Out of the world we are in now. Tell me, what's your lineage?"

"Scottish, Greek, and Italian. My father's all Italian, my mother is Italian, Greek, and Scottish, but both are Italian by way of Rome."

He nodded, his eyes narrowed in assessment. "More the Greek than the Roman."

"My ancestors spent much time in bathhouses, no doubt." He laughed at my joke, but the great difference he was quite sharp in pointing out was that the Roman wanted to conquer the world, whereas the Greek, a philosopher at heart, only wanted to conquer himself.

"In ancient Greece, self-knowledge was the purpose of life. A man was measured, not by his fortune, but by how much his character had evolved throughout his lifetime."

"That seems right," I said. "But don't get me wrong. I wish I could write things that would make me rich."

He threw up a hand to silence me. "Save you the curse."

At one point in the conversation, something quite extraordinary happened. The story I was long ago wrestling with, which I had completely forgotten about, the one I mentioned earlier with the woman's monologue about mendacity that didn't seem to fit the short story or novel form, came to mind. I saw it now clear as day, the woman lit in chiaroscuro—she was in stage lights. The idea was always meant to be written as a play. However, writing a play had never occurred to me, and I'm quite sure I'd never have written one if I'd not met Halvor.

NADIA WAS fast asleep when I'd gotten home. On tiptoes, I eased the bedroom door closed, lit my special incense, prepared my special green tea, placed my cigarettes by the computer, and went to work. Two weeks later, I had a rough draft of my first play, *Nigredo*. The title came from research I'd done after my conversation with Halvor. I was drunk by the time he mentioned alchemy, but I remembered him referring to it as the "sacred science."

"Alchemy? As in the quest to turn lead into gold?"

He smiled. "The lead is the flesh, the matter. The gold is the spirit within. Under the rule of the Catholic church, alchemists were considered heretics and sorcerers. They had to hide the true meaning of their spiritual practice."

Curiosity is the gateway.

The ancient tradition of alchemy, believed to have originated in Egypt, had exoteric and esoteric implementations. While the exoteric, the precursor to chemistry and the physical sciences, was indeed concerned with metallurgy and transforming base metals (lead) into the noblest metal (gold), the esoteric was concerned with the transmutation, purification, and perfection of the human soul. The alchemical process, known as The Great Work, had four general stages: nigredo, albedo, citrinitas, and rubedo. The first stage, the nigredo, introduces the base material—the leaden ego's inferior nature—to the fire for the blackening or putrefaction that prepares it for the next level of refinement. Essentially, as I understood it, The Great Work fuses the material state of being with its state of conscious awareness to create a third state, which is the awakened, spiritual, or Christ consciousness. But the wary few who succeeded in this most difficult and obscure practice found it necessary to hide the secrets of their success from the profane, fearing they would use it for selfish intent. They devised a language of symbols and enigmatic texts that were only decipherable by other hierophants, those who purified themselves of their inferior natures. Yes, there had been many charlatans who put themselves forth as alchemists claiming the ability to turn lead into gold, but the true secrets, as I later learned, are self-protected; what is impure can never touch the absolute.

This revelation about the true nature of alchemy intrigued me, sent me down the rabbit hole. Carl Jung's fascination with alchemical symbolism, which he saw reflected in the archetypes of the collective unconscious, resulted in his correlating the stages of The Great Work to the psychological process of individuation. In this framework, the nigredo represented the psychological state of disorientation known as the "dark night of the soul," when shadow aspects in the subconscious attacked the ego-based consciousness. It was an ideal analogy for my play; the central problem surrounds a glib, wealthy woman's psychological disorientation after learning of the unethical means behind her family's fortune. Hence the title, *Nigredo*.

In the world I grew up in, such things were unheard of; life was mired in the material plane, earning a living, and enjoying the fruits of one's labor. Since the arrival of Nadia, I had opened myself to reassessing my perspectives on spiritual matters, but this process had gradually shifted from the idea of an external divinity, inward to the fount of true power. Was there any truth to The Great Work and what it promised? Was alchemy, a system presented in different terminology, akin to that of the Buddhist monks who obtained extrasensory powers? Was this the secret way to mind mastery?

"Oh, please," Nadia said. I was telling her about alchemy and The Great Work, something that, prior to Navid, would've interested her. "You? The way you are? You're going to become some spiritual master now?"

"What do you mean, the way I am?"

"Exactly," she said. The conversation ended there. Perhaps I was trying to reinvigorate her interest, remind her of how she had brought me back to the fold. Instead, I was left wondering what she'd meant. *Exactly?* But I knew: I lacked the self-awareness required for such an undertaking.

I wrote like a fiend to finish *Nigredo* and ignored all the discoveries I'd made about myself in the process of writing about a person living blindly. After all, I had to write; I couldn't entertain disruptions.

"What have you been working on?" Nadia asked.

"I'm writing a play about—"

She threw her hands up in exasperation. "Now you're a playwright? How do you know how to write a play?"

My gut burned. My meditations had me simmering with the desire for *Nigredo* to exceed all expectations so that I could be vindicated from Nadia's condemnations of my writing pursuit.

Halvor read the first draft, then urged me to get more specific about what I wanted to say. "And then don't actually say it." This meant I could no longer ignore the discoveries I'd made about myself. Who was I beneath the self-image I'd constructed for the world? I had no discipline over my bodily drives—I gave in to all my desires whenever they arose without the thought of refusing them. The contradictions between my words and actions, my thoughts and beliefs, were staggering. Not only was I not in control, I was also completely unaware of what needed to be controlled. This line of self-examination opened me to dark discomforts.

It was no coincidence that the very next day, while Nadia and I were shopping at the food store, we came across Miles. I hadn't seen him in years, since the night I punched him. With the sight of him, I piqued like a lion. We glared at each other across the produce aisle. He'd gained weight and those pale blue eyes had saggy bags and streaks of discoloring like rust stains beneath them. He looked to Nadia, who pretended she didn't see him, then turned down an aisle. Just something about him being in the same world as us made me sick. Us? Yes, like the sky is inseparable from light, it seemed impossible to think of myself and not have Nadia appear.

Later that afternoon, in a moment of clarity, I saw myself as Miles might've seen me, my tough guy self-image. Punching him had nothing to do with his stealing, did it? And he didn't look well; he looked as if he had fallen into decline. By the time I went to bed, I felt terrible regret for assaulting him and wished it had never happened. Wasn't it true? The tough guy was what I gave to the world as if to appear strong, the mask to hide my true vulnerability and fear, to cover my extraordinary sensitivity and my inability to accept life as it was with all its impermanence. Those dark discomforts raised by my self-examination began shaking the tree, and as the leaves fell, I jumped to catch them lest they pile up and cover the green grass beneath my feet.

Three weeks passed. I wrote, revised, and wrote more. I returned with what Halvor agreed was an improved draft. A few phone calls and a handful of emails later, and he'd arranged a group of actors to read what was written, which, as he explained, would change once the actors gave it life. "Be open." The play reading was to be held at The Independent on 8th Street, a small black box theater hidden in the alley behind Electric Lady Land Studios. It was there I met Luciana "Luce" Merola.

9

———

On the day of the reading, Luce, who was cast in the lead role, arrived late. The other actors and Halvor were drinking coffee and discussing a recent theater production they'd all seen. I was seated in the back row of the theater, anxiously cracking my knuckles when the door swung open in a quick burst. All heads turned to the doorway where Luce stood in suspended momentum, clearly questioning if she was in the right place. Through squinting eyes, she searched the faces and when she made Halvor's among them, she threw her arms into the air and embraced him.

I'd watched episodes of her critically acclaimed television series, but her onscreen presence hadn't impressed me. That changed the moment Halvor introduced us. She had wild, kinky black hair and eyes the same color, undeniable eyes streaming what I can only describe as the current of life. Shaped like a '50s pinup girl, her allure was that of the old-world Italian peasant women rooted to the earth. It's fair to say she was rounding out her forties, yet there was not one line in her Sicilian skin. I watched her move around the room, introducing herself to the other actors without any pretense; to one, a young actress, she said, "Love that scarf. Oh, it's so pretty."

I won't get into the details of the first reading—the draft needed work—but after, Luce had pulled Halvor aside. "I want to put this up," she said. Halvor later confessed that by asking Luce to read, he'd hoped for that exact outcome. Her name made it possible to get funded. Though her unmistakable Italian looks and her New York accent had been used by casting directors to typecast her in the sort of role she played on her TV series, he saw her depth, had no doubts about her range. Rehearsals began two weeks later.

Evenings following rehearsals, I'd give Nadia progress reports. She didn't seem to grasp the importance of this new venture. "What's Luce like?"

"Invested," I said. "She says it's in the theater an actor works on her art."

"Well, TV pays her bills," she said. "She can afford her art." She yawned and sent a wary glance to the dirty pots and pans filling the sink.

Writing is a solitary endeavor, as is the fruit of the labor; fiction is meant to be read, and reading is also a solitary endeavor. A play, on the other hand, is meant to be performed before an audience and, while each audience member has a subjective experience of the play, what can be considered solitary, theater in essence is a social endeavor. This aspect brought me out of a solitary creative process into a communal one of discussions and debates with a director and trained actors, who forced me to clarify the intentions behind my work.

I was unused to this sort of specificity. At first, I pushed back. My creative process couldn't be articulated, why I felt strongly about giving a character one action over another, one line of dialogue, so on and so forth. Who is as specific in life? I wrote like a jazz musician plays, improvising, searching, trusting what felt right—the way I lived life. I was never one who could outline and plan too far ahead. Again, I cite Mercury in my 8th house. I was specific about the story world, characters, and conflicts, which came to mind dynamic and charged and were usually the impetus for setting out to write. The rest—how it begins and ends—were general ideas, loose and subject to change. Often, the planned beginnings and endings were adjusted as the ideas matured and became more solidified. I had one rule: every story must end with a sense of meaning that earns the audience's satisfaction.

"You're giving us ideals," Halvor said after reading my new draft. "We want reality."

"What about the myths?" I said. "They inform reality like consequence."

"Reality is consequence," he said. He urged me to allow his critiques to elevate my craft. "Feedback, especially the negative, will not only show you who you are as a writer but as a human being. Use it to stretch toward your potential." His words created a storm in my mind. There was a layer of seeing I was somehow missing, not only in my play but in life.

"So, how's the rewrite coming?" Nadia was smoking by the window.

"It's hard," I said.

"I don't know where you get off thinking you could just write a play."

"Well, I'm figuring it out."

"Your life, man. It's like gambling and needing the win." As I considered this, my heartbeat quickened. I was watching her smoke; she turned, looked me up and down, hissed: "What?" The contempt in her eyes was chilling.

"What happened to the spiritual girl who shunned material things and spoke about God, chakras, and ancient temples?"

"You smothered her."

"*I* smothered? You were smothered before I even came along."

She scoffed. "You're not crazy? I walk on eggshells in public. God forbid someone looks at me. You're a madman like that—" she tried to snap her fingers but didn't quite get the sound.

"That Aries fire, right? What happened? You don't like it anymore?"

"It's ridiculous."

"You want some guy who doesn't give a shit? That it? Like trust fund Charlie who comes and goes as he pleases?"

She crossed her arms and stared down into the courtyard. "I don't know what I want."

"Well, maybe you should figure it out instead of blaming me for your shit."

"My shit?"

"You're unhappy because you're clueless about what to do with your life and you resent me because I found something I love. Sorry it hasn't made me rich."

"Don't fucking psychoanalyze me."

As if the battle with my own negativity and the inner earthquakes of self-discovery weren't enough. Nevertheless, I incorporated the useful feedback that came out of rehearsals and rewrote the play. Still unsure as to whether I'd pulled it off, my consolation was in knowing that I'd entered the challenge and gone to the peak of my ability; the rewrite was the best writing I had done up to that point in my life. Halvor read the new draft on the spot. After the last page, he laid the script aside, pulled back the brim of his sailor's cap, and ran his hand across his forehead. "Theme appears like God appears to the faithful."

"Do we have a play?"

"It pops—*denial leads to suffering*," he said. "Yes, we have an honest play." He was proud of me. "Adversity is your friend." At that moment, I knew my life had changed.

MY FRIENDSHIP with Luce was automatic. It was as if we'd been childhood friends who'd just picked up where we'd left off. Most nights after rehearsals, as going home to Nadia's negativity became less appealing, Luce took me to the quiet bars on the west side, which she chose for their specialty cocktails. I was surprised to learn that she hadn't completed high school; even though she lacked formal education, life experiences had instilled a keen emotional intelligence. We'd sit in dimly lit leather booths and explore the big ideas she was curious about, like whether art imitates life or life imitates art. During these discussions, she weighed my views with genuine interest while seemingly seeking a new level of clarity within herself; she'd listen, digest, respond with utter openness.

Small talk and gossip didn't appeal to her, but we did share stories about our lives. She married young, was divorced by twenty-four, and since, hadn't had a serious relationship. "Can't even remember my last." She confessed that she'd not been dating. I found it hard to believe. I'd suspected her and Halvor had a thing; they'd show up together to the theater, reinvigorated, chugging coffee, sending glances that prompted laughter only one in the know could join. "It's like he sees my soul," she said. "I trust him."

Of her work, Halvor remarked, "It's flawed only in its unparalleled rawness. Humanity without compromise. But sometime the stronger choice is to withhold, let it simmer."

Of course, this came as no surprise; Luce was this way in life. "Acting is living. There's no separation."

I was impressed by her approach to acting, her commitment to the rehearsal process, the character, and the manner she employed when the careful, artistic-choice debates arose. She unpacked her motivations with confidence, spoke freely, not over anyone, just impulsively, and at times with a sort of childlike innocence, while in others that loud, commanding voice somehow seemed to compensate for her poor eyesight. I found it comical when she mispronounced words or misused others. "For all *intense* and purposes, my character is *libel* to go crazy if she doesn't accept the truth about her family." She always managed to come close enough to communicate her point. Much later, this aspect of Luce became a source of my embarrassment. I'd always given too much power to the opinions of others.

You see, there were two Luces. One was professional and constant; the other was unabashed and flighty. In restaurants, any public place really, she'd ask questions with obvious and readily apparent answers that, had she taken a moment to consider, she wouldn't have asked. Once, we were at an art show in Beverly Hills with Picasso ceramics and Max Ernst paintings on display, and she yelled to me across the crowded gallery, "Look, an Earnest!" drawing glances from all the highbrow connoisseurs. She was a recognizable actress, after all. I cringed. "What do you care? Screw them." She found my embarrassment hysterical. "So serious."

Then came the test. Halvor had arranged a staged reading of the play for potential producers. The actors were seated in chairs on the stage with Luce in the center. They read the entire play for an audience of five; the four producers Halvor had invited, and yours truly. The reading flew by. I remember feeling that the play underwhelms. I also remember thinking, *Who are you to write a play? Mister tough guy.* After the reading, strung by insecurity, I lingered at a distance as Halvor conversed with the producers. Once they'd left, Halvor said, "Well...wasn't the response I'd hoped for, but we didn't get an outright no, so..."

THE FOLLOWING evening at The Coffee Shop in Union Square, Halvor sat in that false, moody light cutting an undercooked egg white omelet. His sailor's cap was on the seat next to him, his ascot loosened. He seemed uncharacteristically quiet, defeated even. The sparse crowd somehow made the low-playing Miles Davis bluer. Perhaps I was projecting; the unsettling truths that writing the play had unearthed—questions about how well I knew myself, how well I knew Nadia, and whether I was any good as a writer—were lately and increasingly vying for my attention.

Halvor cleared his throat and broke the silence. "Got some news today." He kept his eyes on his omelet, carefully cut a sliver, and folded it onto his fork. "Spoke with one of the producers," he added, lifting the forkful to his mouth, a glob of egg whites that looked like a mass of cooling porcelain. He chewed slowly, patiently, as I sat waiting for him to finish his thought, dangling in the anticipation of bad news.

"You're killing me," I said, which sent him into a fit of

laughter, causing him to choke and nearly exhale his food through his nose.

He settled, sipped his beer, cleared his throat, then reached across the table and clenched my shoulders. "We're going up at the Cherry Lane!" He'd been putting on a charade. He shook me as if to wake me. "We did it, man!"

And news such as this, a rebuttal of my fears and doubts, is what kept those dark discomforts from being truly entered and explored. You see, when doubts are met with their opposites, they suddenly lose all their grounding.

10

I stumbled in around three that morning. The apartment was dark, aside from the flickering halo cast by the almond-scented candle on the windowsill where Nadia, posed in her silk kimono, knees to her chest, was smoking a cigarette.

"Baby," I said. "Baby, we're going up at the Cherry Lane." I showered her face with kisses.

"You stink," she said, pushing me away.

"Can you believe it?" I spread my arms, goading her to join me in celebration.

"Where were you?"

"The Coffee Shop," I said.

"That's nice." She stumped out her cigarette and came from the windowsill. "With Luce?"

"Halvor," I said and moved to kiss her. Again, she parried me, this time warning me off with a raised fist.

"I know what that bitch is up to."

I chuckled. "Are you crazy—"

"You're all impressed with her. She's so invested."

I squinted to join the two Nadias wavering before me.

"This is great. For us, I mean. After the run, it'll probably get published. That means royalties." Braving her fist, I wrapped my arms around her and whispered things that failed to soften her, so I burrowed my nose behind her ear, and she twitched from the tickle, giggled, squirmed to escape, but drunk as I was, I carried her to the bedroom with her arms wagging so that the kimono slipped away from her left breast, and like a silly fool, I suctioned it with my mouth and made fart sounds.

Adversity *had* revealed me. Walking into my fear made me strong. How quickly the whole thing—the play, the rehearsals, the venue—came together. I remembered what I'd read in the spiritual books about synchronicity and resistance: when we are living in alignment with our true purpose, there's little to no resistance from the outside world. *All is mind.* And to this point, I couldn't help but wonder about my intentioned meditations, stoked by the burning desire to have the play exceed all expectations. It seemed I'd manifested my writing career. Had I tapped into the source? Of course, being a playwright was not what I'd envisioned, but it's said, *We get what we want, only not as we imagine it.*

THE NIGHT before the play opened, as the dinner I was cooking neared completion, I was gazing over the blueish tones sinking into the courtyard below, uncorking a bottle of cheap cabernet, when my eyes brushed the windowsill. I froze. Next to the almond-scented candle was the mosaic bowl, the white porcelain interior juxtaposed by three turquoise fragments. I leaned closer. The ring I'd years ago placed on Nadia's finger was now in three pieces that no longer resembled a ring.

"It broke," she said as we sat at the table. She said it as if she was talking about a cheap mug. "It only cost a dollar," she added.

Hadn't we made it priceless with meaning?

Opening night, Nadia and I watched from the back row of the theater, a vantage point that allowed me to gauge the audience's reactions and engagement in the play. Throughout the entire first act, I hardly watched the stage in deference to the backs of heads and profiles filling the seats in front of us. I realized my hands were gripped to the armrests and all parts of my clothing in contact with the chair were sweat-dampened. Nearing the close of the second act, after Luce's monologue, her realization that she is a stranger to herself, I noticed Nadia sobbing. She wouldn't look at me. Then, halfway through the third act, I felt her glance. I was reluctant to meet her stare for fear of disapproval, but when I finally gave in, she smiled. It seemed a concession born of newfound understanding, as though she'd made a discovery about me through the writing. *She likes my play.* Her reaction, which I hadn't even imagined in all that I was imagining and hoping for that night, made me giddy. It wasn't the standing ovation the actors received, but Nadia's tacit approval that sanctified my effort.

11

———

The Cherry Lane was sold out for nearly every performance. I was interviewed by several newspapers and magazines, which pegged me as a "fresh voice representing the disillusionment that bridges generations." The truth is, during these interviews, I found it difficult to talk about the play and felt a bit like an imposter—especially when asked what playwrights had influenced me. My knowledge of playwrights and their works was lacking. Nevertheless, *Nigredo* earned generous reviews, as did Luce, whom critics said, "finally showed her true range." During the run, Halvor pulled me aside to say that he would consider directing one of the classical Greek plays after all, but only with Luce as his lead and only one play. "*Medea*. She alone has the power."

Closing night, Jeff Nesse, a Hollywood literary agent, attended the show. "You should write movies," he said, sidling up to me in the lobby of the Cherry Lane. He joined us for cocktails at a nearby pub, where he explained that he worked for a mid-level agency in Beverly Hills, and to sweeten his pitch, teased the idea of "options" and all sorts of fees writers received in Hollywood. When I asked him about his interest in fiction, he said, "Not unless you think you're sitting on a bestseller." He handled screenwriters and television writers. "Come to LA. I'll make it worth your while."

The shift from obscurity to public awareness was jarring in its suddenness, to say the least. I had no idea what I would write next, nor did I have any clue how to write a screenplay or a television series.

As it happened, after the run of *Nigredo*, Luce decided to sublease her New York apartment and rent a railroad apartment in West Hollywood. "There's more opportunity there," she said, urging me to consider Jeff's offer. "What's the worst that can happen? You get tan?" *Go with the flow.* Opportunity was knocking. Though I'd always meant to be a fiction writer, screenwriting was still writing, and if I wanted to make money so Nadia and I could upgrade our lives, screen-writing was certainly my best chance, as it was the most lucrative path for a writer.

Nadia nearly came out of herself when I mentioned a trip to Los Angeles. "What do you mean? For how long?"

"Only a couple weeks."

"How am I going to do that?" she asked. "I just started my new job." She had recently left a hostess position at a chic hotel for another at a newer, chicer hotel. Her mouth was agape when she understood I meant to go alone, which seemed to imply a presumption that our journeys would always remain in tandem. This naïve expectation struck me with tenderness for her, while at the same time, an acknowl-edgment that I was expanding, and she was contracting.

The morning of my flight, fear besieged me. I was entering unknown territory—separation from Nadia. I feared the endless possibilities that came with venturing out of the nest, those I was only now aware could change the life I had with her; no matter what, leaving, because it required some demystification of expectations, would change things for better or worse, even if I returned without incident. With my bags at our feet, I held her by the front door, doubting my decision to go.

"It's just for a little," she said, wiping my cheeks. "Right?" She seemed fine with my decision, fearless even.

"I promise," I said. And there on the windowsill was the mosaic bowl with the fragmented turquoise ring in its center.

CHOICES. One must understand why he makes the choices he makes. Until he does, the reality he lives in is not the reality he thinks he's living in, nor is he the driving force in his life. My foray into spirituality had taught me this: self-knowledge requires unflinching courage in the direction of honesty and a dogged commitment that painstakingly earns the necessary degree of awareness to begin to know oneself. There is a test to determine one's courage and level of self-awareness, but it isn't for the obstinate or faint-hearted. Examine the thoughts that come to you over the course of an hour. If you can commit to this process, you will see you are host to the whims of what seems multiple beings inhabiting you, and each wants something antithetical to the others. This is where the work begins, as the only outcome, if one hopes to know himself, is to admit that he is ignorant of the moving forces within. And without. For the prideful, such as myself, this sort of thing tips the apple cart.

I've had these moments in life when I just had to do something despite it feeling wrong or knowing that it would, if it came to light, hurt someone else. It's easy to say that selfishness led me to do what on the outside *seems* like a selfish thing, but what about the undeniable impulse that made me cast off my reason and my values to go through with it? When I look closely at these moments, I see my decisions were not conscious choices; they were ordained by an unknown agency, a subconscious force that takes over and displaces rationale. I mean the choices that disrupt the existing order of things, the life-changers. And the order I disrupted? It wasn't what I'd thought it was, and the new order established by my "bad" or "selfish" choice led me to where I needed to be. Despite the initial, inescapable shock of upheaval, the track we are on is always the right track even when it's glaringly wrong—more so, perhaps. What is true in that statement dazzles me, inclines my thoughts toward Bacon's Providence and Deity, or at least to admit that I had no idea who I was or why I wanted what I thought I wanted. But that impulse, that selfish thing? Knowing what I think I know now, I feel tempted to offer an opinion on the age-old debate between free will and predetermination, but haven't I already?

Only later, after Emily appeared and began instructing me in the ways of her "science," did the marauders of my will show themselves to be the bastard children of unruly desires. "Take the self out of it," she insisted. "You must take the self out of it." True spirituality is meant to dissolve the illusion of separation. When one comes to see that Satan is the Lord's highest servant, for it's the fire of hell that forges saints, his sins become blessings.

I'D NEVER BEEN to Los Angeles. I had no reason to go, no interest. I admit I had my chin raised and a chip on my shoulder, that whole New York creative wariness of Hollywood and its schlocky, commercialized industry. Before I'd even gotten off the plane, I saw myself arguing with Jeff at the impasse where artistic vision meets the world of commerce. But venturing to Los Angeles would have little to do with business and all to do with an unwanted transformation.

LAX was a madhouse. I collected my luggage and went outside to the pick-up zone where the concentration of car and shuttle bus fumes made my eyes tear. After looking around for fifteen minutes or so, I finally spotted Luce standing at the curb beside her idling Jeep Cherokee. She appeared to be arguing with a runty officer whose slight frame made his uniform look oversized. I figured he was probably telling her she couldn't park in the pick-up zone, that she had to move her Jeep, so I hurried toward them just as the officer held out his pad and pen. She scribbled something, and as she handed it back to him, caught sight of me. "There he is! See!" She waved. "Hurry. Get in." The officer glanced at me, then down at his pad with a sort of satisfaction. I tossed my luggage into Luce's messy backseat, then hopped into the passenger seat.

"What was that?" I asked.

"Wanted an autograph," she said.

The secret of the ocean lies concealed in the desert. That was my thought as we drove out of the airport and Los Angeles, the subtropical paradise, presented itself. In nearly every view, hills are thrown into relief by distant ranges, blue and pale from a white haze born of smog that diffuses the omnipresent light. Even in shaded spots, light emblazons a cornucopia of colors and textures. Manicured lawns and shrubs. Birds of paradise. Bulbous succulents. Fruit trees. And low stucco buildings that give way to endless sky. Endless, blue sky topping the knobby fronds of tall, slender palms sentenced to a perpetual, hypnotic back and forth sway that seems to emit a gentle whisper, *list-less-ness, list-less-ness*. Oh, I can attest to the mysterious influence of that city, how its spell, spread by the ever-present breeze, settled into my lungs like pixie dust.

"The only thing that's weird," Luce said, "time just flies by. We're used to the seasons back east. Here, they're so *supple*, to a New Yorker they don't exist." *Subtle,* Luce, and yes, they are.

We arrived at my hotel on Hollywood Boulevard, a good two miles east of the famed strip, which I chose for its cheap rate. At the foot of the driveway, pacing in circles, was a suntanned freckled man, shirtless and emaciated with scabby, dehydrated lips. His pants were filthy, shredded to the knees, and out of the tattered sneaker on his right foot peeked one gnarled toe. Sinewy and taut, with the anguished eyes of a saint, he screamed at his invisible tormentor, whom he seemed to clearly see in the air above him. "Welcome to LA," Luce said.

The hotel's stucco, U-shaped duplex was meant to be salmon-colored, but persistent sunlight and the exfoliating dust-washing of the breeze had muted the paint to a mere pinkish hue. The shabby view conjured the smells of moldy polyester bedcovers and the reek of cigarette smoke. Luce glanced around as she drove up to the office.

"Why you staying here? Just stay with me."

"I appreciate it," I said. "I just…"

"I know," she said, "Nadia will have a shit fit." We laughed, then laughed again when we'd entered the substandard room and it matched the images I'd imagined.

That evening, Luce cooked a welcome dinner at her apartment in West Hollywood. She'd certainly reached the point where financial concerns had eased, but the apartment was like something a younger, struggling artist might have. We called it Luce's studio, but technically, it was a railroad apartment. The front door opened on a kitchen that led to the main room, the studio, so to speak, which had stations designated for different life functions. There was the work area with her desk and computer, the living room area with the cherry red sofa, coffee table, and ratan chairs, and the bedroom area with her bed, a lamp, and a small bed table piled with books. Lastly, a narrow hallway branched from the studio, led past a couple of closets, and ended at the bathroom.

In the short time she'd been living in Los Angeles, she'd managed to assemble a bunch of her transplanted friends, mostly New York actors and writers, into what she dubbed the Orange Family, as they all lived around the block on Orange Avenue. And just as families come together in the evenings for dinner, they'd come to Luce's table for her home-cooked meals, some wine, and to talk about their day.

There was Steve, a paunch, stereotypical Italian actor with restless, jester-like energy. Michael, a handsome, gifted, though psychologically imbalanced method actor with an insatiable hunger for women. Paul, the oldest of the bunch, was a former socialite turned self-proclaimed sage whose tiny body and large head somehow made him appear pious. And last but not least, Gabriele the Sicilian, who won a place in my heart. His eccentricities molded him a surrealist poet and filmmaker, and his mod haircut and dress were reminiscent of Soutine. They were all headlong in their artistic pursuits, none were married, and only one, Michael, had a child. On my first night in Los Angeles, in Luce's railroad apartment, I shared a meal with this new bunch, engaged in thought-provoking conversations, and experienced laughter that entered all the compartments of my body.

Impressions of Luce's studio. Lusterless wood floors with deep, dark lines and cracks like dirt-caked wrinkles on a laborer's mug. Original crown molding with the names, initials, and birthdates of previous renters carved into the wood. Iron-ribbed windows, vertical louvers, and pebbled glass through which one could only distinguish if it were light or dark outside. Scuffed plaster walls displaying the works of up-and-coming painters Luce had purchased at art walks, and on the wall above the cherry red sofa, framed prints from photographs she'd taken of gritty New York characters, colorful doorways, and decaying trainyards.

Many nights in the year to come, I'd breathe the fragrance of red sauce and fried meatballs that wafted in from the kitchen while the matron of the Orange Family held court, waxing philosophically, poetically even, misusing words and confusing analogies, yet somehow landing the points in a way no one else could.

Anyone who has gone off into the world to pursue a dream and finds the struggle knows to be alone is to be dead. The fatal flaw in struggling artists is that they confuse their art with their identity and fail to see that their art is only their work. As such, an out-of-work actor or a painter who doesn't sell is lost. Luce understood this; she gave everyone permission to be themselves. She created a scene, mixing and matching her unassociated groups of artist friends, goading spontaneous dance parties that boiled into the back garden and were sure to ensnare random neighbors and their guests. Not only were her gatherings a sort of ventilation from the restlessness brought on by the inherent uncertainty in our career choices, but they were also necessary for the evolution of our hearts and minds, to bring us beyond thinking of ourselves as "professions." There were times during the parties that I awoke into some heightened awareness, before the drink or smoke pushed me over, and a feeling I can only describe as recognition exploded in my being, recognition that I was alive, that I had escaped the ordinary.

In the coming year, Luce's studio would grow enormous in my mind, as important to me as Gertrude Stein's salon was to modern art. And the Orange Family, that displaced troupe of carnival acts? They somehow kept the law of gravity operating in Los Angeles, and believe me, there is ground here. It's been sanctified by the Scorpio's blood.

12

Jeff Nesse and I met for breakfast at the Urth Café. "The play," he said. "Your strength is character. Great characters. But *concept* is everything. Even if you fail to execute on the concept, if it's a good concept I can still sell the script. On the other hand, the execution can be spectacular, but if the concept is only blah, we're dead in the water." His crash course on writing for a market lasted forty minutes. I felt myself bucking against what he was suggesting, just as I did when Nadia suggested I write sellable stories. I patiently listened. After all, I'd made the journey to Los Angeles precisely because I wanted to make money. Then and there, I convinced myself that I could find my window of interest into whatever it was I was writing, and that would justify writing for a market.

"In fact," he said, "television's the new frontier, right?" Cluelessly, I nodded, as I didn't watch television. "I have a friend heading development at Raven. They do all the cop shows. I have a killer concept for a television pilot, but the series arc is a mystery to me. Was gonna give it to this writer I'm developing, but he's got his head up his ass. Writes this dark drama shit that won't see the light of day. It's good but dark. So why don't you take a crack at the pilot?" *Television?* Yes, this was business and business must be profitable, and an agent with a writer staffed on a series makes a consistent commission. "You're gonna blow it out of the water," he said. "You got the chops."

That night, as I was reading a book on television writing, he emailed me the short synopsis of his idea. The final sentence of his email read: *Be sure to include ethnic leads or we won't be able to sell it in the current market.* I agreed to write the pilot on spec, which meant I would only get paid if he sold the series.

THE NIGHT I returned to New York, Nadia and I had dinner at Frankie Yaki. My return had defied my fears; my expansion had proved enriching and the world I'd left for a short time seemed unchanged—well, almost. Nadia's welcome was ambivalent, as though she were feeling me out; I didn't push. Frankie was lively and drunk, and after each of his stories, he slid his forefinger and thumb in opposite directions across his mustache to flatten it and wipe away any debris. "You a star yet?" He grinned and nudged Nadia as if to shake her from her preoccupation. By this point in the evening, I'd assumed she was either dropping into a spell of depression or was on the tail end of one. "You're dating a superstar," Frankie joked. She smirked so as not to be rude.

Nadia remained aloof once we'd gotten home. "I'm not in the mood," she said, parrying my advance. She nestled herself on the windowsill and lit a cigarette, leaving me to lament the reunion I'd anticipated. Seeing her again, the impossibility of her beauty, had me frothing with desire. "Did you meet anyone?" she asked.

"I met lots of people—"

"You know what I mean," she snapped. Before I could answer, she said, "Whatever. Everyone should have secrets."

"What the hell does that mean?"

She shrugged, kept looking out the window. "I wouldn't want to know," she said.

"That's not what you meant," I said, positioning myself before her, waiting for her to give me her eyes. "What secrets do you have?"

Now she was smirking. "None. Big dummy." But her taut smirk formed into the least sincere expression I'd ever seen on her face.

My trip to Los Angeles was the first time we'd been apart. I wondered about her job at the chic hotel in Soho that catered to celebrities and the like—had *she* met someone? It was foolish to imagine she wasn't daily propositioned in such an environment. Ordinary Joes wouldn't have the courage to approach her, but movie stars who believe in their deification, even the ugly ones? Then his face flashed in my mind: trust fund Charlie and his James Dean shoulder pinch. It had been years since I'd heard his name, but that night when he appeared on the sidewalk and told her she looked amazing? Her entire being spoke of their unfinished business. Did she see him while I was away?

The smell of Monoi Tiare oil rising from her skin tormented me. I rolled over on the bed; she was faced away, giving me her back. Even this far along, we were good for it three, four nights a week. We'd been apart for nearly a month, had a couple of glasses of wine; now we're in the same bed and she's not in the mood? *She afraid I'll smell someone else's stink on her?* My skin felt hot as my unrequited desire ricocheted inside me, leaving me at first restless and at last desperate. I could sense she was awake. I blurted, "Jeff wants me to go back out there to write the pilot." She gave no reply. "He thinks it's best. So we can meet to discuss notes." Nothing. I watched her for a few seconds. *Is she sleeping?* My legs kicked about; my heart was pounding. "Would you consider coming out there?"

An unbearable minute must have passed. Finally I reached for her, and just before my hand touched her shoulder, she said, "*This* is my city."

A MONTH LATER, I was in my Los Angeles apartment, the one I'm now in, writing the pilot. Aware that too much change at once is certain to meet resistance, I lied to Nadia and told her I was subleasing an apartment for my three-month stay; that was my intention until Gabriele told me he knew of a great deal on a place.

The apartment was a corner unit in a low-income art deco building that shared a hill with Barnsdall Park. I could rent it month to month without signing a lease. The spacious one-bedroom had a sprawling balcony that faced the section of the Hollywood Hills adorned with the Hollywood sign and Griffith Observatory. The apartment also came with a parking space, which got me thinking. The cost of a car rental for three months was nearly three thousand dollars. To lease a cheap car for a year would cost about the same. If I intended to take three or four extended trips to Los Angeles over the next couple of years, it seemed I was better off leasing.

As I stood beneath the sun taking in the views from the spacious balcony, I somehow didn't hear the mariachi music blaring from the open windows of the neighboring apartments, or notice the chihuahua shit on the walkways, or that there were clotheslines strung across several of the porches, laundry on display. I saw blue sky, endless palms, hills that ran all the way to Santa Monica. There, the Griffith Observatory; there, the Hollywood sign. I wrote a check on the spot; it was one of those not-even-conscious choices ordained by the unknown's displacing of my rationale. The next day, I embraced irrationality to the fullest, leased a Honda Civic, bought a table and chairs, a cheap mattress, and plates and glasses from a 99-cent store. I had essentially relocated without considering Nadia or my life back east, which I easily justified by taking the view that I had made a responsible decision. Frugality serves a struggling writer.

Now that I was settled, I had work to do. My days were spent reading every available book on television writing, writing the pilot, and planning the series arc. Evenings were spent with the Orange Family at Luce's studio. On some nights, we'd all brainstorm the pilot, and they would offer ideas for developing the characters and plot twists. Michael was particularly good at this, and some of his suggestions made it into the series bible.

Two months in, I'd completed my first draft, which Jeff met optimistically. I spent another month rewriting based on his notes, and come winter, I was back in New York thawing Nadia, sniffing around for signs that Charlie or some other thief had been in my space. Everything seemed in order. My world was intact. She was even affectionate the night I returned and, in the morning, served me breakfast in bed.

A week before Christmas, Jeff called to say that he'd sold the pilot to his friend at Raven Pictures, who had a production deal with a major network. "I got you eighty for the pilot. Now how's that?"

"How did you sell it without a pitch?"

"Concept, baby. The networks are throwing money at these guys for development, so. Look, I told him you had the bible and were just doing a pass on it. They definitely have ideas. When you come back after the holidays, you'll meet with them." The celebration started with a shopping spree for Nadia—perfume, jeans, and boots—gifts for her compliance.

New York at Christmas time. Garlands strung in rows above the cobblestone streets of SoHo. Holiday-themed shop windows with foam-sprayed snowy corners. Store to store, Dean Martin, Brenda Lee, John Williams, and Burl Ives were belting the classics as we shopped without counting pennies, swept by the energies of new possibilities. *This must be what it's like to have money.* Positive change, as in getting what I wanted, was easy to enter; under these circumstances, fear felt like excitement. Nadia's glow seemed to acquiesce with my thoughts. We hadn't gone down the dream path together since the miscarriage, but over lunch at the Mercer, she talked about the country house we'd buy and her ideas for decorating the living room. Over dinner at Il Buco, we talked about us, about our daughter Ines, and how I hoped she'd look like her mother, and if we had a boy.

"I'm proud of you," she said, smiling, underlit by candlelight.

"*This* is what I've been holding out for..." I paused, knowing I should not say it, but I felt it so strongly, "to take the next step. Us, I mean." I held her stare until she understood what I meant. Her cheeks flushed. I'll never forget what appeared in her eyes; it was as though she'd finally received the acquittal for that crime I wasn't sure she'd committed. She leaned to kiss me. The elderly couple at the table next to us stopped eating in deference to our display of affection; they were all smiles and perhaps reminded of their younger days.

The plates were cleared; we were awaiting dessert. Nadia sipped her wine, inhaled deeply, held me in her stare. "So now what?"

"Well, I'll have to polish the series bible. And we have to see if the network will keep me on as a writer."

"That's not what I meant but... wait. You wrote it."

"Yeah. Doesn't work like that. I don't have a track record. Jeff says I'll take some meetings about getting in the writer's room when I go back."

Her eyes went flat; she straightened in the chair. "You're going back?"

"Nadia, do you realize how hard it is to sell a television pilot? The first one you write? If I'm working and making money like that, we could get a place there."

"Why would I want a place there?"

"Seventy and sunny every day? And you wouldn't even have to work."

"I like my job. And I didn't sign up for a long-distance relationship." The elderly couple at the table next to us had gotten quiet; the woman sent tentative glances.

I leaned forward, lowered my voice, "Neither did I. But this is where we are."

Nadia didn't pick up on my cue. She barked, "You're gonna do what you want anyway, so."

I suppose I believed if I earned a good enough living, Nadia would come out west. She had no ties to New York aside from her job, but it wasn't a career; it was a job. I suppose I also believed that if she loved me, she would follow me where I needed to be for my career. Just as I'd imagined her moving in with me would give me some sort of control, imagining money would soothe our troubles proved to be another illusion.

At the start of the new year, Jeff called with more news. "The network wants to bring on other writers to develop the series. Writers with track records."

"But I'll still have a crack at the writer's room, right?"

"Well, no. The network wants diversity." Those diverse writers with track records? Three realistic, well-developed ethnic leads weren't diverse enough for the market, so they changed all the characters, races, and sexual orientations to suit every demographic and broaden the show's appeal. My first brush with the reality of the business and how, in the hands of a bunch of Frankensteins, something organic becomes a monster, left me disenchanted. In the end, the pilot never got made. Jeff remained optimistic, "What did I tell you about concept? See? We sold it anyway. Get your ass back here and start working on a feature."

It took me a week to find the courage to tell Nadia I'd bought a ticket. I didn't use any tricks, a nice dinner and flowers, to lift her, only to drop her. I just came out with it. She showed no reaction, barely nodded. To my surprise, she said, "Need a vacation. I'll come visit." I was so relieved I bought her a ticket that day, then realized I needed to come clean about the apartment and the car lease. Sensing the time was opportune, I confessed; to this, she reacted. Her face was ugly as she glared. "I'm not coming." For the remainder of the weekend, she'd locked herself in the bedroom. I managed to get us on speaking terms the day before I was leaving, but her resolve hadn't weakened. She admitted to feeling betrayed by my decision to rent the apartment and lease the car without discussing it with her.

"You're not wrong to feel that way," I said. "But try to understand."

"I understand," she said. "But I'm still not coming."

The night I returned to Los Angeles, a draining fatigue somehow brought my faculties of discernment to a sort of black and white simplicity. I took a bottle of zinfandel onto the porch, sat to take in the views. *Nadia.* In the beginning, she was different, exuberant, engrossing. Now she seemed perpetually weighed down, reticent, stifled. We were constantly at odds. We weren't friends anymore. It was even ironic that my interest in spirituality had blossomed while she'd discarded her spiritual practices altogether. We had swapped dispositions. *What is it? Her beauty? The physical connection?* Nothing had ever come close. *But sex is not love. You love her. Don't you?* Of a sudden, the night air felt cold. *Why stay? Because she's your other half. She completes you.* I was now on my feet, pacing, smoking, rolling my shoulders to relieve the ache and stiffness in my neck. Something like this went through my mind: *What she completes is your ego's need to possess such beauty, as her by your side validates your misguided self-worth.*

On the evening before Nadia's scheduled flight, her obstinance remained. "You fucking lied to me," she hissed. "Now you think I'm gonna come there?"

"Fine," I said, "don't come." Later, at Luce's, as I was railing about Nadia's lack of support concerning my career, Luce checked me.

"I don't blame her," she said. "You make a decision like that without running it by her? I mean, imagine if she did that to you." It wasn't that I hadn't put the shoe on the other foot, but somehow Luce's calling me to task made me walk the mile. I'd have been furious with Nadia had she done what I did. In fact, I'd have believed she didn't take me or our relationship seriously.

The following morning, I awoke to Nadia's voicemail: "I land at noon." The car ride from LAX was tense; she didn't speak a word. I thought, *She's going to explode when she sees the low-income building.* To her credit, she only snarled and through stiff lips muttered, "Looks like Beirut in 1970." Cautiously, she entered and moved through the living room, came upon the full kitchen, then went into the hall to survey the spacious bedroom. Upon returning, she said, "Great light." And I know it was the spaciousness, the very thing Manhattan denies, that prompted her to say, "Can I decorate?"

I had only one condition. "I never want it to feel like home." We made love on the new carpet with trimmed fibers adhering to our skin, and later, at sunset, plopped in beach chairs on the porch, we shared a bottle of cabernet under a Van Gogh sky.

That weekend, she picked a couple of club chairs from secondhand stores, one a muted turquoise, the other cadmium orange, and two cheap, glass lamps—one beige, the other lime green, both with white linen shades. From a high-end furniture store, she selected teakwood blinds and a shaggy white carpet. At the fair on La Brea, our final stop, she fell in love with a macramé birdcage; it was big, three tiers. She hung it from the ceiling between the kitchen and dining area, and sure enough, she'd managed to transform yet another living space into a work of art.

Luce prepared dinner at her place in honor of Nadia's arrival. I was excited to introduce her to the Orange Family, as they had become important in my life. Besides, I thought it would set her mind at ease to meet them; outside of Luce, they were all men and she had nothing to be wary of. Everyone welcomed her graciously, Gabriele especially, whose admiration for her beauty couldn't be concealed. But after the introductions, Nadia put on airs. She sat beside me quietly smoking, listening to the conversations, barely contributing unless she was prompted to speak, and even then, her answers were curt. Her energy had crimped the evening, seemed to suck the life out of everyone. When we were readying to leave, Luce protested. "No. Stay." She took Nadia's hand, "Leslie and Emily are coming. Want you to meet them."

Nadia glanced at me. "I'm tired. Jetlagged."

Luce frowned. "Too bad. Okay. Next time."

"Leslie and Emily? Who are they?" Nadia asked.

I kept my eyes on the road, bracing for the argument. "I don't know. Never met them."

She snarled. "Luce's so loud. You're all huddled together like college kids. Dreamers."

"I wasn't dreaming when I cashed the check from the pilot. Those boots you're wearing, they're real, right?"

Our long-distance relationship had unforeseen consequences. Despite financial considerations, it was vacation each time Nadia visited; road trips to Big Sur, Joshua Tree, Palm Springs, La Jolla, San Diego. But for me, the swing of three months in New York, three in Los Angeles had a sort of schizophrenic effect. I went in and out of two completely different realities, peopled with completely unrelated faces. There was something extraordinary in the feeling of living a double life, akin to an injection of surrealism between the eyes.

Whenever I returned to New York, Nadia would have a

hard time adjusting to me re-entering what she now declared, "My space!" I moved around her like a silent servant, diligent with the chores I'd typically shrug off, such as cooking, laundry, and food shopping. Added to her spells of depression, she took to a sort of prolonged daydreaming where, perhaps, she imagined the life she couldn't seem to find in the one she lived. With each return, her withdrawals went deeper, and only when I was set to leave again would she rouse herself as if she could at will escape the mind that surrounded her like prison walls, sneak out to offer herself, even if sometimes she did it begrudgingly.

Curiously enough, the further apart we grew, the more intense our intimacy became; it was as though we were competing against the imagined, secret lovers we'd taken on, me against hers and she against mine, seeking to outdo them and remind each other of the partner that mattered. Those long separations made reunion, at least to me, transcendent. My suspicions and worries would evaporate. I'd lie beside her marveling at the strangeness of intimacy and how the patterns of the universe, knowing nothing of human will, somehow, sometimes, coalesced with the will and when it mattered most.

In the early mornings when I was leaving—I always took the first flight out—I'd wake before the alarm, get ready, and she'd stay in bed until the final minutes before the car would arrive. I'd find her in the dark bedroom, warm beneath the covers, hints of gardenia on her skin. I'd kiss her shoulders. She'd pretend to be asleep until finally she'd turn and kiss me, and her hands would press into the backs of my shoulders as if she knew where to find the dams to release the deluge, send it flooding out from my heart to swell in my throat.

13

———————

Four years passed. In all that time, I'd not optioned or sold any of my scripts. My only jobs were rewrites, one an indie film, the other a studio film. The studio rewrite was specifically for character development, which paid well, but in intervals I still had to rely on unemployment to survive. I'd also written two new pilots, the concepts of which Jeff felt were too abstract to go out on the town, and one feature film screenplay. *River Without End* was a drama about a passionate love affair that ends in betrayal. The script's opening image starts as a wide shot of a window bank with the lonely mosaic bowl on the sill and slowly pans to a close-up of the bowl's white interior, which holds three turquoise fragments. Jeff read it, said, "It's a page-turner. Great twist. But I have some notes."

Autumn of our ninth year, the third of our long-distance relationship, Nadia came for an extended visit. It rained nearly every day. She seemed defeated, looked as though she might cry at any moment. I remembered what she'd said years ago about me smothering her and, "Everyone should have secrets." I also remembered that night when I sat on my porch with the bottle of zinfandel and my fatigued state allowed for the black and white assessment of our relationship, when the voice exposed my egoic need to possess her beauty. Even though I questioned my love for her and whether our relationship had run its course, my desire to keep her was stronger than ever. I went with her back to New York, fully aware that I was clinging to what I felt slipping away. My stay was short and uneventful, plagued by nostalgia for the apartment, even the city.

Frankie threw me a sendoff at Frankie Yaki the night before I headed back. All that week he'd been limping around, suffering from lower back and groin pain, which he tried fruitlessly to stave off with pain killers. "It's the nerve beneath my ass muscle." I could see him counting the minutes, his pallid face wrought and glossed with perspiration. Then he was gone. He'd Irish goodbyed us. Nadia and I followed suit, went back to the apartment where she lit the almond-scented candle, I popped a cork, and we danced to ska music.

I can't help but remember how we went at it, the darker dimensions underpinning our laughter and indiscriminate drinking. There we stood in the throes of a truth that neither of us had the courage to address; it was as if we'd made a pact to obliterate the fear of a future that had already happened. But when the darkness cleared, the birdsong echoing off the brick walls of the otherwise quiet courtyard seemed haunted, infused with the notions of time and impermanence. On the daybed, clinging to each other in drunken solemnity, we were like victims. Ah, and it is my last, my very last good memory of her, good only because she still cared. Fitfully, she turned to me, dawn's light flush in her eyes, took my cheeks in the palms of her hands, held my stare, and said, "Always, my love. My love," and kissed me repeatedly, hastily, before burying her tear-streaked face in my chest.

"SAW FRANKIE GETTING INTO A TAXI," Nadia said, sobbing. "He looked terrible." The nerve beneath Frankie's ass muscle was not the cause of his pain. Just after my sendoff, he'd been diagnosed with stage four liver cancer. It had spread to his bones. "What are you doing?" She asked, her voice quavering. I was standing in the doorway of my apartment with cool rain-splash sprinkling the tops of my feet.

"It's raining," I said.

"Freezing here," she said. "Snow again tonight."

Frankie died a week later. That night, I drank scotch on the balcony and thought about my friend. I wasn't sure Frankie knew how he'd impacted my life. If not for him, I'd never have met Halvor and Luce, or Jeff. Even the bedbug infestation took on new meaning for the changes it had brought about. It's said fate has no past, only a future.

In the days that followed, a feeling came over me, loneliness such as I had never known. The feeling seemed to grow out of the Los Angeles landscape, which suddenly showed itself strange and unfamiliar; I was a long way from home. A sense of dread pervaded my morning and evening meditation sessions, and when I turned to the spiritual books for reprieve, the words that once rang with truth seemed empty and out of reach. Grasping for comfort, as the feeling wouldn't relent, I offered to fly Nadia out for a visit, but she was still angry that I didn't fly back for Frankie's funeral. "You could use it," I said. "Get some sun and escape the New York freeze."

"Can't," she said. "I have to work."

"Then I'll come home," I said.

"Now you want to come?"

I remember the discomfort in my gut, the constricting, gassy feeling. "Is everything okay?" I asked.

There was a long pause, then she said, "I don't know."

Over the next week, there were a series of nights she was unreachable on her cell. I'd call and call into the early hours, and when she'd finally answer, she was already in the fight, impatient with my concerns. *Out all night, getting short at a quarter to six in the morning?* I was on fire. "Everything closes at four," I said.

"I'm in a cab now." Her voice was unrecognizable in its defiance. "Why *you* still up?" she asked.

"Because I need to know what the hell you're doing!"

She scoffed. "I went out. I have yoga early. I'm going to bed."

"You didn't tell me you started yoga classes."

"You didn't tell me you rented an apartment in Los Angeles."

Of course, her confession, that she'd cheated on her husband, that which I'd willfully kept out of my mind, returned with all its accompanying fears. Jealousy-spawned scenarios kept me pacing throughout the night. I found it impossible to write, but boy, could I create stories about Nadia. It wasn't Charlie I imagined, but the character in *River Without End*, the dark European who interferes with the marriage. He isn't handsome; he has unique features, steely gray eyes, a big nose, long, greasy hair. He stops by her hotel lounge for a second time. At first, she denies the attention brought on by the curse of beauty, but he manages to make her laugh. When he comes a third time, she realizes she's grown familiar with the idiosyncrasies of his accent; it amuses her, chips her resolve. The awareness comes, of being alive, that all limits are self-imposed. Her answers to his questions come without thinking, surprise her. When he abruptly leaves, she's annoyed, unable to concentrate on the simple tasks of her job.

Evening in New York. Snow falls on quiet streets. Nadia passes from the heated hotel lobby into a wall of freeze. Prince Street is a wind tunnel. Snowflakes sting her eyes, feel like flecks of sawdust before they melt. The smell of wood fire evokes images of chunky sweaters and steaming coffee. She moves into the white puffs of her breath that disappear as she reaches them. *Another night*, she thinks. Bag tight to her shoulder, hands in her pockets, she rounds the corner into a flurry-laden gust. The amber bursts of streetlamps and the faint glow of candles in the fogged cafe windows conjure the feeling. She wants to be held by a man who makes her mind disappear. Three long blocks trekked, unseen, and she's reached Hester Street with it simmering in her belly. She doesn't know what, but she's trying to remember something she'd said to the European; she said so many things that make her wonder, *Who am I?*

She stops outside her building. Frankie Yaki, closed since Frankie's death, sits in shadows like a memory. The deserted sidewalk is laid with virgin snow, shimmering in the white light cast from the lamps above the lintel. As large snowflakes cross from the blue air into the cone of light, they become luminous like stars, glistening as they trail downward. Entranced, she hears the echo of her mother's voice calling her in at curfew, smells the odor of her stepfather's cologne mingled with cigarette smoke. She sees the concrete where the grass used to be and the unearthed tree her father had planted. Hurriedly, she inserts the key. Six flights she climbs, her breaths coming quicker. The weight of her bag seems oppressive. The worn marble stairs, crooked and mean, blur from tears.

"So what," Luce said. "She went out a couple times? What do you want her to do? Stay home every night?"

Was I overreacting? No, I felt it. "Nothing good happens at five in the morning," I declared.

"You hang out all night," she said. "You're not doing anything, right?" Luce was preoccupied, antsy, twirling her hair in her fingers. We sat through a long silence. "I have a girl crush," she confessed. "I'm not gonna do anything. Just, you know."

"Who?" I asked.

"Emily." At the very least, I was surprised. Luce didn't go with women, but she once joked, "You swing both ways, you get more hits."

"Who's Emily?"

"You met her!" she said. "The Brit. The actress." I shrugged. "Her and Leslie just moved here."

"Who's Leslie?"

"The Aussie. You met them. I know you did." I shook my head. "Oh. Coulda sworn. They're *both* gorgeous. But Emily?" She waved her hand as if to fan herself.

Shortly after Luce left, I smoked a cigarette on the porch, watching the mass of gray clouds tumbling in from the east snuff the last light and turn the unillumined windows of the houses in the hills flat and dark.

Then Nadia called. "I'm confused," she said. "I need time."

I WAS a madman boarding the plane to New York. Oh, the betrayal, the deception. Scenarios were playing out in my head: me attacking the dark European I'd imagined, the fictional character from *River Without End*; attacking Nadia after she admits her infidelity, righteously beating her for her act of betrayal. I was unable to sit still through the torturous duration of that flight. My aisle pacing unnerved several passengers; a flight attendant guided me back to my seat. Then, in the taxi from JFK, I realized I was mumbling to myself, wringing my fists as though preparing for battle. When the taxi exited the Holland Tunnel, I was suddenly thrust into what seemed a maze cut from the angular faces of the clustered, towering buildings. A bout of vertigo sent waves of nausea through my gut; saliva pooled in my mouth. My hands were trembling, my heart pounding against my chest plate. I lurched forward, mumbled something to the startled driver, who glanced back over his shoulder. I motioned for him to pull over at the corner of Varick. "Here! Good!" I barked. I pulled my bag from the trunk and walked the rest of the way, let the adrenaline burn off in the fresh air. I recalled quotes from the spiritual doctrines, tried to fuse to the truths within them, but I now saw that intellectual understanding had no power over my emotions, over the great surge of energy wedged in my core.

Darkness behind the retractable windows at Frankie Yaki. *Only March*, I thought as I withdrew my keys, then froze on the spot from the impact of a thought that seemed absolute in its truth: Frankie's death was an omen. My life here was over. *No, no.* Slowly, I climbed the crooked staircase, endured the stabs of fear, thinking myself like Caesar in his moment of reckoning.

I entered the two-room apartment. The color explosion —reds, teals, browns—drew me deep into associations. A stream of smoke trailed from a stick of incense on the holder. I examined the room, was immediately struck by how she had rearranged our things. The daybed now sat under the windows that looked onto the courtyard. The round, marble tabletop and iron-ribbed frame I rescued from the garbage when we lived in the studio on 10th Street was now against the wall. A large suzani, a new addition, Indian red with cream-colored patterns, nearly covered the entire wood floor. Several dirty coffee mugs and wineglasses cluttered the sink. On the refrigerator, a magnet held a picture of her from India that Charlie must've taken. She's smiling, arms opened wide, spreading the red poncho she wears as she stands next to a bull on some dirt road. She's told me she was never as happy as on the day that picture was taken.

Creaks from the hallway, then she appeared—archetype of beauty, my other half. Her cheeks were still rosy from a morning session of hot yoga. The green sleeveless t-shirt and tight, black jeans revealed weight loss. Those eyes, intensified by black eyeliner, held my stare a moment before she dropped her head and hoisted herself onto the countertop. The scent of gardenia oil lingered in the air. Now she faced me with down-turned lips—voila! She appeared a sorrowful child. I was wobbled by the air of false humility I detected, as when she'd return from one of her spells, knowing she has inconvenienced me. I sensed her hesitancy, felt strained by mine. Our awkward conversation covered unimportant details about my trip, meaningless questions, *Have you eaten*, et cetera. Hunched on the daybed, rigid in my dishonesty, my attempt to appear strong by not saying much or exposing my need to touch her, added to the emotional strain of the past three weeks, and the anxious plane ride home—all at once, I withered.

It's hard to say how much time passed, but when I woke, her body was wrapped to mine, a python enfolding a lamb.

Her lips moved across my neck. The surge, the very thing I feared I'd never know again, overtook me. Passion nearing vehemence arose to reclaim my fleeting ideal and *our* intimacy, earned over nine years. I took her beneath me, a half-obsessed fury, but before it went further, I stopped, pushed up on my hands, and hovered above her. I needed to know. She blinked rapidly from the force of my stare. "Were you with anyone?"

"No," she whispered and tugged me toward her. My present need outweighed my desire for truth: nothing was more truthful than my need. My mouth, in warm gasps, she consumed, starved as I, and this, not her answer to my question, was enough to allow me to continue. At last, surrender exfoliated my resistance as we, as one, transcended the hurt of our minds by physically annihilating the space in which it existed.

Come morning, I heard keys jingling in the other room. Fears rushed my mind like a mob, propelled me from the bed into the kitchen. She was gathered by the door with her yoga mat and bag, just about to leave. "I thought we'd have breakfast," I said. "Talk."

Her face twitched: she seemed afraid of me. "I'm going to yoga," she said.

I moved toward her. "I think we should talk?"

"I don't want to. I can't." Her hands were shaking so badly she was unable to grip the doorknob to open the heavy door. "I just... I want to go to yoga! Why are you trying to stop me from doing what I want!" The moment the jagged sounds of her words expired, I saw that she knew her reaction was excessive, uncalled for. Nevertheless, she recommitted herself. "I'm going."

I had to make a stand. "I won't be here when you get

back," I said but my threat went unacknowledged, and the door closed behind her.

I looked around the room as if to take it into memory. Her reconfiguration of our things bathed in the clear, morning light. The shelf displayed the framed black and white photo of us from the jetty with our initials graffitied on the rocks. New lovers, smirking. I stumbled through the memories of when it was new, held fast to the idea of our cosmic love, but there in the quiet, seated on the daybed, from that space, the open, empty space of the room, I could not deny what spoke.

Hours passed. The lock on the heavy door popped, and as the door slowly opened, the high-pitched creak of the hinges raised the hair on my arms. She was startled to find me there sitting on the daybed, a reaction that betrayed her hope that I'd be gone. The door glided across her fingertips and closed. She laid her bag and yoga mat on the floor. My hands shot up to hide my face and it started again, my torso heaving, bobbing. She stood above me until my pathetic state infected her, then sat beside me, wrapped an arm around my waist, and caressed my hair. Her gesture contained a transmission; our tears were from different sources. Hers was the deep cry of resolve, acceptance of the sadness in all that is unfair, of previously failed attempts at love, and the recognition that ours was yet another. The chain was broken.

"Let me talk," she said. Her hands trembled as she lit a cigarette—merciless beauty; I wanted to steal it, soar into the heavens. She said she had lost the ability to feel. "I'm terrible, I know, but I don't know who I am anymore."

"I'll come home," I said. "We'll get married."

"It's too late," she said. She moved across the kitchen, withdrawing her appeasing warmth.

"There's someone else," I said.

"I haven't cheated, if that's what you mean. It has nothing to do with that. I don't want *this* anymore."

And suddenly, she was unrecognizable. I was dizzied by her hollow eyes, repulsed by the crooked arch of her shoulders as she stood at a distance waiting for me to leave. *How is it? My other half no longer?* But she wasn't a stranger, was she? I was only seeing her as she always was, inaccessible. What stared back at me was the truth I'd forfeited in favor of my ideal. By some grace, strength I suddenly possessed, I stood, grabbed my unpacked bag, and walked out the door.

BOOK 2

14

———

Death is certain. Rebirth confuses me.

As I've said, Los Angeles was never meant to be home, at least not by my design. I came here to write, not to bear witness. There, the Hollywood sign on the darkened hillside. If ever a word was polysemic. H-O-L-L-Y-W-O-O-D, the universal term for the entertainment industry, signifies a dream for some, a destination for others, but it's no coincidence that sign is perched at the top of a hill, the apex of a hiking trail that actors, writers, musicians, and all the dream-chasers hike. How does one not think of the hill-climbing metaphor often applied to the arduous journey of goal attainment? When I'd first reached that dusty precipice, sweating, sucking wind, I stood in shock: it was all façade. The letters are cut from a thin, flimsy corrugated metal, tin maybe, overlaying wood, moored to that dry slope by pylons. I'd expected solid letters carved from stone, marble maybe, something with weight and depth, but no.

Here, in this paradisiacal, subtropic garden sick with dreams, they come from all corners declaring the legends in their minds, things of visions. What most find is their inglorious mediocrity served by endless rejection and cruel indifference. The dispossessed breed madness in her valleys. Each night from the starry boulevard come the cries of broken souls, a collective voice echoing its hungry ghost monologue. Land of sun and stars. The city of angels.

It's become common to hear people say that they don't believe in God or religions but are spiritual, nonetheless. Though I'd believed something of the sort myself, I'm not sure what that means. Even after twelve years of Catholic schooling, nine years reading Nadia's spiritual books, and half a dozen years developing a meditation practice, I was still lost in secular ambiguity.

All movement starts in the soul and by the time we become aware of the distance we've traveled, the destination, often unintended, is in sight. Adding this layer of confusion to life seems like a gimmick from a sick sense of humor. Why should this snare of self-ignorance exist?

You don't get what you want; you get what you need. How accurate. I'm left baffled. *What we think we need is often the very thing we must let go of to get what we really need.* The italicized words are axioms from the trendy sort of spirituality that emerged out of the mishmash of self-help literature and Eastern philosophies which were circulating in Los Angeles at the time of this story. People talked about *manifestation, spirit,* and *love*; it seemed everyone was seeking the formula for manifesting happiness and success. As such, Los Angeles was a petri dish for cult phenomena, from the strange allegiances surrounding certain acting teachers and their techniques to the exercise and diet trends promoted by movie stars—big business in a town humming with insecurities. Out west, the gold isn't in the earth; it's in the dreamseekers, the endless rush, the new infusion of strivers. When success eludes, they somehow believe they are spiritually deficient, that some vibration within needs to be aligned, then success will come. For this dilemma, multifarious spiritual groups and New Age churches await, touting their nondenominational gurus who regurgitate ancient wisdom as if they themselves had discovered the keys to salvation; they kept them in the garage next to the keys for their Bentleys.

THE NIGHT I returned from New York, I sat on this balcony in the same wood chair, staring across the rooftops above Franklin Avenue at the wildfires consuming the hills. Billowing smoke, black ropes of it, snaked across the sky and thickened the air with ash. What the drought had forsaken, the fires claimed.

Those findings I'd shelved about Nadia, the dark discomforts writing *Nigredo*, had awakened, staged a revolution. Blitzkriegs from my subconscious attacked my ego's base values; voices raged, cursed, pleaded, all but one that kept repeating *denial leads to suffering*, the theme of *Nigredo*.

My veil of ignorance had lifted like a stage curtain, and there was Nadia and I acting out our tragedy. There weren't scenes but vignettes, instances that spanned our nine years together showing the precise moments I chose to look past reality, past what my intuition was telling me because it didn't suit the reality I wanted. The denouement seemed blatantly obvious. Nadia *was* the gateway to my soul, the dark night of my soul.

For a week straight, night after night, the wildfires raged in the hills. Strips and patches of white, orange, and red ribbons like jagged teeth bit into the darkness above. Griffith Observatory on its flaming perch looked like a castle under siege and I, sitting on my porch witness to the destruction, felt equally scorned.

It's hard to know exactly when it was, but at some point during that first month of my return, feeling desperate to escape my mind, I made the mistake of going to Luce's for one of her parties. Gabriele was plying me with Peroni, curious to hear my thoughts on French New Wave cinema. Michael was on about his relationship troubles with Chloe, and Steve kept searching for an ear to extrapolate his theory about UFOs mining human souls. Luce just wanted to drink and dance. There wasn't room for any of it; conversation required an effort I just couldn't summon, and eye contact overwhelmed. The mention of sex or love, even words relating to them, jabbed me like sharp objects. Until then, I'd been unaware of how often these subjects were the topics of conversation. I hid in a corner like some misanthrope, longing to regain the tough-guy self-image, but I couldn't seem to locate the conventions of that persona. As I was sneaking out, I came upon Michael alone in Luce's kitchen. He was standing beside the table with his back against the wall, eyes screwed, mumbling as if he was interrogating someone. It took him a moment to acknowledge that I was there, and even when he had, my presence didn't interfere with what was occupying him. I assumed it was Chloe. "You, okay?" I asked. His eyes shot to me, looked me up and down, then scoffed as with disdain; it was as if he looked through me, as if I didn't exist, or if he couldn't tell whether I was real or not. I've never felt so insignificant. Then his attention went back inside to whatever it was he was working out in there, whatever was troubling him. This was the first time I'd witnessed his condition, what the others called slips. It was, in fact, unsettling; Michael was a strong, fit man and when he was like that, rage bubbling beneath the surface, he seemed unpredictable. After that night, I ignored the Orange Family's invites and locked myself in my apartment.

When Halvor called, I was too raw, too unprepared for the additional shock. He'd gone to a Yoga class at Kim's studio where he saw Nadia with Javiar Desiderio, a young actor on the rise. "They were definitely together," Halvor said. "Thought you should know." Barely a month had passed since it had ended, and she'd moved on? *Was I just a book she'd read and tossed onto a pile?* Suspicion consumed me. *Was Javiar the reason for her late nights, her ignoring my calls?* My Aries nature flared. I wanted to tear her down, destroy her so that she would fall in a heap next to me. Javiar? I would've reached into his chest, torn out his heart, and sank my teeth into it before it stopped beating. Wasn't I, the fire sign, meant to set the earthy Virgo ablaze? Remember that conversation? "Or I'll smother you," she'd said.

Months passed. My hair had grown wild; patches of gray and white thickened my beard. It wasn't only assumptions about Nadia and Javiar that tortured me. Something far more serious compounded my mourning process. Everything I thought I knew was being challenged—all my ideas of self, love, sex, purpose, God—leaving me with one certainty: my ignorance. Self-loathing came over me like a hood. There wasn't a minute's peace in all that time. I could hardly do anything other than pace my living room while grunting and wailing like an injured animal. But then it started.

When I'd try to collect myself, close my eyes and breathe, maddened or enraged faces appeared in my mind's eye, demonic faces, screaming, gnashing their pointy teeth. The realness, the details of their faces, the veins in their eyes, the texture of their skin—I could only conclude that these entities existed inside of me. Then I began to feel them. The force of their influence. I imagined them as energies I had unwittingly strengthened by fueling them with violent and negative thoughts and feelings. Not so much imagined them in this way but conceptualized them as such in an effort to understand what was happening. Were these my demons? Jealousy, Envy, Rage, impaling me upon the double-edged sword I'd forged to protect myself against vulnerability?

There was no escape, not even in sleep—when I was able to sleep. Bizarre dreams, haunted nightmares disturbed my rest, left me guessing at their meanings. I began seeing patterns in numbers, like Nadia's birthday repeating on clock digits, license plates, and receipts. I was in the darkness of outer space, not the serene outer space, the quiet expanse of peaceful nothingness we see depicted in movies, but the reality where the warring forces of planets, blazing asteroids, and gaseous comets battle.

Pain is inevitable; suffering is a choice. When Nadia first introduced me to Eastern philosophy, I gripped the edges of the magic carpet, but I wasn't in need then; I was curious. The tides had turned. I ran to the books of the spiritual masters: Meister Eckhart, Osho, Thích Nhất Hạnh, Krishnamurti. Front to back, I read book after book, and after completing one, I'd lay it beside me feeling I had just found *the* answer, as each book offered bits of wisdom that rang true and temporarily brightened my outlook. But it only took a day or two to completely lose hope in *the* answer, in which case I'd dive into another book seeking the shortcut, the formula that didn't exist. Or did it?

15

Jeff managed to option my feature script, *River Without End*, to a producer named David Guptman, who guaranteed he could get A-list talent attached. He had recently produced a movie with a couple of good actors, and two or three movies with not so good actors, but the reception of the good movie made him, so to speak.

"How much is he paying for the option?" I asked.

"His contacts." Jeff assured me Guptman's relationships were worth more than an upfront fee. "Just be patient," Jeff said. "Hey, this works. We sold your first pilot. Optioned your first feature script."

But Guptman canceled our "notes" meeting. Instead, he called to discuss the changes he wanted. "Sorry to cancel," he said. "Been dealing with the wedding plans, blah, blah, blah." His canceling in favor of a call was a blessing for me due to the state I was in. We'd met once, shortly after Jeff had called about the option, at The Ivy. Picking up on my inability to make eye contact, Guptman, the portly, hairy-necked ape quipped, "Hey, you with us here?" This came just before he delivered his lengthy monologue expounding the virtues of "tits," which ended with his cutting our meeting short to entertain a "pair of beauties" on some pretty actress, whom, I presumed, was looking to get into one of his movies. He even said, "Honey, I don't make those kinds of movies," then whispered, "for the public," and *she* giggled.

"So. We need to rethink this," Guptman said. "You ever see *Iniquity*? I think you need to go more in that direction."

"But that's a thriller," I said. "*River Without End* is a drama."

"Thriller's an easier sell. Hell of a lot easier to pitch. Dramas don't see the light of day unless they're adapted from bestsellers."

"You're talking a page-one rewrite," I said.

"Yeah, a page one," he said. "Let's overhaul it. I think it can be bigger. Set pieces, extravaganza, you know? Ticking clock kinda thing. I really love this Frank Ransone character. I can see him as some covert operations guy in a dystopian society. You know what I mean? Studios and A-listers love that shit."

It was an effort to remain calm. "Will I be paid to rewrite it?"

"You'll get paid when we go into production. But I can't do anything with it the way it is." In defiance, I cited the coverage Jeff had gotten from the readers at his agency, a solid recommend, but Guptman countered, "Readers don't know shit. They're kids out of film school."

I called Jeff straight away. "Sit tight. Let me talk to Guptman." Sit tight? Had I been tighter, I would've snapped like a dry twig.

∼

"WE HAVE A FEW PERONI." After months of isolation, I finally allowed Gabriele—he wouldn't accept no for an answer anyway—to talk me into a night out. "Just a few Peroni." As I sank into the worn leather seat of his antique Porsche, I was already second-guessing my decision. "My man," he said. "We have a little fun." He shifted gears and sped off, raising the volume on the radio so that the melancholy Italian peasant song he was singing along to didn't have to compete with the loud engine.

As we drove along Hollywood Boulevard, something in the way the white light cast by the telephone poles that paled the asphalt and created a stark contrast to the fluorescence of the marquees and storefronts painting the sidewalks had awakened a sense of the macabre, à la the perverse horror of the Grand Guignol. Also, the cacophony of different kinds of music, the bass from the nightclubs clashing with the rock and roll from the bars, added a nightmarish layer to this sense of the unusual. I tried to ward it off, but it only intensified as I watched the slow-moving cars that packed the lanes of the boulevard. They seemed like prowling animals with beady eyes staring out of their windows, combing the teeming sidewalks for prey: the clubgoers, junkies, swindlers, and tourists.

Gabriele, completely unaware of what was happening inside me, was in good spirits, nicely dressed in the calfskin blazer he made when he lived in Santa Fe and owned a tannery. Sicilian by birth and blood, he was raised in Belgium, but his English had a French accent. He spoke in metaphors, used words as though they were symbols. In entering his thoughts, one found the world reflected by funhouse mirrors. Graduate of the Accademia di Belle Arti di Roma, Gabriele had studied sculpting, even shown natural ability. His condo was decorated with white marble busts, one on the piano, one above the China cabinet, and one inside. He'd proudly indicate, "Molière, Dante, Goethe."

When I asked why he'd given up sculpting, he shrugged and said, "La mamma." His mother couldn't bear the thought of her oldest son starving for his art and insisted he needed to earn a steady living. Obedient to her wishes, in the '80s, barely a man, he came to the land of plenty where he began working as a car mechanic. At the time of this story, he made his living as a construction contractor, but in the evenings, he wrote poetry. He'd also written, produced, and directed a series of short films which were well-received at Cannes and Venice. His style fell somewhere between magical realism and surrealism and left viewers disturbed. Of course, the Europeans lauded his poetic brutality and raw sensuality.

Nights were long with Gabriele. He had stamina that only Europeans seem to possess, a sort of disregard for time, for adhering to a schedule imposed by a job. Living was what mattered. When you first met him, he'd face you as if assessing a block of stone for his work. Enigmatic statements would come from his mouth, *Fantastico!* or *Scopare la miseria!* You'd hesitate as if you'd suddenly become the butt of a joke, only to find yourself amused by this strange man's passion. It took me some time to understand him, to follow his conversation and fish the meanings from the Dalí-like images his words created. It was worth the effort.

"So. You are in the shit, my man." He nodded his head as his thick fingers closed around a Marlboro. "You know when everything happened with Olivia, I fell, man." Olivia was his ex-wife and the villain of his short film trilogy. "My mind was a tornado. I was looking out of my asshole, not my eyes. I didn't know what the fuck was going on. Like a shark in a fire. But you know, time just brings you back. Time is like the milk of la mamma."

We arrived at a trendy bar with a Russian name on Santa Monica Boulevard. I followed as he bypassed the long line of waiting patrons and marched directly toward the velvet rope. On the other side stood a doorman wearing a fedora and a car coat, making it a point to ignore those waiting in line. Never mind my aversion to the whole waiting-to-be-picked pageantry, in the state I was in, the thought of being rejected by this doorman was more than I could stand. I grabbed Gabriele's elbow. "You know this guy?"

"It's all good, my man," he assured, then planted himself before the doorman. "Buonanotte!"

The doorman nodded in a way that made it clear he didn't know Gabriele and that he was put off by his confident approach, perhaps wondering if he'd become the butt of a joke. His girlish eyes, complete with eyeliner, indicated the long queue, mostly men like us. "You on a guest list?" came out in a dismissive exhale.

Gabriele said, "Ah, no. We are going to come in and have a few Peroni." The doorman stood there staring into Gabriele's firm baby blues. Yes, his approach had flustered the prick. Almost reluctantly, he opened the rope for our entry.

"You see, my man," Gabriele said. "I am stronger than him." Chin high, he peeled back the curtained doorway—a rush of voices burst from the low-lit barroom. I was high on a dose of anxiety, but he smiled, waved his hand out over the mass of people as if it were a feast. He bounded directly toward the bar, moved aside the bodies obstructing his path, and summoned the bartender.

"Two Peroni." The bartender, who looked to be in her twenties, had the rockabilly style with jet-black hair tied up in a bandana and vibrant ink covering her arms. "She's nice. Wow," he said. "She would have loved me back in the day. I had a pompadour, man. Big. Just like this." He created the visual with measured swipes of his hands around his head. His chin shot up and baggy eyelids, smoker's eyelids, closed in around his eyes, made him look like a conspirator. "In the town I come from, there is a monument to the greatest Sicilian man ever, man. Do you know who is Salvatore Giuliano?" I shook my head, doing all to maintain composure amid the sensory onslaught of scents, faces, and sounds. "Oh, man. He was the greatest bandit ever. Fantastico. He is to the Sicilian what Robin Hood is to the English." Across from where we stood, a group was deserting a table. Gabriele moved quickly to claim it and I skimmed the wake of closing bodies he'd barreled through.

Gabriele went on about Salvatore Giuliano, how he intended to make a movie about his life. I listened with one ear, aware that sitting had not quelled my sensitivity to the crowd. In fact, it gave me a spectator's view of the social scene I had no interest in reentering. All I could think of was Nadia being wooed by Javiar, and who knows who else. Twice, I even believed I saw her there in the crowd. That whole damn show seemed staged to mock my despair—kissing couples, possessive arms slung over shoulders, the excited, flirty banter of those meeting for the first time. But what hurt most, in all those faces I saw dishonesty, traces of the thoughts behind feigned laughter and interest, covering the true needs those empty social cues betrayed.

"Look at that." Gabriele motioned toward a dark-haired woman standing by the bar in a revealing black dress and red high-heels. "Oh, man." He seemed angry, not aroused. Sucking his teeth, he folded back the soft collar of his leather blazer and pulled himself upright in the chair. "You okay, man?" he asked. I stared as he gulped his Peroni. His free hand laid a gesture of piety. "I know where you are. The dark room. They take our soul and say you are not good enough. Then your legs, you are a puppet. A midget with the torso of a normal man." He balled his calloused hand into a fist. "In America women think to be strong is to be like a man. They want balls. This? No good. The womb is greater than balls, eh? A bird is not a fish." He sighed, sipped his Peroni. "My mother was stern, but she loved me. I only want to give that love back. But American girls say *vaffanculo*. They want your soul and only for a toilet. I say, *no, you fuck you*." His disdainful eyes bobbed in the emotional flood his thoughts had triggered. "When I first came to Los Angeles, I was a dove descending into a bowl of chocolate. A clown arriving at the abandon circus. There were two ways to go. It was like this," he lifted his hands as if to indicate the length of something, "or like this," he closed the gap between them. "Do you understand what I mean?"

"Is that your soul opening and closing?"

That wasn't what he'd meant, but he nodded. His mouth curled as he gave it a second thought. "Maybe, yes. Fuck, it's your soul or your asshole, man. That is just what I see, you know? There are no words." He enjoyed a bout of laughter. "When I first came to this city, I met a woman. I was not crazy about her, but she like me, you know. Amanda was her name. Amanda something. She was a Jewish girl. So, one night, I take her to a nice dinner. After, we go back to her house. I had a lot to drink, you know. She starts to get hot. But I was not liking her in that way. I didn't want just to sleep with her. I told her I would sleep on the couch, but she said no." He paused to relay utter shock. "She told me to leave, man! Looking in her eyes, I was like hit by a truck. This was backwards. I could have taken advantage, I maybe even wanted to, but I didn't. She should have not wanted just to sleep with me and instead given me her bed and she sleep on the couch. *That* is a woman. But no. Then I knew what this place was, man."

"Hi." Two young women, a blonde and a redhead, were suddenly before us.

"Buonasera." Gabriele stood, extended a gentleman's hand to each.

"What are you guys doing?" The blonde asked.

"Discussing clowns," Gabriele said.

She looked to the redhead. "Clowns?"

"Yes," he said. "We are all clowns in the abandoned circus."

The blonde, the crinkles on her face, made me wonder if she thought they'd made a terrible mistake by approaching us. To my horror, she turned to me. "Are you a clown?"

I wanted to scream, to run to the edge of the earth and jump off; how had I ended up in this predicament? My eyes raked her; the outfit, the too-tight mini-skirt, the excessive bronzer and make-up, the painted nails, and the enormous breasts breaking the confinement of the too-small top.

"Are you a clown?" she asked again.

I met her eyes, grinned, and said, "Pagliacci." She grimaced.

"Fantastico!" Gabriele exclaimed, clapping his hands.

"What's that?" the redhead asked the blonde, who shrugged, unsure and even more uninterested.

"Here. Sit. Have a drink with us." Gabriele gestured toward the empty chairs. The girls exchanged a glance.

"We have to meet our other friends," the blonde said, clearly the mouthpiece of the duo. She quickly took the redhead's hand, and to my relief, they rushed off.

"You see. They can't accept truth," Gabriele said.

"Have to get out of here," I said.

"Yes," he said. "We try someplace else."

"No. I should go home."

"Okay," he said. "We try someplace on the way." It was no use arguing with him.

La Poubelle, a dimly lit French bistro on Franklin, reminded me of a place I knew in the West Village. Both had atmosphere, good food and wine, and walls covered with crookedly hung paintings. We finished our first round at the bar and just as I decided I was going to leave, walk home, Gabriele lured Imelda, an attractive make-up artist, with his clown talk. The lively twenty-something was game, but after a few minutes of Gabriele's surrealistic metaphors, which managed to confuse the hell out of her, she seemed bent on prying conversation out of me.

I busied myself by peeling the label off my Peroni bottle. She was yammering about the project she'd just finished when mid-sentence, she paused. I glanced up. "Nervous about something?" She indicated my preoccupation with the label, which I now folded into a sort of weather dial. "Why don't you look at me when I'm talking? You look everywhere but at me." I handed her the finished product. "What?"

"I made it for you." She inspected my creation for some hidden trick.

"What is it?"

"It's art," I said.

"This ain't art, honey." She tried to hand it back, but I was already busy peeling the label off the back of the bottle.

"I'll make you another." I rolled the label into a tight, tiny ball and handed it to her.

"You're kidding, right? This is art? Explain," she challenged. I held out my hand for her to place the art into my palm, the width of which seemed vast as that tiny ball dropped and rolled to a stop in the crease of my lifeline.

"My world," I said.

She shook her head. "That's just...stupid."

"It's profound," Gabriele said, lips pursed. "Bravo. I see it, man."

"Should I play my violin?" she said.

"Sure," he said, then under his breath, added, "Se ti aprirà la mente."

"Mia mente è aperta," she refuted, startling Gabriele with her Italian. "My father's from Assisi," she said. She snarled, snatched my little world from my palm, and dropped it into the empty beer bottle. "So much for your art."

I nodded, stepped away from the bar, and announced my departure. "I will take you, Vic," Gabriele said.

"No, stay. I'll walk."

Imelda stood from her stool. "I'll drop you off," she said.

"No, it's okay—"

"I'm ready, too," she insisted, reaching for her purse and cell phone on the bar top. "So shy."

I looked to Gabriele for help. He winked, "Just the thing. Wear your clown nose."

Once outside, I turned to Imelda. "Look, I prefer to walk. Get some fresh air."

"Who walks in LA?" She shook her head, grabbed my hand, and dragged me along.

She drove an Audi coupe with tinted windows. The interior smelled new. The music was too loud, some sentimental singer-songwriter stuff which she unabashedly sang along to, but it saved me from having to speak beyond the occasional directions I shouted. The dissonance was in some ways comforting, a distraction from my thoughts. As we pulled up outside my building, she cut the volume. "Where should I park?" She misread my confusion, leered at me. "Why you so shy?"

And just then, looking at her plump lips, it occurred to me: *She's attractive. Nadia's moved on... I'm a free man.* I pointed to a parking spot up ahead. "Park there."

Imelda took her time viewing the photographs on my walls, those I'd taken while on trips with Nadia. The bluffs in Big Sur. A sandbar splitting the Pacific in Gualala. A tarantula from Joshua Tree. Fingers laced, palms resting on her slender belly, she sidestepped from frame to frame as though she was in a gallery. *Her profile is striking*, I thought, hoping to fuel my desire, which was yet to arrive.

Once she'd sufficiently viewed the last photograph, she let go her hands and shrugged as if to say, *Well, now what?* She plopped next to me on the sofa, watched me smoke, making it clear I was supposed to be doing something else. Impatience resulted in her plucking my cigarette from my mouth and taking a drag. "Nasty," she said and thrust it back at my face. The quiet felt heavy, and only then did it occur to me to play some music. "Jesus. You'll put us to sleep," she said regarding the instrumental playlist I'd cued.

"So, you pick something."

She was looking past me, "That's beautiful," she said. "Wow." The macramé birdcage Nadia had purchased at the Goodwill store. I crushed my cigarette in the ashtray and headed to the counter, poured two glasses of wine. I felt it, that I wasn't up for this, but I refused to succumb to my feebleness.

Zeppelin's "When the Levee Breaks" kicked up just as I returned with the wine. "I don't drink," she said. "I was drinking club soda all night. Didn't you notice?"

"You had a beer."

"That was your bottle."

"Are you sober?" I asked.

"Yes. Well, I never had a problem. I just don't like it. I don't need it."

"Very good." I emptied her glass into mine, took a long pull. The glow from her cell lit her face as she messaged someone, granting me the unimpeded opportunity to let my eyes wander her body, yet delightful as it was, nothing stirred in me.

She dropped her phone onto her purse and looked up. "You're weird," she said. "You just look at me. That makes me uncomfortable."

"Before you said I didn't look at you." The contempt I'd developed for my pain and my resistance was at its height about then, redirecting into a sort of disgust for her willing-ness. "Isn't that what everyone wants?"

"What?"

"Attention," I said.

"I guess, but you don't say much, and you're not supposed to say that either." She pulled herself up, moved closer. "You wanted to hang out, right? And now I'm here and you're like not even doing anything." I was puzzled by how she'd interpreted our interaction. "Do you want me to leave?"

"If you want," I said.

Ding. Someone messaged her. She ignored it. "Why are you so...above it?" She placed her hand on my knee. Her eyelids fluttered as she leaned toward me. It happened fast —the kiss, then I was seamlessly straddled as if by a Brazilian grappler. I reached to place my wineglass down but missed the coffee table. The glass shattered, sending fast-moving streams of red wine across the fake wood floor toward the shaggy white carpet. I moved to get up; she tightened her thighs. "Leave it."

I couldn't match the gusto of her kisses. Oblivious to my state, she pulled my shirt over my head, tossed it aside. She was rubbing against me, moving my hands to her places. Because I didn't, she tore off her tank, and inches from my face were the perky nipples of perfectly shaped C-cups. I could tell she valued them, her prized attribute, as if she had, since they'd fully formed, not missed a day before the mirror to esteem their symmetry. She was waiting, studying my reaction, expecting what others had surely confirmed. To escape the pressure, I dove into her breasts, murmuring, sobbing, but I only managed to entice her. Now she pulled at my belt, and in seconds my jeans were on the floor. Sounds of rippling static popped and crackled as her leggings shimmied down her legs and past her feet in what seemed a sort of choreographed pirouette, and the leggings, featherlike, floated through the air and soundlessly landed on the rug.

At my eye level was a manicured patch between flush, shiny thighs. I understood I had to end this once and for all. I pulled her against me, held her tight so she couldn't move, but her jagged restlessness broke my grip. She threw herself down, pulled me on top of her, and I had to bury my face in her shoulder to dodge her kiss. She pushed up again, hissed, "Whaaat?" Then covering her annoyance with a strained smirk, she sprang at me, all lips and tongue, but I nudged her away with my forehead. "What the fuck is it with you?" Her narrowed eyes searched me, then widened with suspicion. She plunged a cold hand into my underwear. Suspicion confirmed, she withdrew her hand, sat up, and tucked her knees to her chest. Her cheeks reddened. "That's never happened to me before."

"Me neither."

"I'm going to leave," she said.

I hadn't said anything by the time she'd finished dressing, nor when she turned a look of madness as if I'd just told her Santa Claus didn't exist. The door slammed behind her.

I must have sat there for an hour, calibrating the unintended consequence of my disorientation: impotence. Me? In the hands of beauty? Then it became clear—all those times in my life that I'd gone through with it when I really didn't want to, when I was drunk or bored, clear that the highest in me, the guiding voice was telling me I didn't want to, that I was only doing it because *it's what men do* and because *look at her*. How many times had I misused my sexual energy, shared it unwillingly and took on that of others without understanding the consequences? And now, that which was highest in me had drawn the line, taken away the ability lest the motive was not properly discerned. Withered, I finally stood to clean the broken wineglass from the floor and was glad to find that the streams of red wine had not reached the carpet. I knelt to collect the broken glass and suddenly paused at seeing my fragmented image reflected in the shattered pieces.

The very next day, I received a notice in the mail from the Department of Motor Vehicles. On my approaching birthday, my driver's license would expire. Now that I was a full-time resident of Los Angeles, I had to relinquish my New York State license for a California license. It may seem insignificant, but when you suddenly don't know who you are and you're grasping for pieces of your shattered identity, such a simple thing seems cruelly ironic, like dying of thirst while stranded at sea. The universe, as I vaguely thought of the All then, wanted my dissolution on record. Victor Cerrone from New York was dead.

16

———————

This was all before Emily drew my birth chart and declared that Saturn's opposition to Pluto cursed me with the philosopher's disposition. "Your passions are meant to destroy you," she said. We were at the round table in Luce's garden. "Only passions have such power. But this is necessary if you are to take control of your life instead of living as if you are helpless. By integrating the shadow, you give up the outer world of effects and move to the inner world of causes." She sounded like the gurus in Nadia's books. Emily's guidance bent my mind toward new perspectives, turned me away from my self-absorption to see and appreciate the apparent yet overlooked miracles of everyday life. This is the first practice, to enter the moment by seeing it for what it is; to honor each experience, good or bad, instead of shading it with memories or ideas about what we believe it should be.

My whole life had been preparing me for Emily. From my childhood wanderings in the woods in Staten Island, feeling watched by some unseen entity, whose image I conjured from Giger's profane album covers, to Catholic grammar school and sneaking girls into coat closets for kisses, and much later, becoming a rakish prowler in the East Village, to the nine years with Nadia, who introduced me to Eastern philosophy, and the bedbug ordeal that led to Frankie and Halvor, I was being moved steadily through the stages, crucible to crucible in preparation for my teacher.

THE SMELL of red sauce drifted down Fountain Avenue. Luce opened the door wearing a cooking apron over her tight, white I Love New York t-shirt. "He's alive! Didn't think you'd come." She hugged me, then stepped back to the stovetop with her wooden spoon and gracefully stirred the bubbling sauce.

The kitchen had been repainted since my last visit: lemon-yellow walls with brilliant white molding. Newly purchased artwork in cheap frames was on display. At the table beneath a hanging paper lamp sat Paul, that tiny middle-aged man, an aureole of light reflecting off his large, bald dome. Socialite by trade, the self-proclaimed sage had renounced his predilection for the dark-skinned men of Washington Heights that roamed the summer streets shirtless and sweaty. He was now celibate and, as such, renewed. He sang along to Chris Isaak's "Cheater's Town" blaring from his cell phone speaker. *"You stood there, you smiled, you opened your heart and you liii—"* respectfully, he dropped off Isaak's high note. He wore his white suit, the same white suit he always wore, which was at least a decade old, but somehow still crisp and white like the freshly painted kitchen molding. His cotton t-shirt was also white, tucked in at the waist and showcasing his prominent potbelly.

"Paul," I said. He bent forward, offering his hand as a

Victorian woman might for a kiss. Tiny, soft fingers, like a child's, lay across my palm. To complete his mock formality, he lowered his chin, leered up through his spiky lashes, and said, "Thought we lost you."

"Steve's inside," Luce said, tossing broccoli in a cast iron pan. "Everyone else is running late."

"*Oh, baby, you lied to me, you lied to me...*" Paul was on his feet with the music, his hands pressed to his heart. "*You opened up your little black heart and you smiled and ya liii—*" again, he dropped off the high note.

Steve was splayed on the cherry red sofa when I entered the studio. He rose swiftly, received me with a smile and a brotherly hug. Despite his rough skin and thinning hair, he was handsome, though not in the classical sense. He had charisma, a personality ideally suited to the extra pounds he carried. He understood who he was in the social order and often said things like, "If a woman ain't taken by your physical appearance, the ability to make her laugh is the next best thing, brother. A woman laughing is a woman conquered." He'd let that settle, then add, "But she might, by the grace of God, find me attractive."

"Haven't seen you since you went back home," he said.

"Not home anymore," I said.

He frowned. "See what women do to us?"

"You do it to yourselves!" Luce yelled from the kitchen. Steve winked, waved her off. "New York isn't New York anymore," he said. "All the real New Yorkers pushed out. Who can afford it? Ask me, it's an elitist conspiracy." Conspiracy theories were Steve's obsession. He believed he knew who really killed Kennedy and Hoffa, or that a cabal of secret societies was creating a New World Order with the help of Satanic aliens. He could tie Reagan to the apocalypse and Manson to the CIA, and even though his logic took copious liberties, his belief in his theories was absolute.

He had a surprisingly sensitive side, too. For instance, he lamented the feminist movement because he believed their progress had made life more complicated for the women of his generation. "They put career over reproduction, security over love." His sister was a perfect example. She flourished as a corporate attorney only to arrive single and childless at her fiftieth birthday party. That night, she confessed to her family that she felt empty and unfulfilled despite all her hard-earned money and prestige. She recalled an epiphany she had one morning during her commute. She'd remembered herself as a child playing with dolls, saying, *All I want is to be a mother*. Of course, in the world she was growing up in, she was made to believe wanting so little for herself was less than she should hope for. At fifty, odds of conception had dwindled, and if she still wanted to be a mother she would most likely have to adopt. She hadn't aged well either. Despite the laser treatments and chemical peels, the tummy and face tucks, the breast implants, men no longer took her seriously. "I'm a fuck puppet." Steve would often fall into depression after speaking with her; it wasn't only his compassion for his sister that got him down, thinking of her being used by men, it was that he was headed in the same direction, and he couldn't use his career as an excuse. He hardly had a career, and he'd never stopped searching for the woman with which to start a family. Perhaps this is why he fell into conspiracy theories; no matter how outlandish they seemed, theories of oppressors were more digestible than groping through a hopeless reality and being forced to accept harsh truths, like the reasons his life hadn't turned out as he'd hoped.

Luce entered with two glasses of cabernet, the silent-moving Paul in tow. She handed me a glass, then queued an old disco song. "Aww—remember this?" And, perfectly attuned to the beat, she did the hustle across the floor without spilling a drop from her wineglass.

"These'll make you laugh." Steve thrust his iPhone forward to show me two photos. In both, he wears a proud smile and has an arm strung over the shoulder of an aging movie star. A second glance and Steve's smile seems tinged with irony; he's mocking the aging stars. "Pissa, right? He still looks good."

"Where was this?" I asked.

Paul scoffed. "Tell him."

"Went to network at Sundance. One night, there was like a crew of fifteen people trailing into the Sony party. The bouncers were holding the ropes open, not even paying attention, so I joined the back of the line, followed them right in. No questions asked. These two dinosaurs happened to be there. They both had comeback films premiering."

"And you exploit them on your social networks," Paul said, "to make it seem like your life is more interesting than it is."

"Lighten up." Steve clutched Paul's shoulders and shook him. Paul didn't like being handled. "It's all in the image, pal," Steve said. "My friends back home see my Instagram, think I'm living the life. Who cares, right? It's fun."

"For scheisser und giggles," Paul teased.

"For scheisser und giggles, pal!" Steve hugged him. "We're having fun tonight!"

"Doesn't S look spiffy?" Luce meant it, but Steve seemed reluctant to take as a compliment what sounded facetious. By now, I'd gathered that he was in love with her. I think everyone knew, but since she didn't feel the same way about him, her opinions weighed more than any. He moved to the mirror to tuck in the back of his tailored shirt. A knock came at the front door. "Here's something that will wake you up," Luce said, winking at me as she scuttled out of the studio.

"Oh, these two." Steve bit his fist. "The Aussie and the Brit. Knockouts." He bent toward me, "Remind me to tell you about the one I met on Tinder—forget it."

"Maybe she saw the pictures of you and the dinosaurs," Paul said.

"Enough." Steve stabbed him with a stubby finger.

A serenade of alluring accents spilled in from the kitchen. Anticipating what, I don't know, I placed my wineglass on the coffee table but when I leaned back on the sofa, I was unable to settle into a comfortable position. I was shifting about self-consciously as the gallop of boot heels neared. Steve and Paul went to the doorway and bottlenecked their entrance. I stood just as Leslie burst from the jam and came toward me like a comet—bright, gleaming green eyes, tanned skin, and sandy, highlighted hair. I recognized her.

"Hey, mate. Leslie," she said, holding out her hand.

"We've met," I said, still unable to recall when. She took a moment to process my face. I did the same, and then it came. "Years ago," I said. "During the play."

Then it came to her. "*Nigredo*! Right," she said, then realized, "You wrote it!" She did a little happy dance.

Luce shook her head at me. "See, I knew yous two met!"

A sudden sensation of heat on my right cheek caused me to turn. I found myself the focus of shy, lavender eyes that, now discovered, seemed exposed beneath the severe black bangs of a punky bob cut. She was tall, slender, with milk-white skin. A toss of her head and the deceptive bob let loose long, silky tendrils that swept her cheeks and hid her eyes some. She extended a hand. "Emily." Her voice was husky, toneless.

"Victor." Her hand was cold.

We held each other's stare a moment before she forfeited the thought of a smile and withdrew her hand. "Well, then," she said, "as you were." She moved past me, leaving behind the scent of raw amber, which swirled into my nostrils.

Everyone had a glass of wine, music was playing, conversations were branching. I still hadn't found my comfort zone and felt somewhat alienated from the pockets of discussion, so I feigned distraction by busying myself with my cell phone. Something about Emily had disrupted me; yes, the premonition that we were meant to share in some experience, whatever that might be. I watched her unawares; what seemed inborn sophistication in her mannerisms contrasted the strange beauty she possessed, like models I've known who have androgynous faces and a slight awkwardness in their bodily proportions that makes their limbs appear insect-like.

Michael and Gabriele arrived. Michael grinned when greeting Leslie and Emily; the grin was creepy due to his indelible tension and the psychotic strain in his green eyes. His talent and good looks had brought him early success as an actor, but something had gone wrong. It was said he was never right again after he'd subjected himself to a sleep deprivation exercise in preparation for a role, four days without sleep. We'd all witnessed him slip, when his behavior became aggressive and frighteningly impulsive. We wondered if he'd slipped in the wrong company and the word had gotten out. He'd also seduced the wife of a famous director he'd worked with—an ex-wife, but still. That had to have harmed his reputation some. At the time of this story, barring the slate of epic films Gabriele intended to make with him one day, his career was nonexistent. His primary pursuit was luring women back to his apartment on days when his five-year-old son was with his ex.

"Let's eat!" Luce yelled.

The men dragged out the long folding table. We claimed chairs and I found myself seated between Michael and Leslie as handmade ceramic dishes filled with steaming pasta and gravy, meatballs, and sautéed vegetables were passed from hand to hand and nearly emptied before they were finally set down.

"Anything with the script?" Michael asked as he arranged his plate.

"They want a rewrite," I said.

"Of course," he answered. He disclosed his latest trouble. He had broken it off with Chloe. She was only twenty-two, fair, waifish, not at all what one might imagine for him; he was forty-two, but he believed age was no barrier to love. After a tumultuous year together, they'd decided to take a break—well, she had. Only one week passed before she came back. In the interim, in a drunken state, he'd taken home a random girl from The Den. When Chloe arrived anticipating a reconciliation and asked what he'd been up to, he told her the truth. As she ran out of his apartment, swiping his son's Lego castle and bashing it to pieces, she screamed, "I hate you!"

He shrugged, pulled on his chin, "I told her the truth, right? You'd think she'd respect that. Because I slept with the other girl doesn't mean I don't love her." Though I disagreed and found myself in cahoots with Chloe, I was aware that my ideas about love were so confused I dared not speak. In truth, my attention was elsewhere.

Emily hadn't said a word throughout the meal. Sitting

with good posture, unnaturally still, she listened to Luce weigh the pros and cons of doing *Medea* in New York with Halvor directing. Though there was plenty of room at their end of the table, they were nearly on top of each other, shoulders touching.

Then the table was cleared and folded away, and the lights dimmed. I was on the cherry red sofa across from Emily and Leslie, who sat on rattan chairs hand-rolling their cigarettes. "To acknowledge the new energies that come into play this time of year and use them as aids," Emily said.

"But why do we burn them?" Leslie asked.

"Fire represents the conscious will. It's an offering."

They were discussing the vernal equinox ceremony Emily had come to perform. I hadn't heard any mention of it until then. We were all to write vows or declarations on pieces of paper and, during the ceremony, offer them to a flaming censer to consecrate the intentions of our wills and realign with nature.

"It's spring. The time of regeneration."

Outside in the garden, we were seated in a circle with our petitions folded in our hands. The night air had a chill, and above us, the breeze caused a gentle shimmying in the limbs of the grapefruit and avocado trees. Emily held a lighter to a tear of paper, then used it to kindle the twigs she'd gathered from the garden and stuffed into a bronze censer about the size of a soup bowl. As the twigs caught, the flames swelled against the censer's interior walls, made the polished bronze appear golden. We sat in reverent silence, all eyes fixed to the fire as the golden light burnished the foreheads and cheeks of Emily's congregation.

Now she was standing earnest and upright in the center of our circle, eyes closed, whispering incantations. Ceremoniously and by degrees, she turned clockwise, bowing to acknowledge the four cardinal directions and corresponding elements: north, earth; east, air; south, fire; west, water. She didn't say any of this, and we didn't exactly know what she was doing, but no one questioned the theatrics. Perhaps it was that the rituals of our ancestors lingered in our blood. It could've been that the ambiguous neo-spiritualism circulating in the world at that time, especially in Los Angeles, had made such things fashionable so as not to seem outrageous, particularly among a group of free-thinking artists. It could've been that we'd all been desensitized by a yoga or meditation class where some eccentric instructor mentioned such things, or at some Hollywood party, where a lost soul high on cocaine was yapping about bioenergy healing and reptilians. Or maybe it was just that each of us, seemingly impotent in creating the careers we desired, needed to believe in the efficacy of rituals, in the ability to call upon the help of Unseen forces. I know I was transported to the 10th Street studio where Navid performed the healing ceremony for Nadia, still clinging to the belief that the healing would've had lasting results had she not uncovered his trick and withdrawn the power she granted him. I was still undecided about whether I'd manifested the play or if it was just in the cards; I'd also lost Nadia and had certainly not tried to manifest that. I was willing to espouse any practice in exchange for a belief that would heal me.

Emily instructed us, one by one, to approach the censer, commit to the vow, then place the petition on the fire. "Believe," she said. Instantly, the voice in my head reminded, *Belief is key*. It was interesting to see how the intentions held in my friend's minds affected them as they approached the censer with their written vows. Luce was timid, emotional; Michael tense; Gabriele stern, nearly vengeful; Paul serene. When my turn came, I was self-conscious; I wanted to be as focused as the others, to believe in what I'd written on my petition. "It's all the same," Emily said. "The magic is in writing the words." She motioned toward the glowing censer, and I placed my vow in the flames, watched the pure, white paper blacken, curl at the edges, and fold in upon itself.

Then the ceremony was over. Luce's was thumping with blaring disco classics. Luce, Emily, and Leslie danced without reserve. Michael and Steve danced at a distance as if there were a border separating them from the women. Paul occupied a corner of the studio; his impassioned dance recalled forays at Manhattan after-hours clubs or the blue-lighted bars in Harlem that popped up on dark streets next to industrial yards. Gabriele stood like an eager player on the sidelines, sipping a Peroni, head clucking, every so often giving over to a dance move that seemed more like an involuntary spasm than anything inspired by musical beats.

"Luce!" Steve, face drenched with sweat, shouted over the music. He wanted her to watch his dance moves that were now outdated and as such comical, but she ignored him in deference to her own moves. He shook his head, waved her off, and disappeared into the kitchen.

"Vic!" Luce yelled. I was on the sofa, contemplating the vow I'd placed in the censer. "Look at him sitting there. Get over here, you!" She grabbed my wrists, pulled me from the sofa, and twirled me into Leslie, who straddled my thigh and entrapped my rigid, confused body in her dance. I'd crashed-landed into an all-too-physical reality and tried to step away, extract myself from the situation, when suddenly Emily came up behind me. She and Leslie locked hands and I, inert and wooden, was sandwiched between them. "Come on!" Luce yelled, protesting my resistance with a shove that nearly toppled me. "Oh, to hell with you." The embarrassment was excruciating; I slid out from between them, went for my wine, drank the glass down.

Emily made her way to where I stood recovering. Her head tilted to the side as if to address a child. "Doing good, mate?" She could see I wasn't. She bent to retrieve her tobacco and rolling papers from the coffee table when her lighter fell to the floor and slid beneath the sofa. "Par for course," she said as she reached under the sofa, groping for the lighter. I noticed a small tattoo on the underside of her left wrist, a symbol inked in black. She peered up at me, her face lunar, aglow; her smirk was like a match strike, no trace of shyness in those lavender eyes any longer. "Nothing's easy, eh?" She finally came up with the lighter.

Leslie was asleep on Luce's bed. The others had left. It was around three in the morning, but Emily, on the cherry red sofa, and Luce, reclining on the floor before her, were deep in a discussion about art, whether life imitates art or art imitates life. Just beside them, I was seated on a ratan chair —their audience—watching and listening.

Emily paused to find the words, eyes trailing to the ceiling. "It's necessary to define ourselves," she said, "so we present an image for the world. An idea of who we think we are and how we want to be perceived by others. The catch is, we become attached to the image. We identify with it." She could see Luce trying to reconcile what she'd said, held up her finger. "For instance, actors, writers, doctors, lawyers, whatever—are not who we are. They are what we *do*. Services we provide. But when we live to serve an idea, an image, nothing we do is authentic. It's conventional, imitative." Grasping her point, Luce hesitantly nodded. I watched Emily drag on her joint, exhale, and found my curiosity tweaked. "With social media, reality television, fake news, all of it feeding us opinions and lies, who has a truly unique thought anymore? We're afraid to speak what is true because what is true is true only for us, right? Truth is subjective to some degree. We guard what we discover about the nature of our minds and hearts out of a fear that we'll be ostracized if it doesn't fit the popular narrative. But if you look, you can't agree with the way things are—everything has become commerce, about money, and those who make all the money have the rest of us mired in bullshit issues that distract us from the fact that we are being fleeced. Therefore, uniqueness equals dissent, in the real sense."

She paused: she seemed to have real feelings attached to what she was saying, as if the tragic downfall of society she was describing was her personal mission to correct. "But the controllers even have a monopoly on dissent—the fake kind. Clever bastards have managed to orchestrate dissent and use it for their cause. So, we live in an objective reality and try to fix the world based on objective ideas. This is what differentiates Eastern and Western approaches to philosophy. The East is all subjective. That's why there are so many problems in Western societies, at least in the social and spiritual realms. And it's worse for us, for artists. Today, everyone thinks they're an artist because they have some talent. Talent is fuck-all. Everyone has *some* talent, but most people don't know what their talent is and if they do, they aren't grasping it as a means to understanding who they are. They simply want to quantify it. To gain money, fame, because, objectively speaking, money and fame equal success. All they're really doing is regurgitating what brought others success and ignoring their own unique experience. Nothing new comes out of that approach. That's art imitating life."

"Well," Luce said, "what's life imitating art?"

Emily sat upright as if inspired with new thoughts. "If we can agree on this—that the purpose of art is to elevate, then art must have transcendent qualities, strive for perfection. Without this, what we call art is merely *artful*, as in mediocre. There's no real vision. The person who created the wheel didn't imitate life, but forever changed it. *Vision* adds to life what we didn't even know was missing. And the one who discovers who she is and creates out of necessity creates something new, changes existing paradigms. That is when life imitates art."

Luce glanced at me as she digested that. "But if God created the world, which is what *I* believe, then the world as it is, is what it's supposed to be. It isn't supposed to be perfect."

Emily didn't skip a beat. "God? Okay. That's interesting. That's another conversation altogether, but. Okay. What is God?" Luce stared at her. Emily said, "Exactly. So how many people do you know who actually have faith—true faith founded in a personal experience of God?"

She waited for Luce to grasp what she was saying. "I know lots of people who have faith, but—"

Emily interjected, "Forget that. How does one achieve true faith? That's what we're really talking about. We can only have true faith when we discover who we really are. By shaking the given ideas of God and faith and the wrong conclusions about morality. By surrendering to what is. With striving, the meaning in our experiences will undoubtedly reveal what God is. Then, if we are lucky, inner union comes, perfection. And I don't mean the God of religion, although *She* is submerged in all *those* doctrines, I mean

God who invites us to participate in creation. The person seeking to understand himself is really seeking to find God in himself. This is what art is all about. So, the real question is, what gives life its meaning?" She awaited an answer, but Luce came up blank. Emily turned her lavender eyes on me, grinned at my uncertainty, and said, "Vision gives life its meaning. A vision of union, perfection. When art is created from this understanding, the world changes. *Life* imitates art."

THAT NIGHT I dreamed I was sitting in the front pew of an old church, staring at the burnished crucifix hanging behind the altar. Atop the altar sat two censers letting streams of frankincense. The doors at the back of the church opened and blinding sunlight filled the doorway; so bright it was that it seemed the sun had dropped down to earth just outside the church. As I squinted from the intense light, a figure materialized in the doorway, a distorted silhouette, then it retreated. Somehow, I knew I had to follow.

When I stepped out of the church doors, the light instantly dissipated, and I was standing at the trailhead of a forest. I walked the trail until I came to a wide clearing blanketed by autumn leaves, yet all the trees were flush with summer-green leaves. Just then, it occurred to me that I was dreaming. A sense of playfulness came over me and I bent down, scooped a handful of leaves, tossed them into the air, and watched as they fell around me. Then she was there, Emily, across the clearing draped in a long, white muslin gown, hands cupped and pressed to her chest. The yellow, orange, and red leaves beneath her bare feet made it seem she was hovering above flames. The sense was that I knew her intimately; I trusted her. She whispered into the cocoon of her hands, raised them above her head, spread them, and a black finch flew off through the trees.

I woke instilled with the belief that there was a reason for my ordeal, that the disorientation I'd been experiencing had far more significance than I could have guessed. What was yet to become clear was that my desperate foraging into varying spiritual paths to find one that could free me had inadvertently supplied me with the intellectual understanding required for Emily's mentoring, which was about to begin.

"Thoughts are determining the quality of your reality," she insisted. "Illusory thoughts." I heard it so many times, read it that many more, but it was her husky voice, the certainty of its tone that brought it home. "We can't face the traumas of life because we don't accept them. We stuff them down, deny our emotions, and end up neurotic, trying to control anything and everything that threatens our comfort. But suffering is essential to growth. Welcome it." Emily came with a halo, not horns.

17

———

She called it research.

On the morning of the day it began, my Chinese horoscope, shaken from a can of sticks, read, *a foreigner will enrich you.* An hour later, Luce knocked on my door, accompanied by the lavender-eyed Brit, who trailed in behind her with the languorous gait of a forlorn poet, suede ankle boots clomping on my fake wood floor. Weeks had passed since the dinner at Luce's. I'd gone back into isolation and I was averse to company, but my resistance melted the moment I saw Emily.

Sprawled on the shaggy white carpet of my living room floor, the three of us shared Emily's hand-rolled cigarettes and finished the bottle of cabernet they'd brought. With the teakwood blinds drawn, blocks of clear light carved our bodies in shadows. Muffled traffic sounds from Hollywood Boulevard crept over the rooftops of the adjacent shopping center onto my porch and drifted in through the open door to fill the spaces of our silence.

I'd soon learn that Emily was bent on changing the fixed ideas of things. She'd ask questions or make enigmatic statements that at first seemed random or nonsensical, then later, when busied in some mundane task, they'd resound and hit with purpose, meaning. She'd call to light a conviction of mine and not only present the opposite point of view, but a median, and somehow make both seem persuasive in their truth, thereby redefining the perimeters of my conviction. Her Promethean talent opened my mind, stretched it beyond its normal range, a process often calling for changes I wasn't quite prepared to enter.

She was telling of the meeting she'd had the day before with a Danish director to discuss the role of a sex-addicted sugar babe. I knew little about her at this point, only that she was a year and a half out of a serious relationship and was now carrying on an affair with some famous actor whose name was yet to be revealed.

"I haven't really been active," Emily said. She was talking about her preparation for the role and how to find the truth of sex addiction in herself.

"Oh, please," Luce said, waving her off. "You and him?"

"That's only here and there," Emily said. "But it hasn't been."

"Sex-addicted?" I asked. "What kinds of things is the character doing?"

"Men, women. Two men," Raising an eyebrow, she smirked, nudged Luce with her elbow, "Two women."

"What's the film called?" I asked.

"*Les Trois Six.*"

"A horror film?"

"Psychological thriller," Emily said. Luce's face scrunched. "Would you pass?"

"I'm careful with the sex stuff," Luce said. "Depends who's directing, producing, all that. I mean, if it's tasteful, I'm more open. But not if it's just for effect."

"Right," Emily said.

"How can you best serve the character?" Luce said. "Start there. Sex is not who she is, right?"

"Hmmn. Right." I remember how Emily's lips twisted to one side as if considering the work that lay ahead; then, the moment her wit arrived, how her body straightened one vertebra at a time, culminating with the lift of her chin and the narrowing of those lavender eyes: "Research?" She looked to Luce, then to me. It was a suggestion, not a question; Emily understood the power of suggestion. I'd swear I saw the word emerge from her mouth, form in the air, float away ~~*R-E-S-E-A-R-C-H* ~~ What she implied flooded the attic of my mind with warm light, with what felt more like a memory than something that was yet to happen. There was an ensuing silence, lingering smiles, and Luce dragging her fingers across the carpet.

Her pun was wildly clever; research is the essential work for actors and writers. Just like that, she'd taken a word that usually referred to some tedious chore and transformed it into a scandalous action verb. Her talents were remarkable.

The memory of Emily on that afternoon—blue wool cardigan slung from her shoulders, those slender legs crossed to prop her odd-angled recline, the smirk arching her pretty mouth—will never fade. It's strange looking back to that moment, knowing now that she'd cast one of her spells on us.

AT SUNSET, we left for Luce's. The warm evening drew Emily and me into the garden for a smoke. My first time alone with her.

"Luce says you're a good writer." She was observing me

authoritarian-like, with her head slightly forward, chin cocked. Emily had many guises, could one moment look like an innocent waif, the very next an executioner. "What do you write?"

"Everything. I mean, started with poetry and short stories. Haven't published anything in years though. I wrote a play. Luce was in it. That's what brought me out here. To write movies though. But I think it was a mistake." I inhaled and silently chastised my nerves. She saw that I was shrinking. Her face morphed into an expression of adoration such as one might reserve for a child. She touched my hand with what seemed pity, and promised, "Mistakes are wonderful."

Unable to endure her penetrating stare, I found the beauty mark just above the right corner of her mouth. I felt I needed to redeem myself, talk confidently about the great fiction I intended to write. "I have this thing in my head about the kind of writer I want to be," I said. She nodded as though she understood precisely the kind of writer I wanted to be.

"If the desire is born," she said, "the ability exists. It's good you fancy writing meaningful things as opposed to shit. I'd like to read something of yours."

"Do you read often?"

"Every night before bed."

"What do you read?"

"I'm terribly shallow." She pinched her shoulders, batted her eyelashes. "I like mysteries. The writing is shit, but I'm a sucker for a good story."

"Hey, there are some literary mysteries," I said.

She sipped her wine, paused, listened. Only then did I hear the joyous chatter of the birds in the trees and the trickle of the fountain above the koi pond.

I was eager to say something, but I didn't trust anything

that came to mind; I was painfully aware of my need to impress her. That was just it—I became self-aware in her company. And *I* was terribly shallow because I remember thinking, though entirely different in every feature, Emily's beauty was a fair trade for Nadia's. I'd have gone south to north in the exchange.

"Do you believe things happen for a reason?" I asked.

She laughed. "Not for the reasons we imagine." She leaned toward me. "Tell me. What does Victor's perfect life look like?"

Instantly, Nadia came to mind, images of the Hester Street apartment. I exhaled and said, "A published novelist. A paid screenwriter living in a house in the hills."

"So success to you is in material things. Validations."

"Well, I want to make a living writing."

"Aren't you? And you *have* an apartment close to the hills. You *are* writing screenplays. Maybe you already have what you want."

I'd not come around to this perspective; nothing about the word "perfect" described my current life, outside of my health perhaps, but happiness seemed more out of reach than ever.

She filled a cigarette paper with the tobacco she'd pinched from her pouch. "Perhaps that's the reason," she said, then ran her pink tongue across the glue strip of the paper. I shrugged, unclear as to what she was referring. "Your breakup," she said, giving the final fold to her cigarette. "Think of it as an offering. We have to give to get. It's the law."

THAT NIGHT, I had another dream—a nightmare.

Flickering torchlight threw shadows on decaying brick walls as I ran down a narrow corridor in what appeared and felt like a dungeon. Nadia and Kim were chasing me, sick with need, like junkies. I reached the end of the corridor, which opened into a sprawling, candlelit room. Shapes emerged, structures built of wood, like medieval torture devices with manacles and chains. All at once, the space was seething with female bodies, coiling, undulating, and stretched on the wooden machines as the chains and bindings twisted their limbs into positions for orgiastic delights. Slithering movements and deep moans aroused me against my will. I was desperate to escape, but the corridor I'd entered vanished. There was no exit. A chorus of whispers beckoned me to join the orgy. Women in various stages of ecstasy reached for me, to pull me in, but there was something in their eyes—more than human. Nadia appeared beside me, naked, fiending—it was in her eyes, too—and pulled me toward a wooden throne on which she spread herself. A hand grasped my face—Kim's mouth covered mine, took me rising in her hand. My resistance withered from her kiss, and just as I was about to surrender, my gut tightened; I suddenly comprehended deception at play and the need to withstand my desire.

I pushed Kim away, only to see Nadia, crowned with a tiara of colorful feathers, spread on the wooden throne and being consumed by two women. "FINE!" I yelled, now ready to indulge. I grasped Kim by the shoulders, kissed her like mad. She was naked, forcing my hands between her legs, only I couldn't find her entrance. There wasn't one. I realized then, jealousy had blinded me. Again I was doing what I really didn't want to do; I'd fallen for the deception. I balled my fists, shook them in the air, defiantly shouted, "NO!" All motion in the room instantly ceased. Many agitated eyes stalked me. A hiss broke the murderous silence. Another. A half dozen became a cacophony. The women slithered toward me and I had nowhere to run. Then a voice called, *Victor, wake up.*

I was back in my bed. Aside from the light bleeding through the parted curtains onto the wall across from the bed, the room was dark. But...the wall. There was writing on the wall, letters in thick, black paintbrush strokes. I leaned up to read the words when suddenly a force swelled in the air around me, what felt like a diabolical presence about to consume me. Again, the voice called, *Victor, wake up!*

At last, I awoke in my bedroom. My eyes darted to that same wall, lit as it was in the dream. There was no writing but before the relief of knowing I was only dreaming could set in, my skin bristled, my spine went cold; something was in my room. Utterly still, senses piqued, I scanned the darkness. Listened. Though I saw and heard nothing, every atom in my body warned I was not alone. Carefully, expecting to be pounced on at any moment—by what exactly I don't know—I slid from the bed and went into the kitchen, where I sat smoking cigarettes until dawn. When daylight came, I saged the apartment, a useless endeavor as the nightmare twice recurred.

It's said the mind self-corrects in times of psychological instability. The psyche is trying to work out the traumas to regain normalcy. Emily had a different explanation. After the evening in Luce's garden, she disappeared for a while, but later, when she resurfaced, I told her the details of the nightmares. She plainly said, "They were attacks. We refer to our negative traits, which are really repressed impulses, as demons for a reason. Lust is a dark energy, and you were a gratuitous host. But now you've seen its truth and are withdrawing your invitation. It made a play for you."

The term *succubus*, coined in the fourteenth century and derived from the Medieval Latin *succbare,* meaning *to lie under*, was used to describe a demon that assumes the female form and has sexual relations with sleeping men. The succubus steals his sperm to impregnate unsuspecting women, who then birth deformed babies. Repeated contact with a succubus can adversely affect a man's health. In dreams the succubae appear as beautiful seductresses, but during the sex act, their true nature shows in some grotesque detail. For instance, the succubus may force a man to go down on her, and her anus may suddenly prolapse. These demonic entities weren't only relegated to folklore but were mentioned across Hebrew, Islamic, Christian, and Buddhist traditions. In the modern era of psychology, the succubus shook its diabolical significance; the deceitful sex act from which men awoke only to find themselves pinned beneath the demonic entity was scientifically rendered and termed sleep paralysis.

I couldn't write off the influence of my ongoing disorientation as the possible cause of my nightmare, nor could I deny the data from my senses, which clearly believed the presence from the dream, the thing inhabiting Nadia and Kim and the orgy women, had permeated my reality.

I WAS SITTING with Paul in Luce's garden in the shade of an avocado tree. "Think about it," he said. "You were probably a little boy who discovered his hard-on. What is this thing, right? They were called privates then, remember? Or you're too young." His raspy chuckle gave way to a coughing fit. "Your parents tell you, *no, don't do that* when they catch you. Then you go find a place to hide so you can investigate. It feels so good, but now you think you're doing something you're not supposed to be doing. Bingo. Sex becomes stigmatized—taboo. And human nature? We love doing bad things. It's instinct, to rebel against being told what we can and can't do." We sat quietly for a while as Paul drifted into what seemed ironic thoughts. "Imagine if sex-ed taught us the true purpose of sex, that it's a divine act? It creates life. Sex is holy. I mean, the sexual energy, if used properly, it heals the body and sustains vitality. But we're so hung up about sex in America. One camp tries to stop us from doing it, the other promotes it as liberation, for sheer pleasure. Believe me, honey, I went down that road." He chuckled again, sighed as if grateful. "Like all things, the answer lies somewhere in the middle."

Reflecting on what Paul said, a chasm opened in my mind and the poisonous elemental thoughtforms rooted to the mineral imbalances in my blood seeped up into awareness. Throughout my grammar and high school years, I constantly daydreamed about sex. Procreation, what made the sexual act holy, was above all the greatest fear associated with sex at that point. As it happened, when I was seven or eight years old, my father's uncle passed away, and he bequeathed his collection of *Playboy* magazines to my father, from the first issue up to the month he died in the mid-'80s. It didn't take long for my brothers and me to discover the many boxes in the attic. I can't describe the strange terror and joy my boyish mind derived from viewing the female form in those spreads. The women had thick mounds of pubic hair, and all the breasts were real, some perfect, others sagging, but real. Depending upon the theme of the spread, the women were smiling or faking arousal; some had the look and pose as though they'd been caught doing something naughty; others smiled proudly, usually the Midwesterners, as if it were a graduation photo they were taking. Soon after we'd discovered the *Playboy*s, stacks of our favorites were hidden in the drop ceiling of the basement, conveniently located next to the downstairs bathroom where my burgeoning impulse for the opposite sex was conjured and consecrated on the voiceless, two-dimensional images of stark, nude objects.

In Catholic grammar school, I'd sit in class thinking about the girl at the desk beside me with the knee-highs and plaid skirt, the two of us disappearing into the coat closet during lunch hour while the nuns were away. My pining wasn't relegated to one specific girl, but to all who in some way reminded me of the *Playboy* centerfold models. I even fantasized about the attractive lay teachers and took every opportunity to peek down their blouses when they bent over to get a glimpse of their developed breasts. Mrs. Nivolla, a twenty-something, sensual Italian English teacher, never wore bras. The year I was in her class she'd managed to summon the gross profit of my lust—even years later when in a slump, needing arousal for a masturbation session, I'd find myself recycling Mrs. Nivolla. Sunday nights, after a trip to the downstairs bathroom, I'd lay in the dark, imagining professing my love to her. I actually believed she was attainable, married or not. One might have guessed my penchant for writing love letters resulted in a few to Mrs. Nivolla. Thankfully, I lacked the courage to hand them over.

Around the age of twelve or thirteen, I received my first live-action glimpse of the female form. One summer day after hours of swimming in James Egan's pool, without provocation, the confident, fourteen-year-old Cara, a Staten Island neighbor, took me to the side of the house, closed the gate behind us, and in the shade of the slotted fence, unzipped her one-piece bathing suit to show me her ripe breasts. The images I retain: her black curls, matted with chlorinated water, frame her slightly tilted face; sparkling brown eyes awaiting endorsement. Merely fourteen, she already knew her power. That autumn, this time hidden by the slotted fence on the side of her mother's house, Cara taught me how to French kiss.

As it was told to me by the older boys, the popular boys that everyone looked up to, the treasure was hidden and not easy to raise. They spoke of buttons and clits, tongue techniques and angles, all of which were quite confusing. "Spell the alphabet with your tongue. It always works." Despite my concerns over the church's dogmatic stance on premarital sex, because I was still god-fearing at that age, I adjusted my antenna for the signal cast by the eager girls, who, like me, took advantage of any opportunity to find places for experimenting. Our houses were too risky as parents back then were wise to the spells of silence that came from rooms occupied by adolescents of the opposite sex. Besides, sneaking stifled progression kept it to short kisses and rushed gropes that left me frustrated and unable to sleep. Thankfully, my neighborhood was surrounded by Green Belt reserves, stretches of woods that provided perfect cover for such escapades. Over the next five years, until I got my driver's license, the woods served as my airy boudoir.

My first time was in freshman year of high school. It happened in my older brother's bedroom, in his bed, with Andrea Russo, my first real girlfriend and first heartbreak. At this point, I needed to reconcile the contradiction between my desire and my religion; it seemed impossible to control my yearnings. Why would God make me this way if He didn't want me to be this way? I'd reached the age of reason. Need I say more? From day one I was passionate. A young Aries is an exploding star spewing a trail across the universe.

But Andrea Russo, a Capricorn, was a spirited girl. We argued over everything, as everything was a contest. In the end, she won. Only two days after she finally caved to my persistence and we had our first brief, confusing experience together, she broke up with me. She'd transferred her wild obsession with Bon Jovi to Eddie, a high school senior who lived on the same street as Andrea's family. With his long, feathered hair and fluorescent weightlifting pants, Eddie did resemble the Jersey rocker. I was devastated, still reeling from the sensations of her interior, when at a freshman football victory party, she emerged disheveled from a nearby thicket of hedges with Eddie and his proud smirk. The idea that he had soiled my object of desire enraged me. Neither saw me coming, but I think I grunted or something because just as I was upon them, Eddie turned and my wild, swinging fist caught him on the chin, knocked him out cold. The ego surge left me feeling powerful, redeemed, but it was a short-lived victory. Andrea never spoke to me again. A long spell of remorse, accompanied by feelings of inadequacy, followed.

The sudden re-emergence of these memories not only awakened painful feelings, but a bitter truth: from the very start, I'd mistaken lust for love. I saw visions of myself in the downstairs bathroom with a *Playboy* on my bare thighs, staring at a spread of some gorgeous, naked woman, thinking, *I love you,* repeating it over and over until finally the expression of that love appeared.

And Andrea? Yes. It was there still. I'd not thought of her for two decades, yet there it was, my resentment for her. Somehow, it was bridged to the suffering I'd been experiencing since the breakup with Nadia; the feeling after both breakups was identical, the same torture only amplified by the deepened infection of that unhealed wound. After all, I wasn't lamenting the candlelit dinners with Nadia, the walks in the park, the heart-to-heart conversations, the loss of her friendship; I was festering over the sickening images of Javiar, like Eddie, soiling my object of desire.

This barrage of realizations was accompanied by instantaneous emotional validations that surpassed any need to question what I'd come upon, leaving me in a state of chastened humility. You see, I had always known, in some deeper region, that I'd erred, that I'd given undue value to sex, to beauty, which simultaneously prompted a desire and a need; a desire to possess what seemed perfect and out of reach, and a need to destroy it in utter defiance of its sway over me, reduce it in bestial acts and bring it down to the animal level on which I roamed. I remembered Nadia pulling me up from between her legs, "Baby, you sound like a dog!" then pushing me down to finish. Or when we were drunk, and I'd stalk her from across the room, "Your eyes— like a wolf!" Howling, growling, I'd chase her, and she'd run the same route of escape that always failed her, only to throw herself onto the bed, snorting, bracing for my pounce. Or when depression took her, and I'd sense that inaccessible dimension lurking behind her hollow kiss; feeling cast out and unwanted would drive my need to possess and control her. Like a hound, I'd fix myself behind her despite terse glances to reprove my intentioned presses, a steady seduction that never failed and left her pressing back even more desirous than I, allowing mutual sickness to dominate and deceive, making us both inaccessible despite seeming splayed, gutted.

Like a cold needle through the forehead came the sting of accountability: I'd placed the curse of my erotic hegemony on Nadia. All my relationships proved to be acquisitions to secure objects of lust rather than the mutual exchanges requisite for love. What folly it all seemed. Especially when Andrea and the "loves" before Nadia, for whom I felt nothing now, not even tenderness for what we'd shared, seemed like experiences from another person's life, like abridged memories of secondary characters from stories I'd long ago read.

A bizarre thing happened next. I recalled Emily's words: "Lust is a dark energy and you were a gratuitous host." Then a verse of scripture followed, a verse I couldn't recall ever hearing or reading. It wasn't the whole verse that came to mind, just a part: *the spiritual forces of wickedness in the heavenly places.* I Googled those words. Ephesians 6:12. St. Paul says: "For our struggle is not against flesh and blood, but against the rulers, against the powers, against the world forces of this darkness, against the spiritual forces of wickedness in the heavenly places."

I kept reading the verse only to discover, beneath my intellectual understanding of the words, their intuitive resonance was pulling proofs out of my previous experiences to back St. Paul's assertion. The eyes of the orgy women in my nightmare, the presence in my room when I awoke, the demonic faces that appeared in my mind to derail my attempts at meditation. Even the presence I'd sensed as a child when I was alone in a room.

Emily was the only person with whom I felt I could discuss my realizations, but she was still mysteriously absent. My curiosity over her whereabouts fermented. I knew it wasn't an acting job that had taken her away. If I remember correctly, at that point, she'd had a series of callbacks for the role in *Les Trois Six* and was in the mix, as they say, down to her and a 'name' actress. I'd overheard her telling Luce that if she'd gotten that role it would break her six-month drought and help her to maintain her work visa. The last film she did, which was meant to be her breakout role, came and went without any public or industry awareness due to the way the studio had released it, which seemed as if they'd meant to sabotage it, write off the production as a loss.

18

———

Luce, impatient with my wound-nursing, and without an acting gig to occupy her, was on a mission to revive me. In a span of three weeks, she took me to a dozen coffee shops and cafes, cooked half as many dinners that were crashed by an Orange Family stray who happened to wander in just as we sat at the table; she dragged me to social events, film premieres, and art shows, literally dressing me and leading me by the arm to the venues, adding a pace to my life, the impression of "moving on." And at each of these locations, when fans or industry people recognized her and asked to take photos or just complimented her work, she gave them her undivided attention, at times gave too much, I thought. I couldn't imagine what that was like, to be recognized by people everywhere so that privacy no longer existed, but if anyone's disposition had been designed for such a fate, indeed it was hers.

Always a breeze in Los Angeles. The hills came up around us where we laid beneath a sprawling beechwood in

Griffith Park. Out there, far right, charred tree trunks and branches, remnants of the wildfires, broke the smooth lines of the slopes. Three hawks circled above. Luce seemed equally affected by our surroundings, glancing here, there, letting awe-sighs. Her chin rested on the propped fist of her right hand. She looked elegant, witty even, like a black and white headshot of a '40s starlet.

"Thank you," I said.

"For what?"

"You've been a good friend."

"Please," she said. "What have I done?"

I dropped my head back on the chair, found the hawks again; they appeared fixed in that endless blue, wings spread, not flying, just being. *Yes. Like that.*

That night, Steve crashed our dinner at Luce's. After we'd finished eating, he pulled me into the studio. "What goes on with you two?" he asked.

"Nothing," I said.

He stared into my eyes as though trying to uncover a lie. Placing a hand on my shoulder, he leaned closer. "You know me and her, we have our thing."

"No," I said. "I didn't."

He nodded, put a finger to his lips. I smirked, waved him off, certain he was kidding. "No. Really," he insisted. "So." He waited for me to nod that I understood.

It was in that burlesque bar on Melrose, after I watched Luce cheer on the dancing girls and drain a Russian Mule, that she finally mentioned her. "Emily's back tomorrow," she said.

I tried to be nonchalant. "From where?"

"The Virgin Islands." *Emily in the Virgin Islands?* She shot me a look, was grinning ear to ear, "You like her."

"She's *your* girl crush."

"Yep," she said.

"She doesn't seem like the kind to vacation in the Caribbean."

"The actor she dates. He's doing a film on St. John's. He flew her out."

"Who is it?" I asked. Luce shrugged, turned away, began fixing the collar of her sweater. "It's nothing serious. Just sex." *Just sex.* Those words, a reminder of my last attempt at *just-sex* with Imelda. If the opportunity with Emily came, would I fail to rise to the occasion? I quickly cut this train of thought as I didn't want to feed my fears in that direction. Luce glanced at me, and I'd swear she meant it as a warning: "Emily's not one for relationships." Just then, jazzy music erupted. Luce hooted and raised her glass as the burlesque dancers burst from behind the red velvet curtains onto the stage.

Emily returned the next day and that evening, met us at Luce's. She greeted me with a hug and a kiss meant for my cheek that caught the corner of my mouth. "I was excited to see you," she said. As we settled in, I noticed that her complexion was paler than it was before her island getaway, that she now had dark bags under her eyes. A jealous sensation coursed me. *She must not have seen much beyond the hotel room.*

But the night ended abruptly. Luce was rambling on about what, I forget. I was eagerly waiting for the opportunity to get Emily's opinion on demonic possession and to hear her interpretations of the traumatic memories I'd unearthed like sarcophaguses in the Valley of the Kings. But she was fading. She looked exhausted. Finally, she stood. "Run down from my trip," she said, pulling her sweater closed to ward off a chill. She quickly gathered her tobacco pouch and rolling papers, stuffed them into her bag.

"You're going?" Luce asked. Emily nodded, and without a word, somewhat unsteadily walked into the kitchen. We heard the front door open and close. Luce turned to me. "I say something?"

"No," I said.

"Weirdo," Luce said, shrugging it off.

On my drive home, I got that feeling that has now become a mainstay in my catalogue of moods. In this instance, it was caused by my impression of the permeating luminosity in the night sky, how it was dark and light and made pure darkness, as in the absence of light, seem earthbound. Like the rich darkness laying on lightless, tree-lined streets that became absolute blackness beneath the hedgerows. Something about *that* darkness terrified me. Adding to this fright was the staid movement of the silhouetted palm crowns against the night sky, which somehow spoke of indifference and the existential hell of eternal returns.

"WHAT ARE YOU DOING?" Luce was on the other end of the line. "We're coming to get you."

"Where we going?" I don't know why I even asked. If she'd said, *The sewage plant*, it wouldn't have mattered.

"The beach. See you in ten."

We took the 101, exited at Las Virgenes, and drove west through scenic Malibu Canyon. In the hillside, sunlight-bleached patches nearly stripped of color stood in contrast to the cool blues and greens of the shaded patches. As we drove the narrow, winding road, my eyes traced the edge and its precipitous drop into the canyons below. My stomach lurched from vividly imagining Luce's Jeep taking a fatal plunge, a tension that only lessened as we passed Pepperdine University and descended toward the foothills. The Pacific came into view, metallic and shimmering all the way to the horizon.

"Fuck off!" Emily blurted.

Luce found the last spot in the crowded parking lot. I carried her beach bag as we walked a dusty trail cut through dense thickets of low bushes. Nearing the beachhead, the view opened to the crescent shoreline that stretched to Santa Monica. The farthest point curved like a horn and the constant milk-white foam of waves crashing the rocky formations appeared still, rendered like a painting.

"Fuck off!" Emily whispered.

Luce and Emily scurried onto the expansive beach. I stopped on the pavement to take off my sneakers and socks. My feet sunk into the cool, fine, white sand. I inhaled, could taste the salt in the air as I followed the turned-up sand, Luce's and Emily's trail that led toward the back of the beach, away from the other beachgoers. Up ahead, they approached two women on a blanket, who stood to greet them; both wore floppy-brimmed hats and sunglasses. I wasn't told we were meeting anyone. Only when my shadow was hitting their blanket did I make one to be Leslie. Her slender, darkly tanned legs nearly matched the beige of the deconstructed sweater she wore over her bikini. "Mate." She hugged me, pressing a sun-warmed, coconut-smelling cheek to mine. "This is Isla," she said, motioning to the fair-skinned girl sitting on the blanket, who held the brim of her hat as she peered up at me through mirrored lenses. Fiery-red hair spilled onto her freckled shoulders. On the blanket before her, tarot cards were spread. Leslie promptly brandished an expertly rolled spliff from her leather-fringed bag, lit it, took two puffs, and passed it around. Luce pulled four oranges from her beach bag, tried unsuccessfully to juggle them, then rolled one across the blanket to each of us.

By the time I settled in, Leslie was concluding Isla's tarot reading. She looked defeated as she turned to watch a couple passing hand in hand. "I hate him."

"Who?" Luce asked.

"The short stack," Isla declared. It was an inside joke the women found amusing. Apparently, she interpreted her tarot reading in regard to her relationship with some guy. "He wants to devote all his time and energy to acting," she said. "I'm fine with that, but why does it mean I have to get cut out?" She balled her fists, puffed up theatrically, and cursed the short stack; her rejection was all too familiar. She tore off her sunglasses and piercing aquamarine eyes, topazes set in milk pools, rolled up to deflect oncoming tears.

"You can't take it personally," Leslie said, rubbing her shoulders.

"It's so fucking personal," Isla said, wiping a tear.

Emily, half-snarling, half-smirking, watched Isla. "What did you think? Love lasts forever?"

"To hell with them all!" Leslie hooted. She gathered the tarot cards, reshuffled the deck. "Want a reading?" She asked as she sucked her orange and spread the cards face down before me. "Choose three." The impulse was to choose my cards carefully, but before indecisiveness could cripple me, I hastily picked.

She flipped the first card. Seven of Pentacles. "This is your recent past," she said. She flipped the second card. King of Cups. "This is your current shit, mate." She flipped the final card. The Lovers. "Your future." I glanced at Emily, who seemed to be calculating my cards. "So… Seven of Pentacles," Leslie said, searching for an explanation of the card in the manual that came with the deck. Emily leaned onto my lap, and in an affected British accent, said, "It's a time for reassessing. The end goal is within reach."

Leslie, reading the manual, nodded. "She's right."

"How you know that?" Luce asked.

"Boarding school," Emily said.

Leslie continued. "This is your current shit. King of Cups. *A man fiercely protective of his loved ones. Success in the creative arts. Capable of receiving and giving love without the restrictions of youth. Lessons have been learned. Ready for deep commitment.*"

"And this is your future," Leslie said. "The Lovers. *Intense business or love relationships. Masculine and Feminine aspects intertwined. Possible soulmate on the way.*" Again, I glanced at Emily, this time hoping to catch her eyes, but her attention was on the seabirds gathered at the tidal pool behind the beach.

My hastily selected cards seemed tailor-made. I wondered about the mind, how it sees what it wants or doesn't want in what it sees. What it does or doesn't need. If nothing else, Leslie's reading offered hope, and I wanted and needed both.

My attention was pulled to a couple on a blanket maybe thirty yards away. He was reading a book and her interest in her magazine was waning. She glanced around the beach, then looked to her man and slid her sunglasses to the tip of her nose for an unfiltered view; the expression on her face was priceless, but with his attention on the book he missed the tender moment. She reached for his hand, and when he still didn't look, she interlocked her fingers with his and tugged his arm. He allowed her this, but kept reading, so she rolled onto him, knocked away his book, wrapped her arms around his neck, kissed his lips, his nose, and giggling, threw her face into his chest to at last earn his return affection.

Shutter clicks resound. Luce snatching photos. I turned and looked directly into the lens. She barked, "Don't look. Keep doing what you're doing."

Just then, a ladybug landed on my sweater. I watched it crawl the length of my arm to my wrist and up along the ridge of my index finger.

"Name her," Emily said.

"You." I extended my hand to pass off the ladybug.

She held out her index finger; the ladybug climbed aboard. "Lilith," she said, lifting her hand closer to her face to watch the ladybug traverse her palm. "It tickles." We were close, seemingly apart from the others. With her palm face-up, the tattoo on her left wrist was on display, a series of interconnected lines, rune-like.

"What does it mean?"

"It's a sigil."

"What's that?"

Her eyes shifted to mine, briefly moored in suspicion, then looked away. "It has meaning only I know. Deep meaning."

"Like a vision board?" I asked.

She smirked. "Not quite."

"What are you two looking at?" Leslie asked. Emily held out her arm to show them Lilith the ladybug, but she had flown away.

Come sunset, nearly instantly, the breeze off the ocean cooled. Dressed as we were, the beach was no longer welcoming. Leslie suggested we go to her place in Holly-wood. I rode back with Luce, hiding my disappointment that Emily chose to ride with Leslie and Isla in Leslie's Range Rover.

LESLIE'S ACTING CAREER, much like her life, avoided slumps. She was no spelunker; she didn't have the heart for the dark places. Her work in Australia earned her celebrity status, which quickly parlayed into top representation in the States. At the driveway of her building, a tall, electric gate soundlessly opened. We drove in along the upward slope of a smoothly paved driveway and just around a shrub-lined bend, the view opened to a gleaming, metallic façade with an arrangement of sizeable balconies.

Leslie answered the door and led us into a spacious living room, Pottery Barn bohemian and unremarkable, out through sliding glass doors, and onto the balcony. In the corner of the outdoor sectional, legs tucked beneath her, Emily was smoking and stargazing. Isla had gone home. Leslie poured us wine, then sat beside me on the sectional. A sudden curiosity bordering flirtation propelled her to ask question after question about my experiences growing up in New York. She even held the cigarette we shared to my lips when it was my turn to drag. I won't lie; the attention from the beautiful young Aussie felt good. "Give a hand, mate, yeah?" She jumped to her feet, took my hand, and led me inside, explaining, "I bought this sculpture to hang above my bed, but it's too heavy for me."

We entered her sprawling bedroom with the sounds of our footsteps on the wood floor echoing off the high ceiling and sheet-rocked walls. The room was empty but for the king-sized canopy bed of Indonesian palm in its center. It had tessellated vinery in the posts and sheer magenta curtains draping down that nearly touched the underlying cowhide rug.

Light from the walk-in closet spilled across the floor. "It's here." I stepped into the closet. "The attachment's already in the ceiling above the bed. Need you to lift it so I can attach it." She gestured to a crude iron sculpture with cage-like twisted bars enclosing a hollow center. It looked like the skeleton of a rose that had never opened. "Cool, right?"

When I emerged from the closest carrying the heavy sculpture, Emily and Luce were lingering in the bedroom doorway. "That thing," Emily said.

I slipped through the curtains, stepped onto the bed, and held it up so Leslie could attach it to the metal plate affixed to the ceiling. She strung the wire over the canopy and tossed the remaining length bearing the plug to Luce. "Plug it there."

A moment later, white light burst into my eyes. Leslie cried, "Yay!" I sank into the pile of satin pillows below where the white light, diffused by the sheer magenta curtains, bled through as a vermillion haze. The red sheen on the creamy, chocolate-colored satin sheets appeared a sea of blood, ebbing and cresting beneath the shifting weight of Leslie's feet.

"Oh, beautiful," Luce said, slipping through the curtains to lay beside me.

Emily crawled through, turned onto her back, took it in, and said, "Now you've a proper whorehouse."

Luce recognized an opportunity. A commotion ensued as she scurried off the bed. She'd run into the living room to get her camera from her bag. In Emily's closeness, I felt the rise and fall of her ribcage. I rolled my head, found her face inches from mine, but Luce, cradling her Canon Rebel or whatever camera she had, dove through the curtains and landed on top of us.

"Be careful!" Leslie yelled.

"Bitch," Emily charged, rubbing the spot on her forearm that Luce's knobby elbow just visited.

"All right." Luce was standing above us, gauging the light. She stepped over Leslie to frame Emily, who knew how to be in front of a camera. There was nothing gratuitous in her eyes, no tension in her face or lips. "Ooo, that's sick! This light is great!" Luce said, checking the viewfinder to be sure of her settings. Without a pause, she spun toward Leslie, whose face was in profile. Lying on her belly, that tanned, slender body outstretched and the beige sweater cinched gave us a glimpse of a perfect half-moon ass cheek outlined by the black bikini bottom.

I sensed the camera lens would turn on me next, so I began sliding toward the edge of the bed. "No," Luce thrust out her hand. "Girls, come around him," she demanded. "On your backs. Go head-to-head." Leslie and Emily shimmied closer. "Pretend like you're in your own world. Like, you know, in a separate reality. The aftermath of some encounter."

"Gee," Leslie said, "what could that encounter have entailed?"

I felt Emily's breath in my ear as she whispered, "Research." Her fingernails pinched the skin between my thumb and index finger.

Luce waited for the smirks to dissolve. "Em, Les—come on, you got a man next to you." In jarring suddenness, warm hands moved across my chest, my neck, through my hair. I twitched. "Relax, you," Luce whined. I inhaled and exhaled to dull the sensations of their touch and felt the accumulated weight of our bodies pressing the mattress.

"Look at Emily," Luce said. My head rolled right. We were eye to eye. I felt exposed yet utterly present, denying my instinct to flee. My heart pounded in sync with Luce's shutter clicks. Emily seemed to be enduring the same inclination to hide. Then hair brushed my left cheek. There was a warm exhale on my neck as Leslie's lips skimmed my ear. Emily's lavender eyes seemed to lurch to keep my attention, and having succeeded, narrowed with a sort of impish satisfaction.

ON THE DRIVE HOME, Luce was contemplative, as was I. She finally broke the silence. "I haven't been with a man in two years." I recalled what Steve told me about him and Luce, how he had touched his index finger to his lips. Why would he lie? And what about Halvor? I'd never gotten the score.

"That's a long time," I said.

"Believe me," she said, "it's by choice. If I want to, I will. Just haven't wanted to."

Then, it occurred to me. "What about a woman?"

She looked crookedly at me as if I'd said something completely outlandish. "Are you nuts?"

We drove for a while. "Someone had fun tonight," she said with a wink. "Which one would you pick?" *Was it so? I had a choice?* She looked from the road to me, then back again. "Well?"

"You know," I said. She nodded. It got quiet again. "What about the actor?" I asked.

"He calls her, she calls him," she said. "It's nothing more."

"Two weeks ago, he flew her to the Virgin Islands." She waved me off. "Who is it?" I asked.

She kept her eyes on the road, made a gesture, a nod to imply that what she was about to tell me was top-secret. "Tom Seals." It just kept getting better. Not only was Tom Seals handsome, he was also talented. But I remembered Leslie's half-rate tarot reading, the card pertaining to my future shit, The Lover, and the moment on Leslie's bed when Emily had revealed herself.

Luce looked at me. "What are you laughing at?"

19

———

The perfect Saturday. My initiation.

Luce had agreed to babysit the children of her close friends Rhoda and Aldo. They were movie producers and their new film was premiering that night. Me and Emily tagged along.

We arrived at the Spanish-style house in Larchmont Village during magic hour; golden light washed the raw sienna stucco, enhanced the colors of the rose bushes and the blooming bougainvillea vines streaming the wrought-iron fence. Rhoda and Aldo were dressed and waiting by the door. They quickly introduced us to their son and daughter. Rhoda instructed Luce on feeding them. We wished them good luck, then they left.

Darkly stained wood beams ran the ceiling of the rear portico. Embroidered pillows were slumped on the built-in benches, on every horizontal thing. A steady breeze with hints of gardenia and magnolia gently churned the ceiling fan blades before entering the open French doors and breathing life into rooms with art-laden walls. Luce's voice tumbled out from the kitchen, followed by the children's giggles.

Sitting lotus position on Spanish tiles, Emily played with the children's watercolor set. Increasing commitment shaped her whim, and soon she was painting as if it mattered. *I could spend every day with her.* I wanted lodging in her mind, to occupy her like a room and know her as one comes to know the secret hiding places. In a surge of inspiration, I reached for the piece of sketch paper on which I'd earlier sketched Emily's profile as she smoked and gazed over the yard, and a charcoal pencil Luce left behind from her abandoned effort at sketching me. I wrote a poem I later gave to Luce after Emily suggested we make an offering to each other, something personal to empower the friendships.

Emily looked up, found me scribbling romantic longings. "Perhaps," she said, "the things we never get to express won't die with us. They aren't ours, after all." She resumed painting, and while I contemplated her words, the shifting sunlight scaled the east wall of the yard and a shadow darkened my lap.

By midnight we were back at Luce's. Worn from the children, she was already asleep in her bed. Across the way, before the cherry red sofa, Emily and I were sitting on the floor. "We aren't subject to the whims of the planets," she said. "Our relationship isn't one of cause and effect. It's more like how the hands of a clock tell time but don't cause time." She awaited my acknowledgment. "The positions of the planets in your chart map the psychic energies at play in your mind. When I name certain planets, I'm not talking about actual planets floating around in space but the energies and principles they engender." Again, she awaited my nod.

I was a bit confused. "So," I said, "in this scenario, 'time' is the mind and emotions and the planetary energies are like the hands of the clock?" She impatiently waved her hand, placed her laptop on the coffee table, opened to a website that required her login and began. The website graphics stood out: it wasn't a schlocky money-grabbing astrology site with prices strewn across click bars, *$20 Locational Astrology, $30 Manifestation Astrology*, but a well-designed display with complicated symbolism.

"March 29th is your birthday. What year? What time were you born and where?" She filled in the information bars on the webpage, clicked send. A page opened displaying the zodiacal band, a circular chart that was divided into twelve sections with corresponding degrees and aspects of influence. For example, 00° Mars 04'. Inside the zodiacal band, twelve sections denoted the twelve houses, and in each were the symbols of the planet affecting that house, the degrees and aspects of their influence. Inside that band was a third circle with blue and red lines drawn at precise angles to show how the planetary energies, their degrees and aspects, connect to and influence each house. What I was looking at was the alignment in the stars on the day I was born.

Emily ingested the chart. "These sections explain your personality. You're born under Aries, a fire sign, but your ascendant, descendant, so on and so forth, may influence tendencies that overshadow some Aries aspects."

This, I grasped. "What is my rising?"

"Leo," she said, smirking. "Aries, Leo—you're all fire."

We read the lengthy report that explained the chart and used terms like *trines* and *squaring* to describe the relationships; it was way beyond my comprehension. Then, pertaining to each section were the characteristics and traits one such as myself would embody. Quite specific things: *You're fiercely independent; you must be first in everything you do; you rush in where angels fear to tread; your dreams and fantasies are important to you; you have an unstable and unconventional approach to relationships; in the realm of art you are attracted to the bizarre and unusual; heavily involved in investigating and idealizing foreign and exotic intellectual systems and religious philosophies; you rarely get involved with anyone unless he or she has something very practical to offer you.*

She glanced at me. Without a word, she reread the report and when she finished, only said, "Ah." She seemed confused, looked me over, then studied the chart again. She pointed to a red line denoting Pluto's aspect. "Hmm." Again, she looked me over.

"What?"

"Pluto's transit is in opposition to your sun," she said.

"Is that bad?" I asked.

"Pluto deals with your power of transformation. When it's found here, as it is in your chart, it points to inevitable change, usually radical changes. And, no surprise, changes in your attitude toward relationships." My exhale was heavy, burdened by the accuracy of the reading and all the recent changes in my life. "But it's calling into question your destructive influences," she said, "your ability to transform and rebuild." She read more. "This is...interesting." She pointed to another line. "Saturn's in 180 degrees opposition to Pluto. Polarized energies facing off. Fuck. You're getting it twice as hard. They say it's the worst possible aspect between two bodies."

"Fantastic," I said, trying to make light.

She warned, "These are powerful forces. Saturn presides over the material world. Oversees all order and structure. It's resisting the change Pluto's forcing. You want to let go, but you can't." I swear I saw concern in her eyes.

She seemed to possess some superior knowledge and a greater understanding of me than even I had, yet she was reluctant to share what she knew, as if to protect me from something I was not able to comprehend. Sensing this about her, that she held knowledge I wanted, right then and there I discerned her value in my plight. Dare I say, she became necessary. I remembered the Chinese horoscope I drew on the morning of the day she dubbed us as research: *A foreigner will enrich you.*

What did I really know about her? I was the shadow of a man, grasping. She seemed learned despite her excessive pot-smoking, the purpose of which she claimed was to lift the bindings of the egoic structures. "It gives the other perspective that the assimilating ego doesn't see—by choice. It flips reality on its head and with it, your sense of balance. It also enhances reality by making connections to the divine." Her uppity accent and the things she spoke about seduced me, made me believe she had what I needed to acquire. I even granted her the benefit of a superior education. She sounded smart, so I presumed intelligence, pedigree. I'm telling you I assumed it was earned, a byproduct of that blue-blood estate and its legacy of worldly successes. Because that's what I'd imagined, her ancestors rubbing velvety or tweedy elbows with the upper-class English society to produce something like the effect of genies being released from magic lanterns. That's how influential her people were in the world. They had to be.

Consumed by all that she'd said, I clasped my hands and hung my head as she went on to explain that the planetary alignments of my chart weren't only acting upon me, but humanity and all life, albeit in different ways, as all were an inseparable whole bound by natural law.

"We're living in a very special time," she said.

"The age of AI," I said, which earned a shove; this was no time for jokes.

"I'm serious. This world is fucked. Batshit. The hermetic prophecy states: *A day will come when man will no longer care for the earth and the Gods will depart and leave earth in primal chaos.* Does that not seem like what's happening now? Look what we've done to the earth, how we treat one another. But there's still hope. Chaos *is* the energy of transformation." Her earnestness amused me, and that annoyed her. She grasped my shoulders, shook me, but I was giddy from novelty.

"What do you want me to do?" I said. "I can't even control my thoughts. I'm going to change the world?"

"You *can* control your thoughts," she insisted, then lowered her voice, "and those of others as well." She released me, turned away from the fruits of her statement now ripe in my eyes.

"How?" She ignored my question, reached for her tobacco and rolling papers. "How?"

She exhaled, assessed me, what seemed a gauge of my intentions. "Do you dare?"

"Dare?"

"To become master of your reality?"

I knew it was a trick question, so I let it sit. "What got you interested in all this?"

"What sparks the interest is never a choice," she said, intimating that ours was a predetermined destiny. "If it's in the stars, you are called. Will you go, or will you stay?"

"But if you stay, then isn't that your destiny?"

She shrugged. "Depends. Destiny may take more than

one life to fulfill. Not all are called. But for those who are, for me, in this life, there is nothing else."

And her calling? Her renowned acting teacher didn't teach classes on how to act. He held a mirror before his students, told them not to trust the reflection. *Don't look. <u>See</u>.* "In class, we practiced 'being,' a state of remaining present without the conditioned influences of habits and defenses, which my teacher called 'masks for the more specific emotions we're too vulnerable to show.' An actor must first become human before attempting to know the heart and mind of a character she wishes to play. And becoming human means recognizing that all potentials are within you. You must enter the shadow. When you discover the murderer and the cheat in your own heart, then you can forgo judgment.

"I began to see that I'd *received* my views. I was spouting the shit my parents and friends said. So, I challenged myself. Back then, abortion was a ripe issue and I'd believed I knew where I stood on it, but when I properly opened it up in my mind, I saw that I didn't really know how I felt. There were good arguments in both directions. Extenuating circumstances. What was my personal view?"

At first, the discoveries she made about herself unsettled her and sent her searching for spiritual grounding, only to discover similarities, connections between the acting technique and the esoteric systems she now practiced. Both relied heavily on the power of the imagination, refining emotions, and overriding stored sensory impressions; the aim was to understand the nature of the mind and how it works, the nature of emotions and how they create reality. Both acting and the spiritual path required discipline and held the promise of liberating one from what seemed the unintended consequences life unfairly thrusts upon us. She likened her impetus for transformation to the process I was going through, only I still contended that mine was forced on me while hers was voluntary.

"Not the case with either of us, is it?"

"I didn't choose this. It's Pluto and Saturn." I laughed.

"Right," she said. "But the things you want out of life perhaps clutter the space for the things you need. It's the greater thing in us that guides. Of course, it seems forced. Your ego's rebelling. Your illusion of separation. You're holding on to something you believe is vital."

Her words triggered sensations inside me, what felt like affirming, emotional responses at hearing indisputable truths. I wanted more. "So, acting was a catalyst?"

"Water seeking its level," she said. "Whenever I got specific in my acting, whenever I had a life experience to supplement for the imaginary circumstances of the script, my performance went to next-level real. But there isn't always a life experience to draw from that suits the circumstances the character's in." In such cases, the acting technique taught the use of the imagination to create the circumstances, the magic "as if." Imagined relationships with people and objects—how they look, feel, sound, and smell—would then be supplemented. "And it works. Because this practice contains a great secret. The mind cannot distinguish between what is real and what is imagined. Commitment to the reality of what's imagined is key. It's like faith.

"Now do you see the power of the imagination? How many times have your assumptions altered your reality? We create illusions and believe them! It's insanity. But this strange play between fantasy and reality points to the nature of the mind—this is what must be examined if you are to take control."

Later, the "strange play" between fantasy and reality, or fiction and nonfiction, especially regarding what I wrote, would leave me questioning the artist's responsibility in the works he creates and the chicken or egg scenario of life imitating art and vice versa.

As she sipped her wine, the orange-hued lamplight glinted in her eyes. "I have to confess," she said. "I read your play on the beach in St. John. I wanted to know about you, about your mind. It's a prophecy. I know now, after doing your chart. Were you aware that you were writing about yourself?"

"No," I said, but then I remembered the dark discomforts that emerged when I was writing *Nigredo*. Even how she'd just demonstrated her previous point: on her trip to St. John, I'd imagined she was in her hotel room having sex with the actor the whole time and that shaded my reality, how I felt about her on the night she'd returned. In reality, she had taken time out of her trip to read my play. I'm sure she also had sex, ate and slept, and went for walks while in St. John, but my shortsightedness, my wound actually, failed to account for the hours in a day and how one might fill them in deference to diagnosing only what threats might exist to frustrate what I wanted.

"Your character," she said. "She's not meant to live off an inheritance. To be conventional, even. But she's set to do just that until she learns her family's fortune was earned through unethical practices. Suddenly, her identity is disproved by reality. Her dissolution is her calling." She waited to be sure I grasped the correlation. "Only, you failed to redeem her. She resists the truth and meets a tragic end." I blankly stared at her feet as my gut slipped out from my center. Here she was redefining something I'd believed I was resolved in understanding, something I'd created seemingly without knowing exactly what it was I'd created, showing me that my level of awareness wasn't even operating on the surface, that it was submerged.

"That means Saturn wins the battle. Is that my outlook? My unconscious belief?"

She shrugged. "Do you fancy yourself weak?" I felt weak; a bit dizzy at this point. "But what's most interesting, you wrote yourself as a woman. Do you know why?"

"Do you?" I asked.

"I couldn't possibly," she said, "but the feminine energy resides in the subconscious mind. Not only is it the seat of creativity, it's the link to the divine. Remember your nightmares of the sex-crazed, demonic women? By empowering Lust as you had, you'd distorted your ideas of women and sex, kept them base, material. Women as objects, sex as a taking, not a mutual experience. Your suffering was due to your inability to face these misconceptions and consciously let go of them. But the mind is always seeking to assimilate and correct, so what you can't face in waking life is presented in dreams. When you're asleep, the ego, so to speak, and its rigid structures step away, and the mind attempts to release the built-up energies from all that you avoid in waking life. That is why women appear in your dreams as they do, and the dreams become nightmares. Even in sleep, you're unable to face the phantoms of your misconceptions. So, perhaps in writing yourself as a woman, you were attempting to correct and assimilate these energies in a wider context.

"The mistake lies in believing there is a division in the mind." She paused, as her mind took account of what seemed a complicated problem. "In truth, and I know this sounds contradictory considering what I've just said, there's no conscious and unconscious mind. There is only mind and in mind there is what one chooses to see and what one rejects. What we choose is conscious, what we reject becomes unconscious, repressed. I'm sure you've come across this in all those books you've read." Despite feeling grossly outmatched, I nodded. "The key lies in our attitude toward experiences. This is the meaning of free will—the concept of free will is misunderstood. If God, or whatever you want to call the unifying principle, but God beyond our limited personal understanding, created all things, things being energetic experiences, then God is in all things. There is no good and bad. There are only experiences which we, due to our personal preferences, label good or bad. And this labeling process is usually the result of either frustrated or fulfilled desires from our past. Impressions that either *feel* good or bad. We then choose to avoid something that reminds us of discomfort or pain and embrace something that reminds us of comfort and pleasure." She scratched her forehead and waited for an indication that I'd understood what she'd said, but I just blinked and stared. "What we accept remains conscious and what we reject becomes unconscious. The fall from grace is in favoring our self-discernment and rejecting that God is in everything."

"I don't completely follow," I said.

"Consciousness is often referred to as light. The light of attention. Light reveals things to the eye. Think in terms of things we accept. The unconscious is often referred to as the shadow, the unknown. We can't see in the dark. Darkness is ignorance, and we remain ignorant of all the things we reject. The differentiation causes the illusion of separation. To come into the light, we must accept our ignorance. We must invite the phantoms out of the darkness, assimilate them in order to erase the illusory division and enter our ideal state. Union of opposites. The divine union is what being whole means."

There was literally a bell chime in my mind and it came. "The *Symposium*," I said. "The Androgyne myth?"

Her lavender eyes narrowed. She hesitated. "Yes, the deeper meaning"

My understanding coalesced: a perceived *separation into two halves, conscious-masculine, unconscious-feminine. There is only one. All is mind.* "Is it a matter of the will?" I asked.

"Our will is always being directed. The trick is to know this and take control. Otherwise, the enemies send you about."

"The enemies?" I found my opportunity to ask her about St. Paul's verse. "The rulers, the authorities, the cosmic powers over this present darkness, the spiritual forces of evil in the heavenly places?"

She was staring at me, lips parted, weighing my sincerity. "That's for later," she said. "First, see how the past is constantly repeating and determining your life at present. This will show you whose will you are really fulfilling."

"But if it isn't mine, then whose is it?"

"Well, if accepting reality is God's will, then whose would rejection be?" My smirk earned an indifferent shrug. "But again, this is hard to comprehend when you see things dualistically. No good and bad, right?" She lit her cigarette and exhaled a plume of smoke.

"And how do you know that's the case?"

"Will alone," she said with a wink. "And believe me, once you learn how to assert your will, it can be used for more complicated endeavors." The way she ended that sentence, the look in her eyes, the subtle opening of her torso toward me, seemed an invitation. Yes, we were coming together.

"You guys are still up?" Luce called. She leaned on an elbow, squinted to make us in the candlelight. "What the hell are yous doing?"

Yes, I know. If her character seems overwrought or her teachings come off as pompous, fabricated even, the fault is mine. I'm trying my best to render her objectively, an effort that can only fail. Know this: she was not the spiritual kind typically found in Los Angeles, the stripped screw dangling from pressboard. What I now know of her, this can be said: she was an esoteric anthropologist, a student of myth, a psychic pioneer. She scoffed at the law of attraction and the other hokey New Age chicanery for manifesting desires. "How can we want when we don't even know who we are?"

Like a Chinese box, her perfectly timed revelations hinted at the infinite, a character that couldn't be known. Our everyday world and its attempt at objective realities were not her prisons; our boundaries marked her points of commencement. While meditating on the tarot's hermetic symbolism, she claimed to have reached higher states of consciousness and, therein, received techniques for manipulating energy fields. *Received.* She'd made contact with something other, proof that prolonged efforts of the will made anything possible. Even her diet clung to a discipline, only freshly juiced greens, salads, raw pine nuts, and herbal tea concoctions. "Live things for their energy," she'd say. "Chlorophyll, not blood."

See? I still want to exonerate her.

20

———

Emily began instructing me. I must note something I found curious, which wasn't immediately apparent and only became so as I got to know her. During the instruction sessions, she seemed to become someone else; there was a nearly imperceptible shift in her eyes and in the tone of her voice as though she'd come under the aegis of a channeled being. Words were readily at hand with rarely a pause or search for a next thought or proper terminology. Effortlessly, concisely, it all flowed out of her. Perhaps she was shifting into an alter ego, I don't know, but whatever was taking place was genuine, not contrived.

Luce would sometimes participate, but she had neither the patience nor the impetus to engage in this kind of work. Only when the exercises seemed entertaining would she join. During this time, she'd had a few business meetings that required preparation, one for a new television series and two for film roles. She'd read the scripts then go for long walks alone to let the story run in her head, see what associations were made to her experiences, then bridge the known, the specific with the fictional story world. The truly creative aspects of the work are what she most enjoyed.

My lessons resulted in homework, books Emily insisted I read, which we'd then discuss to be sure I understood why she had me read them or to clarify anything that I might have found confusing. By this point, I'd gained an intellectual understanding of my struggles, past traumas, and misplaced values, but she insisted I needed to go deeper, to leave the mind and get into the body. "Emotions act as the magnet which draws to us what we desire. Until we heal our emotional wounds, we can't change the negative pull of our energetic patterns."

The first stage of her instruction consisted of exercises to strengthen my concentration. For unbearably long periods, she'd have me sit with my eyes focused on mundane objects or spots on the wall. The point of the exercise was to discipline the body in stillness and bring it under the mind's control. "You must see that you have a will in order to possess the will." But the purpose of this exercise was to see what thoughts and images appeared when I was still, those that made me restless. This sort of mental engagement, to use my mind rather than have it use me, was beneficial.

The second stage consisted of breathing exercises. "Healing exercises help clear the plate. Tension from past traumas blocks the inward flow of energy and disrupts the micro-orbit (the flow of energy through the energetic centers or chakras). Emotional blockages must be acknowledged and cleared." At the start, I'd be on the floor lying flat on my back. "Breathe," she'd command. "Let the breath locate the tension in your body. Breathe into it." As I'd breathe, she'd press on specific meridian points she somehow knew contained my blockages. They'd be tender, painful beneath the pressure of her finger. "Breathe into my finger. Pay careful attention to the images that come to mind." Sure enough, images arose that exposed some hitherto unrealized emotional pain; for instance, a memory of feeling humiliated. Memories, mostly from childhood, would awaken, those that had reappeared from time to time for no apparent reason; suddenly, by way of feeling, I'd discover a form of trauma in the memory. As she explained, trauma is not necessarily caused by an event but by how one experiences an event. Besides the obvious traumatic experiences, say some abuse, trauma could result from the most innocuous thing, such as a child not getting what it wanted, maybe a cookie, in a given moment.

The first thing I located was the origin of my need to control. Previously, I'd traced it back to Andrea Russo, only now, I saw that it went much further back. When I was four years old, my maternal grandfather passed away. I'd spent much time with him and the pain I experienced from his sudden disappearance caused me to have night terrors. As a child who couldn't understand death and what had happened to my grandfather, I'd concluded that the world is an untrustworthy place where loved ones disappear. But the issue was compounded by losing my mother, who in her grieving, became emotionally unavailable. A four-year-old, especially one as sensitive as I was, needs his mother, and though she was physically present, I felt the absence of her attention. My need for her affection and love resulted in trying to find ways to win her attention, to rescue her from grief, fix her, and bring her back to life. But these erroneous conclusions I drew as a child sent me out into the world seeking emotionally unavailable women in need of saving. An impossible task because it was me who needed saving, to be fixed once and for all and quell the frustrated needs of the child I no longer was.

Emily explained that the unconscious desire is always stronger than the conscious, so even if I consciously wanted something different, for instance, if I wanted to trust a woman, the unconscious desire is what my experience validated. After a few rounds of this painful cycle, the need to control became compulsive. Also, my competitiveness, the need to be the best now showed itself as my pride's assertion of false power, a refusal to accept the limits of my capabilities. But the breathing exercises elicited more than just images.

Emily would continue pressing the meridian points. "What do they sound like?" At first, I was unsure what she meant. "The images. When I press, exhale a sound. This is how you release." I did so, a stifled sort of baritone exhalation; I was still resisting the public display of vulnerability. "Don't control it," she said. "Let it be." So, I'd breathe, and she'd press and the discomfort would branch, spread as a caustic warmth across my chest and throat until I'd begin weeping and making sounds, moaning like a donkey trapped in a ravine.

After the first breathwork session, I felt high, woozy, and at once, weightless and awake. The meridian points in my chest remained tender for days. Emily made it clear that the exercises and techniques required practice if they were to have lasting effects. Discipline. "The very nature of the work relies on the interest and attention of the one who attempts it, on his earnest desire for change." Mine was earnest, and the work was transformative. I began experiencing moments of spontaneous joy, which of course, bolstered my belief in Emily and her *science*.

THE REST of the Orange Family found a locked door for a time. One Sunday after Luce's macaroni and meatballs, Paul and Emily had an argument over what song to play. "You always play that morbid shit," Paul snapped. The sage had been testy that day.

"It's better than gay country songs about little black hearts."

Paul went upright. "Excuse me, bitch?"

"Fuck off, little man." She stood her ground.

Steve got between them and cracked jokes to ease the tension. I looked on, thinking, *These are spiritual people? I took it all seriously; one had to be what he believed himself to be.*

That evening, Paul, in his rich baritone voice, said, "Our failures are attempts to achieve ideals in an imperfect, material world." The insight seemed harsh coming from that tiny man who looked like a deformed child dragging on the Newport perched in the perfect V of his short fingers. I can honestly say he didn't want anything from anyone, just the occasional company, but he did have opinions. He was wary of the sway Emily had over Luce and me. "Wants to be the queen. Has you two following her scent."

"She's insightful," I said.

He waved his hands wildly as if to scatter a bunch of gnats. "Please. What do you think? She figured out the things that baffled great minds for centuries? We're human and imperfect, that's the secret. Life contains everything between happiness and sadness. That's what's beautiful. Enter it, accept it—there's the lesson. Why follow her into her dark shit and end up crazy confused."

"You think she's confused?"

He scoffed, looked around to be sure no one else had come out into the garden. "A basket case."

His warning fell on deaf ears. There was no cause to

doubt Emily. Her teachings were producing results, making what was vague in my mind and emotions specific; my feet were touching ground again. But after Paul's attack on Emily, Luce withdrew her open-door policy for a time, kept the rest of the Orange Family at bay.

Once the clutter vanished, we—Emily and I—became fixtures in Luce's apartment. The dynamic amongst the three of us resulted in a precarious sort of intimacy; we'd opted out of autonomy to become extensions of one another. On a superficial level, it's easy to understand. We were occupying ourselves, weathering the slumps in our careers. Our industry was in flux. Previously, the industry had catered to a mostly domestic audience, but as digital streaming platforms emerged as independent studios catering to a global market, the traditional paradigms were disrupted. The effect was similar to that of a zealot contesting religious dogma. In retaliation, the major studios exhibited their might by swiping up all the big-budget franchises independent studios weren't quite ready to tackle, which also served a global market. The result brought shit film after shit film, from shit scripts that were overly structured and action-packed, to the box office. Even the simplest sort of viewer grew bored and uninterested. Why pay money to see a shit film when you can binge-watch great television, hours of it, series after series, in the comfort of your home? Nearly overnight, streaming platforms and cable television networks had created a renaissance in television, the new frontier for dramatic storytelling. Movie stars had turned to television, what was unthinkable in the '90s and early 2000s, and the series regular television actors, like Luce, got bumped down to the roles that once went to actors like Emily. In this shifting marketplace, the mid-range dramas I wrote became liabilities, the least likely films to get made.

Emily was right about chaos being the energy of change. Not only was the movie industry prone to the alignment of the planets and energies at play, so was the world at large. The collective desire for change had manifested. Scanning news feeds made it apparent: humanity as a whole was rising in protest against a history of dominance perpetrated by the hypocrisy of staid institutions that had created the worldwide plagues of divisiveness and inequality. Centuries of hegemony ingrained in the collective unconscious had reached critical mass.

Emily would complain, "Law has ruined justice. Religion has ruined spirituality. Pharmaceutical companies have ruined medicine. Sex has ruined love. Property has ruined land. And it goes on and on…" She was right. The duplicitous ideology behind the idea of progress, of technological advancement to increase the quality of life for all, was clearly for the few who could afford it; ironically, the progress that had made others obscenely wealthy had become the destructive resonance, the constant tapping on the hearts and minds of the many that threatened to bring the whole system down. Protests, riots, and looting ensued across continents over issues of race, employment, healthcare, and so on.

But Emily felt nothing would really change. "Who has the answers to the problems? We're too self-interested, too neurotic to restore order. It's a vicious cycle that only turns victim into victimizer. Revenge doesn't bring change. Forgiveness does. The outside world is only a reflection of our inner state. We have to change ourselves. Individual by individual."

Change the inner, and the outer will be altered. This seems benign, doesn't it? Like Buddhist philosophy or many of the New Age adages in all the self-help books floating around?

In the Dark Ages it was the basis of forbidden knowledge, the alkahest of transmutation whose practitioners were burned at the stake.

I FELT we'd been sucked into a vacuum, the three of us in that city of endless sky with days that drifted like cloud shadows through valleys. Days made long and full by our adventures.

Keenly aware of my need, I surrendered to the solace in belonging. Their friendships were all that mattered, friendships spared the poison of sexual relations, which isn't to say I was opposed to things developing in that direction with Emily, just that they hadn't. Only while I was with them was I able to escape thoughts of Nadia, and if they did catch up to me, they were less painful to endure. I'd leave them in the morning to get a change of clothes, but I always rushed back to what had become my salvation. I feared they would grow tired of the routine, and again my world would collapse and bury flourishing myths.

On a Monday evening, Emily would cover the untapped power of the imagination or the esoteric purpose of the sexual energy and how it could be transmuted and used to manifest one's will—once one has achieved a will in the true sense. On Tuesdays, we'd hike Griffith Park, and she'd bend me toward wildflowers and tree leaves to point out the numerological patterns of sacred mathematics in creation, proofs of the Designer. Not only was the human body a five-pointed star, such as in DaVinci's Vitruvian Man, a product of this same divine creation, so was the human psyche. "Thoughts are algorithms." The mystical significance of numbers was a favorite topic of hers. And words? She claimed with absolute sincerity that her "science" enabled her to imbue words and symbols with transformative thought-power. "Never underestimate the power of words," she warned. "Spoken, they seal oaths, cement vows, cast spells."

"Read?" I asked.

She looked annoyed, said, "Well, that is another matter altogether."

Come Friday, her lectures would circle back to the properties of the stars and planets and how they influenced the psyche's push toward individuation, but she never failed to end her lessons without the same punchline, which seemed a reminder to herself: "We create according to our desires. If we're taken by surprise, it's because we don't know ourselves."

As for our adventures, we visited art galleries and museums, went to matinees and beaches, all the while sustaining what seemed a never-ending conversation. I remember walking the Getty stoned, that stark-white structure on the hilltop gleaming beneath the sun, stark white against a cloudless and impossibly blue sky. My appreciation for the Getty somehow left me feeling that I'd finally discovered Los Angeles. When they had their fill and I wasn't yet ready to go, they dragged me to the tram. The three of us skipped down the walkway singing "Hungry Like a Wolf," riotously plowing through a group of Chinese tourists wearing surgical masks and sun visors.

That same week we visited Los Angeles County Museum of Art for an exhibition Emily was eager to see: Haunted Screens: German Cinema in the 1920s. Luce, uninspired by the exhibition, had gone off to view the sculptures on a different floor. Emily and I hovered above glass cases displaying sketches of set designs from the highlighted

Expressionist masterpieces; charcoal renderings of urban and rural settings that used rigid and sharp angles to contrast light and shadow and effect fantastical realms. Next to each sketch was a black and white photograph of the film set built from the sketch. I was amazed at the precise translation and the artistry of both.

At some point, Emily had wandered away. I tracked her amber wake into a screening room with black walls and projector screens showing clips from *The Golem* and *The Cabinet of Dr. Caligari*. She stood riveted, arms folded across her chest, fishing meanings out of the silent black and white images. It was only when we were leaving the museum that she finally spoke. "All those films are about it."

"About what?"

"About everything," she whispered.

LUCE AND I WERE BLINDFOLDED. "It's a trust exercise," Emily said, then took us by our hands, led us out the back door. I shuffled forward, barely lifting my feet as we passed from the hallway into the courtyard.

"Don't cheat," Emily said. She let go of our hands. A sense of freefalling rippled my gut. Luce's screech downshifted into nervous laughter. Though the transference of my sense of sight to my sense of hearing came naturally, it was nonetheless disorienting. I inched along with my hands thrust forward. "Trust," Emily said. I tensed as her breath wiped my ear; her closeness was imperceptible. A moment later, I was again jarred when she said, "That's it," because it sounded like she was at the opposite end of the garden. How did she move so quickly?

Familiarity with the courtyard allowed me to map it in my mind; the layout of the table and chairs, the paths between trees, the open spaces that now seemed infinite without sight building boundaries. I lowered my hands, took two full steps forward and landed on the paver stones as I'd concluded I would. Little by little, I grew more confident, more relaxed in my movements. I was walking slowly now, gauging the nearness of objects by somehow using the sounds of the waterfall above the koi pond, the birdsong, and the chimes in the trees to calculate my trajectory. It was as if I'd tapped into some latent sonar ability but lacked the know-how to use it as freely as the known senses, those I now saw I'd taken for granted. It was all in the sounds, how they traveled the empty spaces or were absorbed by obstructions. The textures of the ground beneath me, what my step discerned, produced images of concrete or grass in my mind. Then came a discovery: the sense of sight was not in my eyes. It permeated being.

"The purpose," Emily said. "Was to experience the dimensions of consciousness." By limiting one sense, Emily had proven that consciousness interlaced all the senses, unified the organism it governs. "There *are* more than five senses." What she masked as a simple trust exercise was in reality a demonstration of the natural abilities we unknowingly possess, those the obstinate clumped into the category of parapsychology.

The same evening, to "consecrate" our trinity, Emily suggested we exchange gifts, "offerings of our friendship." We had to give of our possessions, not make purchases. "Little tokens. Something that holds our energy." She believed objects retained the energy of their possessors. It wasn't psychometry that interested her but something much grander. In theory, personal possessions could be used for telepathic communication. "It's said a bone of a deceased master, in the right hands, could make him reappear."

For three days, I agonized over what to give Emily. I wanted it to be meaningful. Then it seemed there was only one thing to give her. In my wallet, I still carried the gold Saint Christopher medal my parents gave me for my first communion. "Interesting," she said as she studied the golden oval in her palm. "He's carrying a child on his shoulder?"

"The Christ-bearer," I said.

"Brilliant," she replied.

I gave Luce the poem I wrote on that perfect Saturday while babysitting. She gave us both postcards, the kinds with old pictures of famous people. Emily's was a rare shot of Marilyn Monroe in her make-up chair; mine was of Ibsen, old yet robust, wearing a medal around his neck with others pinned to his breast. Emily gave Luce a handmade necklace with a gemstone pendant. She gave me the Fool's tarot card.

"The Fool's number is zero. Why?" My teacher was quizzing me.

"Zero signifies infinite potential," I said, bristling. She smiled.

The fool is depicted at the beginning of the journey facing the unknown. He looks up at the sky, the divine spirit, unaware that he is stepping off a precipice signifying the dangers of the material world. He has the bag of tricks, the staff, all the tools he needs, even the little white dog at his feet to protect him, but does he know how to use them?

"Meditate on this," she said. And I did, often. I still do.

Yes, on the surface, we were occupying ourselves, riding out the wave as they say, waiting for it to break. Perhaps that is why our blurry year together in Los Angeles, which we joked in calling our sadhana, when the drought hit and the hills raged with wildfires, passed like one long season. However, it is true that like attracts like by the principle for which a sympathy can exist between them. According to Emily, several principles had been erroneously combined into the popular ideas of attraction and manifestation, that the primary cause of attraction was what was known as the Law of Vibration. Everything vibrates and therefore, vibration is the attractor that joins in frequency and as such like attracts like. In retrospect, I'd say the vibratory pattern that united us, Emily and me, was held somewhere in the frequency that made self-actualization the purpose of life, a cursed need for the inward journey, to exercise choice and derive some semblance of progress that had nothing to do with our careers. You see, the wave never broke.

Knowing what I know now about all that took place, about how we separated ourselves and waited helplessly for our fates to play out, I imagine us as dangling flowerpots in the path of a hurricane.

I'm still baffled by all this self-searching and how it led me to believe that by coming to understand myself, I was gaining knowledge and understanding of the secret laws of the universe. Whenever signs appeared in the world around me, seemingly tailor-made and awaiting my acknowledgment, or when I became aware of an unhealthy thought or emotional pattern and referenced my birth chart to explain why I was feeling what I was feeling, within a couple of days, life would show me how wrong I was to believe that I could decipher signs, much less explain my feelings. What's more, the strange incongruence between what I imagined the signs were signifying and where their meaning landed was too precise a misdirection to be random. It seemed the energies I was exploring were intentionally mocking me. I'd feel like a fool, a citizen of Babel uttering nonsense, running to Emily for clarification when all she'd say is, "Pluto and Saturn are at war. Death is imminent." Fool I was, I took it as metaphoric speak.

But walking around with our noses in the air didn't keep the outside world away. There were setbacks interspersed while all that I've described was taking place. I remember a mild June evening. Emily and I were sitting in Luce's courtyard drinking wine. Earlier that day, Emily had learned she didn't get the part in *Les Trois Six*. The director chose Julie Sable, an A-lister who was looking to do more character roles. Emily was pensive, gnawing at her thumbnails, a storm behind her eyes. I'd not seen her this way before.

"My sister is getting married," she said. She was bunched up in the chair, knees pressed to her chest. "It's bizarre, actually. My little sis. All my mates from home are married with kids. When we speak, we've fuck-all in common." Her tone was bitter.

"You want those things?" I asked.

She shot me a nasty look. "I wanted that film."

I wondered. If Emily had earned her will and her science was as sure as she claimed, then why was she seemingly unfulfilled, bitter like the helpless masses she'd described who knew nothing about the secrets? I'll put it straight. Why wasn't she able to manifest the part in the movie?

The following morning, I got my answer, well, *an* answer. Luce told me Emily's agent had told Emily that the producers felt Emily's breasts were not big enough for the part of a sex-addicted sugar-babe. Breast augmentation was not the sort of manipulation Emily practiced.

On the other hand, Luce had received a film offer for a movie set to shoot in July. I, of course, had nothing in the works, only an upcoming meeting with Jeff. All this time, he'd been going back and forth with Guptman, who was now ready to revisit *River Without End*. Perhaps *my* work at manifestation was about to pay off.

Something comes to mind. Another overlooked warning. Toward the end of that summer, once the door was reopened to the Orange Family, Paul, in a drunken fit of laughter, took my hand and said, "I can't fail. I have no dream to fulfill." I thought he'd meant that he had freed himself of desires, the cause of all suffering, only I sensed something like self-chastisement in his laughter.

Later, Luce confirmed this: "Paul's celibacy isn't the result of some spiritual attainment. Sadistic bastard gets off on denigration."

"Denigration?" I asked.

"You know what I mean," she said. "He holds himself back."

"Deprivation?" I said.

"He gets off on it," she insisted. "Lets it build, then explodes, disappears for a week."

I heard the refrain of Paul's confession, *I'm holding a hose with eleven holes, but I only have ten fingers, baby.*

21

———

Six stories above Wilshire Boulevard, Jeff Nesse's office gave a panoramic view of the Hollywood Hills. "I can see my house." He pointed to a cluster of homes on the distant hillside. All I saw was splintered sunlight glaring off glass and metal.

"You fell off the map," he said as he settled at his desk. "Writing, I hope."

"No," I said, dropping into the leather club chair across from him. He shrugged, locked his hands behind his head and leaned back in the chair.

"Well, Guptman wants the rewrite or he's moving on." I twisted the cap off the bottle of water his assistant offered me when I'd entered, took a sip, and did all I could: nod. Not to coalesce but to acknowledge that I understood what he'd said. There was a silver lining, I was sure; it was up to me, to my imagination.

"I could tweak it," I said, "heighten the drama a bit."

"No. He wants you to rewrite it. Make it a thriller. I think he's got a point." The glint in his crystal blues antagonized me.

"A completely different genre isn't a rewrite, Jeff. It's a new script."

"Yeah, well. Look, isn't the first time I've come across this, but we have to come up with a solution, right?"

"Your readers did coverage, gave the script a solid recommend. It's a structurally sound drama."

"Budget's the problem," he said. "This would need between fifteen and twenty. The sweet spot for a drama is three to five. Guptman doesn't want to go out on the town with a film that has no chance of recouping."

"But if he got it to his A-list contacts—which was the reason I never got paid for the option—and one of them wanted to do it, that's the best we're going to get by way of a guarantee on recouping the budget."

He shrugged, exhaled exasperation, leaned forward. The words didn't come. He leaned back again and repeated the sequence. "There are other issues besides the genre. The set pieces, they're not big enough."

Jaw tight, I said, "You're telling me the budget's too high. Bigger set pieces mean higher production costs."

"Which is why we're trying to get you to reimagine it as a thriller."

"What if I scaled back the set pieces so it fits the sweet spot for a drama?"

His lips pursed, gave it a moment's consideration, then shook his head. "You know—look at a movie like *Baited*. They have that helicopter sequence and the jet-ski thing on the Colorado River with the cliffs and mountains. It's cinematic. That's what I mean."

He had to be kidding. I was holding out for a wink but he just stared at me. "*Baited* is a comedy, Jeff. Dramas aren't about jet-skis on the Colorado River or big set pieces."

"You're in Hollywood. I told you day-one, *concept* is

everything. You need high-concept, grand set pieces so studios can go to town on them."

"Is it big set pieces that stay with us? Or stories that make us look in the mirror."

"Who wants to look in a mirror?"

"In this town!" I relished my dark chuckle.

"Okay, funny," he said, "but audiences want escape. A thrill ride. They want entertainment."

"How the hell do you know what people want?"

He reared back, tightened his approach. "Because the studios do studies," he said. "There are statistics."

"It isn't my job to give them what they want. My job is to give them what they need."

He smirked, tucked his chin into his throat. "That's awfully...forceful. You're in your own way. You got the chops, but—you know all this. What can I say? Unless you want to start thinking along the lines of exotic lands, something stars might be interested in..."

I couldn't resist. "They going to work or to vacation?"

Again, at the point of exasperation, of frank indifference, he shrugged.

A strange thing happened next: in the span of a breath cycle, I had a vision of a swarm of gnats flying through a window, dispersing in the openness, and suddenly, I felt centered, self-possessed; moments before, I was crashing into disappointment, ready to fight a battle I now saw as meaningless. There was an odd expression on Jeff's face as though he was somehow privy to my inner shift.

I perked up, leaned forward. "How's this? Title: *The Final Goodbye*. A couple separates just before their ten-year anniversary, which was to be celebrated in Paris, a trip they've already booked. Heartbroken, the man decides to go through with the Paris trip alone, somehow feeling it's connected to his destiny. We see him in the City of Light for a couple days, socially awkward, frustrated by the language barrier, but trying. Suddenly, an inspiring realization chisels his pain, and his eyes open to Paris. The next day, as he walks the Rue des Barres eyeing the gargoyles of Église Saint-Gervais Saint-Protais, standing in the doorway of the medieval church, he sees—you guessed it—his ex. She also decided to go through with the trip! She has a new haircut and she's dressed provocatively. Their eyes meet. He looks crazed. She hurries off and he pursues her in what becomes a cat and mouse chase through the romantic streets of Paris. Finally, in the Jardin des Tuileries, she thinks she's lost him when suddenly, his hand slips over her mouth. He drags her fighting behind some trees and hungrily kisses her. She scratches at him, and we think she's going to scream, but instead, she opens her legs—she's not wearing underwear. They hump like dogs right there as oblivious tourists pass on the garden path only five feet away— "

"You got me," Jeff interrupted; he was eager, leaning toward me. "This is hot."

"But they don't leave the garden together. Both know the trip's itinerary and, relying on how well they think they know each other, they let intuition guide their moves. The game of cat and mouse continues across this gorgeous, historic city as they stalk each other and play out their dark sexual fantasies at famous tourist attractions. In one way, they see how well they know each other because they always end up at the same locations. But the sexual fantasies unlock things within them that they didn't know existed, and in this respect, they realize they not only don't know themselves, they're strangers to each other."

"See, keep it on the ground," Jeff said. "Don't get too philosophical—"

"One night, he follows her to the Eiffel Tower, where they elude security and stay past closing (we'd have to figure this part out to make it realistic in the age of terrorism). When night falls, on an observation deck overlooking Paris, things take a turn. She insists they act out her rape fantasy. Reluctantly, he goes along with it, only to unleash his rage over their separation. Sprung from the roleplay, she cries, tears at his face, and screams the only French words she knows, *"Boudin noir! Boudin noir pousse la merde!"*

Jeff's eyes veered to the side. "Blood... *sausage*... pushes the...? Oh, you're twisted. I love it!"

"Disgusted by his rage and the inner turmoil it causes, he leaves her there, dress torn, streaks of mascara running down her cheeks. But once he's away, he worries that he's gone too far. He runs back to find her, but she's nowhere. The next day, while waiting for her to appear at the planned tourist spot on their itinerary, he flashes back to the brutal encounter at the Eiffel Tower. He understands his rage now. It's pent up from years of ignoring what his heart was telling him—she's not the one. He waits until evening, but she never appears. Overcome by guilt from what he's realized, he decides to search for her in the hospitals but to no avail. When he returns to the hotel, defeated and worried, there she is, waiting for him in the lobby. Her face is bruised. They go back to his room and lay down together, but when he tries to explain what he's realized about himself, she seizes on his moment of vulnerability and attacks him. He tries to calm her, but she storms out of the room. He chases her to a nightclub where she throws herself at a group of handsome Arabs who offer her cocaine and molly, which she takes without a thought. He tries to intervene, but she pretends not to know him. The Arabs shove him, warn him off. Soon they have her on the dance floor, grinding her, kissing her. Baited by the challenge, he searches the dance floor, picks a beautiful blonde woman, and starts grinding her. Now his ex's jealousy flares. She charges across the dance floor, pushes the blonde to the ground, slaps his face, and runs out of the nightclub. He gives chase, catches her along the banks of the Seine, where they have it out, saying all the hurtful things they withheld throughout their relationship. In a final comeback, under the influence of drugs, she admits she was sleeping with his best friend—some chump we'll introduce in the first act. It's a knife in his heart. Panicked, she tries to kiss him, but he runs off, leaving her with her face in her hands. The next morning, his body is found in the Seine."

"That's epic! I totally saw the movie! The Eiffel Tower, the cobblestone streets of Paris, the Louvre. A star vehicle. See! That's fucking awesome. Write it."

"Why? It's a thirty-million-dollar drama." I stood from the chair. His puzzled look gave way to contemptuous laughter. I was baffled—what had I done to earn his contempt? Refuse to write for free? I saw myself swiping his desk, smashing him in the face, but opted for just flipping him the bird before I pranced out of his office. *They can take my woman, my identity, but they can't take my vision.*

There was, of course, the voice, *You're self-destructing. You came to Los Angeles with the chip on your shoulder and now you've created the very circumstance you imagined.* "No. No," I cried, garnering incredulous looks from the underling agents toiling in their stuffy cubicles. I told myself, trust in your birth chart, embrace the chaos of change. I reached my car in the lot and found I was uncertain who had won that battle, Pluto or Saturn, but it sure as hell felt good to have asserted my will.

TRUST WAS a big thing for Emily. Well, that we trust her. Implicitly.

"For the three of us to truly bond," she insisted, "we need absolute transparency. If we share our deepest secrets, we're no longer vulnerable. To speak is to be freed." About Emily's request, let me be clear: she didn't mean we should sit down and take turns making confessions. She wanted us to partake in a ceremony.

"Rituals are all around us," Emily said, then licked the cigarette paper, fat with tobacco and medicinal marijuana. Lying on the floor, my head resting on Luce's thigh, I watched her fold over the gum edge and run the transparent seam with her thumb. She turned the narrow end to her lips. I reached up with my lighter. "Cheers." She exhaled a fragrant cloud as she turned toward the window. Inches from the row of clear glass panes, a hummingbird was flitting around, poking at the purple blooms of the bougainvillea intertwining the lattice.

"That's Ralphie," Luce said. "He's always there."

Emily continued, "The Catholic mass is a ritual. The priest approaches the altar with his smoking censer, sways it three times towards the altar, then bows north, east, south, west. He's addressing the cardinal directions and the elements they represent. He utters sacred words to invoke the Holy Spirit, lifts his hands in veneration." She raised her hands to demonstrate; the smoking joint trapped between her fingers made the act seem ritualistic indeed. "The mystery of faith, the transubstantiation of the bread and wine into the body and blood of Christ—a true Catholic believes they are flesh and blood, eats and drinks to ingest the Savior's energy."

"But it's a metaphor," I said. "The sacrifice of the body, of ephemeral, sensual pleasures to find true life in the spirit."

"For the average person," Emily said. "Initiates understand the mass differently. Sacrifice is offering death for true life. There is always a sacrifice required."

"When you say it, like that," Luce said, "seems...what's the word? Blasphemy?" She jumped to her feet, pulled her jeans up from the sides, and edged toward the kitchen. "Have to make a call before we do this."

"It's good she left. What I'm going to say next would surely disturb her."

I sat upright. "I'm all ears."

"The gifts we've given each other. I've told you why they had to be possessions of ours."

I nodded, said, "Because they retain our energy."

She nodded. "Here is the truth about the last supper. Christ literally gave his blood for his disciples to drink. In this way, they took him inside themselves so that he could be conjured at will by those he'd initiated. This is the meaning of the resurrection."

As I've said, she had a penchant for challenging my fixed ideas and beliefs. At times she put forth assertions so apparent in their truth, and well phrased, that I instantly adopted them as new viewpoints. However, there were times like this, when her claims unsettled me. "How could you know that?"

"Because I know of the practice, which predates Christ. Of course, the church could never share such things with the masses. Imagine? I doubt the Christians in Texas would pack into a car on Sunday morning if they understood they were attending a cannibalistic ritual? That is why they are given the exoteric explanation. But the truth is not hidden. It's only there for those who understand."

THE INITIATION CEREMONY took place that afternoon in Luce's studio.

As Emily lit the candles she'd arranged, she uttered sacred words to "hold the space." I was lying on a blanket on the floor, eyes closed, breathing as she'd instructed. Luce sat beside me, holding my hand, humming the syllables Emily had taught her. The rhythm of my breath, the warmth of Luce's hand and her gentle humming, promoted a sense of safety. With each exhale, more of me pressed into the floor. In my mind's eye, a whitish, luminous substance, cloud-like or liquid rather, changed shape like quicksilver then suddenly opened like an eyelid: at first, I was looking at decaying brick walls. Then, suddenly, myself: I was naked, a patient laid on a table beneath a penetrating white light I understood to be the light of consciousness, which now began revealing the former stations of inauthentic identities I'd adopted over the years; it—there was the sense that what was revealing this to me was my true self—showed how my appearance had shifted to suit each "idea" of self. The identities churned and morphed one into another; they were inseparable, making it clear how the tree of inauthenticity grew into the tree of my confusion. There were also the conventions of each identity, the adopted views and misconceptions, those of myself and the world. There was no judgment on any of it, I was only seeing, and the breath seemed to be dispersing any remaining attachments to these former identities and beliefs.

Suddenly, my body spasmed, my attention shifted back to the room; what I felt in my chest, a stab of shock, was no different than waking from a nightmare. Emily was chanting in a strange tongue that harmonized with Luce's humming, one rose as the other fell. The shock was still in me, the urge to open my eyes, and though I resisted, I'd nonetheless retracted my surrender. In slipping away I'd lost control, I'd gone off for what seemed a long time yet all the while they'd remained present. Not only was it that I didn't like the idea of becoming vulnerable unawares, I also suddenly felt the need to be vigilant. For the first time, I questioned the trust I'd placed in them. In fighting the urge to open my eyes, to see what was happening around me, violent heartbeats thrust against my ribs; my heart felt massive of a sudden.

Their harmonized voices enchanted, so I breathed, eased into the sounds, let the guns of defense cool. Soon, Luce's humming dropped off. By degrees, the volume of Emily's voice descended into a whisper that presupposed a coming silence, yet I couldn't discern if she'd gone quiet or if she was still chanting under her breath. My entire body was awake, trembling, my every atom engaged in ecstatic vibration that rendered stillness obsolete. Yes, all things vibrate. Each inhale drew it up, this powerful sensation rising into my center, and each exhale allowed me to assess what seemed the mingling forces of rage, contempt, and cruelty. My need to speak, to confess my deepest secrets, couldn't be restrained. "I hate Nadia. I want to destroy her." A pain cut through me. "I hate myself. Everything I've ever said and done was to win acceptance. I don't love. I lust. I possess. Destroy." Streams of warm tears ran down my cheeks as the pressure in my chest, against my ribs, tightened; incoming air squirmed its way into my lungs.

"Breathe," Emily said, but every muscle in me tensed in resistance to the grief retained in the truth I'd admitted, the grief of self-betrayal and ignorance. "Breathe," Emily whispered. Something wasn't right. My hands were stiff, curled in, as might happen to one who breaks his neck. Even my lips cinched in tension. What a fool I was to trust this, yet at that moment, Emily's voice was the only thing that could allay my fears. "Breathe," she repeated, placing her hand on my forehead. "Breathe." I did as she said, and eventually, there came a release, the tension melted away. Emily later explained that tetany was a common side effect of breathwork.

After Luce and Emily confessed their secrets and the ceremony was over, Luce, exhausted from her emotional spill, had fallen asleep right there on the floor. Emily was smoking, still wrestling with the secrets she'd revealed.

"Do you see?" she asked.

"See what?"

"Where your power lies?" I was uncertain what she'd meant. "All the hate and anger you repressed—that's your vitality. The source of your renewal. But the denial of it made it into a monster. It's only natural. Who wants to admit the evil inside? I assure you, denial and repression are the reasons the world is the way it is."

"So in accepting it, what? It just goes away?"

"If only. No, you must transmute it."

"How?"

"Hate it, not yourself." She let me sit with that until a realization dawned and showed itself in my exasperated smile. "What you've done since the breakup with Nadia is not healthy," she said. "Sex is a beautiful experience." Just the mention of sex and dark curtains closed in around the stage. "You're a double fire sign—you need to be shagging. You were simply imbalanced because you let Lust lead. Just as you had idealized Nadia, you've idealized sex, made it your perfect demon. There's no reason to feel guilty. Ignorant you were but are no longer." Was I frozen in denial of my need for sex because I feared sex would lead to more pain?

As if Emily was privy to these thoughts, she held up a finger to interject. "Remember in Romans 14? Nothing is unclean in itself. But if anyone regards something as unclean, then for that person it is unclean."

This interpretation of scripture was taken out of context and had nothing to do with sex; Paul uses it to instruct on judging the spiritual practices of others. I failed to mention, a month and a half earlier, as we were assuming the roles we'd play in each other's lives, Emily had decided to take me into her confidence. "Just us, yeah?" It seemed she was about to bring me in on a plot against Luce, though it was more like the stranger offering the boy standing at the curb, knock-kneed and with a hair-part, a ride home from school. There were things in my birth chart she hadn't revealed, aspects that occurred in her chart as well. "We have the prevalence of Mercury and Pisces connecting us to the other world. We see what others do not." I was immediately brought to my childhood, the awareness of something other, emanations that made even the most mundane objects seem numinous. Education had made me ignorant to presume I was too sophisticated to believe in such things.

"Cosmic energies have bound us in a spiritual alliance. I knew it the moment I saw you." In candlelight streamed with cigarette smoke, she moved closer, placed a warm hand on my thigh. "I need to tell you." She inhaled through trembling lips; in her eyes, a daub of candlelight was shapeshifting. As I thought this, a moment went unaccounted for. She now looked fearful, drew back to take me in as though she suddenly distrusted me. "No. I've said enough. What am I thinking?"

I threw up my hands, protested, "You can't do that. Tell me."

Her eyes narrowed, she shoved me. "These things aren't meant to be shared haphazardly. They're meant to be sought after. Sacrifices must be made. I don't know why I've chosen you. It isn't fair."

"Starting and not finishing isn't fair."

She looked directly in my eyes, "You'd go mad if I told you what I know." She wasn't baiting me; she was warning me.

"Oh, stop," I say. "Tell me. I want to learn these tricks."

Her face sharpened. "Clowns do tricks." Her upright posture bore a reprimand for calling her science a trick. "Go ahead, laugh," she said. "You think this is a game? I'll test you. Prove it's more than curiosity."

"*You* said it was in the stars. A cosmic alliance. And that's why you're telling me, so."

"There's nothing in the stars but gases," she said. She laughed. "I could claw your eyes out. Promise to respect this." I nodded. She gave one last warning, "It isn't me you'll have to answer to."

She threw her hands around to indicate the room we were in, its objects. "This around us, what you see, is nothing. What we call 'matter' on the dense, physical level. The body is meant to serve the spirit, who works in the subtle, unseen levels of reality. Out from the genitalia, the solar plexus, the heart, the mind, spirit travels, ripples the unseen like drops of water in a pond to reach the shores of our desires. Feed the aether with thought and there are sparks. Feed it with feeling, there is fire. Join the two, and there is a conflagration that moves at lightspeed. But don't approach this work like some beggar, *Oh, please give me this*. Make it earnest. Creation is holy. *You* are God."

There wasn't anything new in this. She'd described, albeit in flowery words, the technique for manifestation that everyone in Los Angeles was practicing as they envisioned their hands wrapped around the steering wheel of their new Range Rover, or the smell of Angelina Jolie's pillowcases as she moves naked toward the bed. Surely, there must be more to her science.

"Everyone knows this," I said, waving her off.

"You don't know anything. Look at you. You're like them! How can you know? You don't even know the words."

"What words?"

"The words that make it work."

A spell. That she had seemingly revealed some esoteric secret, she paused, then scratched her top lip while she assessed me. Was she second-guessing herself? "Are you sure you're prepared to take responsibility?"

"I am."

Begrudgingly, she wrote two short stanzas on a piece of paper, and as I eagerly reached, she pulled the paper away. "I want to bite you. They have to be said correctly. And for the last time, be sure you want what you think you want. The words cannot be taken back." And there on the floor of Luce's studio, she taught me how to say the ancient words she received during one of her heightened state-of-consciousness meditations, then how to breathe as I chanted them. Only after did she hand over the paper. "You can't do it here. You have to be alone. If it's more than curiosity, if I've read you accurately, it will work. Immediately."

I CLOSED MY EYES, breathed in, my body rose, breathed out, my body settled. In several rounds, I'd centered myself. As I chanted the words in the cadence I was taught, I realized I was tempering my volume, worried my neighbors would hear me through the flimsy walls. There were also the ceaseless stream of thoughts I needed to abscond, and the recall of words Emily spoke that I now see disturbed me. "*You* are God." A foreboding notion sprung out of this refrain, vied for attention. *Are you tampering with unholy things?* Instantly, Curiosity countered, *Relics of the old religion.*

I refocused my breathing, committed to a full-voiced chant and soon the words and the cadence, sounds that blended perfectly, vibrated throughout my body. In my mind's eye, in that darkness, an illumined substance showed itself and gave way to a pinhole of white light that flickered and abated. Each time it appeared, my intention reached and I lost it. I was still self-conscious. I went into the breath, followed it, sought the vibration of the chant. When I was finally able to allow the pinhole of light rather than capture it, I saw it had points like a star. In its center was an intricate design, what looked like a chakra symbol, but as my inner eye squinted toward it, it dispersed. I had to let it alone. It came again, glowing feverishly, lingered, wavered, widened. Into the light, I placed my desire, my intention: *Heal.* Thought now joined with feeling and the promise swelled inside. Emily's face appeared, Luce's. Waves of sensations tingled my spine, there were bristling sounds—sounds I imagine Christmas lights, if Christmas lights made sound, would make when they are first plugged in. Glorious hope hummed in me and suddenly, Nadia's face appeared.

I opened my eyes to cut the cord. The remnants of the chant still hummed in the tissues and fibers of my chest and throat. *What's this?* The room buzzed; I could feel my connection to every object—the chair, the bed, the end table

—as a sort of energetic exchange. *Lifeforms surround us.* I closed my eyes, recommitted to my intention, chanted.

When my eyes opened again, forty minutes had evaporated. The feeling was as though I'd traveled a great distance. What struck me was the peace I felt. Though it was after midnight, I considered going back to Luce's and just as I reached for my cell phone to call, it rang. I smirked, *Emily, who else?* It had to be. I glanced at the caller ID and winter fell into my intestines. It was after three in the morning in New York. Phone in hand, I paced until it stopped ringing. Silence never seemed so full. Moments later, a ding alerted a new voicemail. "I was just overwhelmed with thoughts of you. Hope you're well." Her voice was scratchy, tired.

I didn't spend time trying to decipher Nadia's message. Okay, a little, enough to recognize that I still hoped for a reconciliation—but the words Emily wrote on that paper? Of course, I ran back to her to tell her the chant had worked. This proved my interest was beyond mere curiosity. I thought it would've pleased her, but she seemed more hesitant than in the moments before she wrote the words on that piece of paper.

"It's a mystical prayer to evoke the unseen energies," she said.

"But Nadia," I said. "I'm still holding out. I wasn't...she wasn't my intention."

She looked spurned. "I told you to be careful. But... *she* was receptive."

This annoyed her; it was as though she'd been outdone by Nadia. "It's said, 'If they are sages, thought can meet thought, and spirit meet spirit, though oceans divide them.'"[1]

22

———————

As much as Emily's teachings opened my heart and mind, took my narrow views of reality and expanded them into panoramic vistas, the base emotions and negative patterns of behavior connected to my lower self would take time to shake. I recall one afternoon at Luce's, the three of us had just returned from a hike. Emily's cell rang. She checked the caller ID, jumped to her feet, and ran out through Luce's back door. A pang of fear cut through me. *Tom Seals must be back in town.* I felt wobbled as if I'd been on rough seas and was suddenly dropped on solid ground. My mind spun scenarios of how Tom's return would interrupt what had become my new life. Nearly forty minutes passed before Emily, seemingly pleased, came back inside. I lacked the courage to ask who had called. Ducking my head in the sand out of fear that the truth would threaten my attachment, as if not acknowledging it might make it go away, had to be acknowledged.

Miraculously, the following morning, Emily and Luce decided we should go on an impromptu road trip. I literally sighed with relief; the threat of Tom Seals was temporarily diminished. We packed Luce's Jeep and drove up along the Pacific Coast Highway toward Big Sur. Not a cloud in the sky; it was that kind of day. The views of the drive: manicured hills and pastures with grazing cows, blooming wildflowers, and clusters of trees; the shimmering Pacific. In Cambria, we stopped for lunch, then went inland to Paso Robles and purchased wine at one of the vineyards before Luce photographed us on a hillside blanketed with poppies. We resumed the 1 at San Simeon, ogled Hearst Castle from a distance, and by late afternoon we'd arrived in Big Sur.

Luce, energetic as ever, wanted to hike Pfeiffer National Park and see the waterfall before the park closed. A dusty trail led through headlands mottled with low shrubs and pine trees, snaked around cliffs from which the turquoise shoreline came into view. There were hardly any other tourists or hikers on the trail, but when we found the ideal vantage point to view the waterfall, we came upon a group of middle-aged men on a reunion trip, one of which recognized Luce from her television show. She didn't shy away from the attention; she enjoyed it, even agreed to take selfies with the men with the waterfall as the background.

As all this was happening, the handsomest of the bunch —he had a mop of messy, sandy-colored hair and wore Patagonia shorts, hiking boots, and a sweat-dampened bandana around his neck—sidled up to Emily and locked her in conversation. To my dismay, we'd adopted the men; they walked back with us toward the parking lot. Each time that handsome bastard made Emily laugh, I felt pangs of jealousy. By the time we reached the trailhead, I'd overheard that he was a screenwriter from Buenos Aires now living in Los Angeles. "Maybe we could have dinner," he said before asking for her number. I wanted to jump between them, *Hey, there's a line, gaucho!* But Emily said, "I don't think so, mate." I must admit, he took it gracefully, like it was all in jest.

That evening, the three of us had dinner on a restaurant patio built into the coastal bluffs. We sat quietly, listening to the ocean. It occurred to me that my jealousy needed to be dealt with. Then I remembered what Emily had said about repression and denial, that the darkness needed to be accepted before it could be transmuted.

She picked at the salad before her, took a forkful to her mouth and, as she chewed, gazed at the dark water. Something was troubling her. She had that look in her eyes that she'd had when she didn't get *Les Trois Six*, minus the anxiousness, which isn't to say she was calm; she only seemed to be. This is how I began to see her, the real her, when she was unaware she was being watched. Moments such as these are like random stars that, when connected by unseen lines, become constellations.

"I've never seen so many stars!" Luce wanted to capture the spectacle. She found a spot in the restaurant's impressive garden, perched her camera on a tripod, and began adjusting the settings. Emily whistled and waved. I followed her to a trail that branched from the garden and led to the coastal rock formations. A sign read: CLOSED AFTER DUSK.

Ocean spray made the porous rocks slippery. Below, crashing waves retreated, swirled out of the dark grottos in the bluffs, and washed down to rejoin the ebbing tide. Emily was ahead of me, crossing to a lower portion of wet rock from which the waves had just receded. She skipped over them to the other side, climbed to the top of the outermost formation, and stood silhouetted against the indigo sky. Just as I moved to follow, a crested wave slapped the rocks; icy water jumped up, soaked my jeans, and left me hydroplaning. I teetered, nearly took a fatal plunge before regaining my balance. I hopped back to where it was safe. "Come," Emily called. Moonlit, hands folded beneath her chin, she watched the rise and fall of the tide. When it was safe to pass, she enthusiastically waved. I hopped across the glistening rocks without incident and joined her. Together we stood at the edge of the precipice. Twenty feet below, craggy, barbed formations broke the rolling motion of the Pacific, but a mile out it was a glass-top mirroring the heavens, water and sky, both indistinct, became one limitless expanse flecked with metallic glitter.

It's hard to say how much time passed, but we were sitting beside each other when I finally found the courage. "Was it Tom who called yesterday?" Her look didn't hide suspicion, which made me realize I'd betrayed Luce's confidence, and led her to see Luce had betrayed hers.

She covered, "When? Oh, no. God, no. Tom." She shook her head. "Bit dry, that one. Sarcastic. Prickish even." Her appraisal left me sated. We got lost in the view. I realized then that our shoulders were touching; our closeness and contact seemed completely natural at this point. "Aren't we all so alone?" She drew a deep breath. "Oh, I love it here. I don't want to leave."

"Right?" I said. "Imagine seeing this every day."

"No," her voice cracked, "this world." I felt her ribcage hop, and when I turned, her hands shot up to cover her face. *She's crying.* She must have felt my stare unendurable; her hands jumped from her face to mine and hastily pulled me into a kiss. That's how it happened. Our first kiss. No bells and whistles. Just the tastes of wine, salty air, and yes, tears. A kiss for sustenance.

∾

CLOSE TO TEN, we arrived at the rustic bed and breakfast where Luce had made a reservation while we were eating lunch at the cafe in Cambria. There was a main house with three rooms on offer, then four individual cabins scattered on a hillside. Only the main house had electricity and Wi-Fi. We opted for a cabin. For the most part, we'd lost all cell reception once we'd entered the stretch of Big Sur, so it seemed a complete disconnect was in order.

As Luce jogged the photos she'd taken that day, the camera's viewfinder cut a square beam of luminescence through the darkness of the cabin. I was seated on a wooden chair, drinking a glass of local pinot noir, imagining Emily and me as a couple. "We kissed," I said in a low voice. I didn't want Emily, who was in the bathroom, to hear. Luce kept her eyes on the viewfinder.

"You did?" She seemed uninterested, kept jogging through her photos. *Not one question, Luce? How was it? Did you like it?*

Fifteen minutes must have passed when it occurred to me that Emily was not in the bathroom after all. "Where is she?" I asked.

"Don't know. Think she went down to the beach." An hour passed and Emily hadn't returned. After the long, full day, I was struggling to keep my eyes open. *Rest them.*

Luce and I walk the trail we walked earlier that day when suddenly rattlesnakes slither out of the brush, fall from the sky, and surround us. We stomp our feet and wave sticks at them, but there are too many. A cacophony of hisses preludes a flurry of strikes. Both of us are repeatedly bitten. In an instant, the snakes are gone. I know we only have minutes before the venom overtakes us, that our exertion to get back to the road and find help will move the poison to our hearts more rapidly. We panic, waste precious time trying to figure out what to do. But it's too late; the skin on Luce's legs blackens and cracks like mud. She drops to the ground in a seizure. Now my legs are blackening, bubbling, peeling. *Wake up*, a voice says.

My eyes opened. I was soaked in sweat, reaching for my legs. Relieved to know it was a dream, I settled some. There, on the bed in the dawn's light, Luce and Emily were peacefully sleeping. I quietly got up, dressed, and went outside.

The chilly morning's clean air was invigorating. Across the narrow road, a trailhead that led into a forest of sequoias and pines goaded me to enter. Beams of light cut through the foliage, sheets of light here and there. As I walked, I recalled my dream. It was the same trail to the waterfall we'd hiked the day before. Surely the snakes represented my perception of the men on their reunion trip. Especially the handsome one who tried to slither his way into Emily's life. Yes. Jealousy had me perceiving threats in the world around me. Then I felt it, that I wanted Emily.

I emerged from the forest onto a plateau strewn with thickets of bulbous shrubs and velvety shadows drawn in relief to the surrounding blue of ocean and sky. Below and to the right, turquoise waves washed a sandy beach, frothed, then ran until the water thinned, and became clear as glass. High tide had left behind a sort of natural collage of randomly deposited driftwood and kelp fronds that stood in contrast to the only thing of order on the beach: a circle of rocks. In its center was what appeared to be remnants of a bonfire. Nothing remarkable in that. People make fires on beaches at night. It was only later, revisiting this site in memory, that I truly understood the significance of the rock circle, and that I'd wrongly interpreted my dream.

WE SPENT the afternoon picnicking beneath a cluster of pines on a remote bluff with panoramic views of the Pacific. Emily was lying on her back taking the sun, something she rarely did. From behind us came the clicks of Luce's camera; she was photographing the barks of trees, photos she later used in *Skin*, her exhibition in West Hollywood.

"Close your eyes," Emily said. "Hear the wind rustling round the trees. The leaves twirling. Clustering." The sunlight my eyes had just shut out singed my inner vision. By degrees, the intense brightness dissolved and was replaced by a stream of images. "Tell me what you see," she said.

"The woods where I grew up. It's damp and wet. Wind wiping yellow and orange leaves out of the trees."

"Why do you think you see those images?"

"Because of the sounds," I said.

"The sounds? Or my suggestion of the sounds?" I opened my eyes, sent her an inquisitive glance. "I said the leaves were twirling," she said. "Clustering. I suggested what you should see."

"But you didn't suggest autumn."

"I did." Then I understood. To describe leaves as twirling and clustering in the wind suggests that they'd fallen. "What's more," she said, "you heard leaves in the wind. Look around." All around us, rusty pine needles covered the ground. I felt duped. "Always be on guard. If *I* can trick you, imagine? The true enemies don't fight you. They slither into your mind unawares." And minutes later, appearing troubled by some newly discovered truth, she said, "You become the mirror. But I guess that's better than being a mere reflection." She shielded her eyes from the sun to survey the expanse of unobstructed horizon, which appeared to be slightly arced, hinting at the Earth's curvature.

"It's too quiet here," Luce said. "My batteries are dead, and I can't charge them. I can't just sit around." She wanted to leave Big Sur, drive back to Los Angeles. "Thought we were staying another night," I said. She ignored me; she had been ignoring me all day and I wasn't quite sure why. Emily attempted to persuade her to stay the night but to no avail; when Luce got something in her head, that was that.

Night fell on the coastal fields as we came down from Big Sur. Luce was driving, Emily was in the passenger seat, and I was in the back. My cell vibrated in my pocket; we had service again. Three voicemail messages awaited, all from Nadia. In the first, her voice was lively: "I'm thinking about you. Let's talk." Less lively in the second: "Please call me. I have to tell you something." And altogether despairing in the third: "I don't care if you've met someone. I need to hear you. Please. Call me." I remembered her spells of sadness and how I'd hold her as if to take her sadness into me, believing I was stronger. The feeling was pure. Compassion? Or was it that, in the absence of my obscuring lust, which hindered my love for her, only love remained?

Wasn't it remarkable? I'd kissed Emily, and suddenly Nadia called? Was it possible that after nine years together we were energetically bonded so that she unconsciously felt the shift? As if my attention, the force of my emotions and thoughts, was holding her captive until that kiss set her free? And oh, the terror of being set free!

We arrived at Luce's close to four in the morning. Luce collapsed on the bed and was asleep in minutes. It pleased me. I was still annoyed that she'd refused to pull over at a rest stop so I could use the bathroom. "Hold it," she said.

"We have two hours."

She glanced at me in the rearview mirror. "Use some of that mind control."

Emily was on the sofa rolling a joint. She looked like a messy deck of cards, hair tossed to one side, eyeliner smeared.

"Where did you disappear to last night?" I asked.

"To present my case."

I sent her a look. "To what court?"

She laughed. "They are ruled by laws, too."

"Who's *they*?"

During one of her discourses, she'd stated that other lifeforms surround us, but they are beyond our perception; elementals are the spirits of the four elements, earth, wind, fire, water.

"To the elementals?" I said it in jest.

"Precisely," she said. It would be a lie to say that I wasn't eager to kiss her again, but something made me hesitant. Perhaps it was that she seemed to have forgotten that we'd kissed. Not that she was keeping her distance; it's that she wasn't closing it. Part of me knew it would be better to allow things to progress slowly, naturally, that way I'd remain aware of what I was feeling, of my motives. Another part of me wanted to go in with abandon. I'd been bottled up and felt the need to counter the abstracting self-work with a little tangible excitement; get out of my mind, back into my body, raise my blood pressure a bit. After all, she was the one who urged me to embrace my sexuality. But just as this urge was beginning to pin my fear, the stranglehold of duality choked me out.

THE FOLLOWING MORNING, it was all over the news. Julie Sable, the well-known actress who'd gotten the part over Emily in *Les Trois Six*, had suffered a freak accident during a pool party at a hotel rooftop in New York. She slipped, fell, and bashed her head on the tiled patio and was now in a coma at New York Presbyterian Hospital. News clips showed devastated fans gathered outside the hospital in a display of love and support. One report mentioned that principal photography on her upcoming film, *Les Trois Six*, was set to start in three weeks.

Wide-eyed, Luce turned to Emily. "That's one way to get a job." Emily seemed jarred; she resisted our stares, kept her eyes on the television screen. For the remainder of the day, she was quiet, careful in her every word and movement. When in the garden, she remained vigilant, looking over her shoulder every so often as if expecting to be taken by surprise. The entire day was impeded upon by her curious behavior, and Luce's bitter sarcasm. That is, when Luce chimed in to poo-poo whatever was being discussed.

Come evening, Emily had gone inside to use the "loo." Half an hour had passed. Luce and I carried in the empty bottles and wine glasses from the garden. "She's still in there?" Luce asked. Retching sounds echoed out of the hallway. We went to the bathroom door and found it locked. Luce shrugged. "Em?" She called. "You okay?" We could hear her clearing her throat.

"Stupendous," she said, then coughed. When she finally came out, puffy eyed with sunken cheeks, she looked haggard. "The wine." She threw herself onto Luce's bed, where she remained until morning.

Among us, there was no more talk of Julie Sable's accident, but I followed the news. Her condition had worsened. There was more to it, but the details weren't being released. The news reports focused on the liability aspect of the accident. Witnesses said she'd not been drinking and appeared sober. Attempting to avoid a major lawsuit, the lawyers for the hotel produced several pictures of the poolside before and after the accident, proof that the tiles were not "wet and slippery." I wondered. Julie Sable was known for her daring. In films, she performed her own stunts. Then, one afternoon, she forgets how to walk?

WE ASSEMBLED IN THE GARDEN. Luce was back to her old self, dishing pasta salad onto paper plates. Steve was singing a Dean Martin tune and pouring Amarone into plastic cups. When he first arrived, he'd passive-aggressively expressed his excitement over Luce's invitation. Instantly, she challenged his tone and bare-faced, he accused her of flat leaving him. Then he commented on our Big Sur trip, something along the lines of a ménage à trois. "You're stupid," she said. But something in her face, her eyes, lent truth to the secret Steve had shared with me. I wondered.

Emily, not fully recovered from her vomiting spell the day before, dodged the sunlight flitting through the avocado and grapefruit trees. She was in black overalls and a wife-beater, wearing the designer shades I liked less than the cheap green shades she usually wore. I'd suspected it was because the lenses of her designer shades were larger and therefore hid the dark circles under her eyes. I was in knots since the kiss, waiting for the next despite her showing no indication that there would be a next.

"When I first moved here," Luce said, "I used to climb the tree and pick avocados to make guacamole." She waved to a neighbor who had come outside for a smoke. "Megan. Come join."

Megan, an actress, had just moved to town for a role in a studio film.

"Where from?" Steve asked.

"New York," Megan said with a frown. "Left a great apartment on West 12^(th) Street. Had it ten years." She was a true redhead, had a theater actor's demeanor, and wore thick, horn-rimmed glasses like picture frames that displayed her sea-green eyes.

"What kind of role?" Steve asked.

"A writer during suffrage. Falls in love with an old-school union delegate but chooses not to marry him and give up her independence."

"You go, girl," Luce said. "How's it end?"

"Duh. They don't get married," Steve said, nudging Luce.

"Well, it's told in retrospect," Megan said. "The film is an examination of her choice. It opens with her as an older woman being interviewed about her life and career. She's single, childless, and battling cancer. Then it flashes back to her thirties and forties when she'd made the pivotal life decisions. In the end, she admits she should've married the union delegate because even though she'd made history, she never found love again. She has a great line, 'Legacy is no substitute.'"

"That's daring," Luce said. "Sort of a condemnation of feminism."

"Love it," Steve said. "Exactly what we need. Little reality."

Emily snarled at him.

"Well." Megan smiled. "There's something to be said for biology. And the traditional roles. Liberation from oppression is one thing. Denial of reality is another."

"Be careful," Luce said. "You say that in the wrong company, goodbye career."

"Please, she's a woman," Steve said. "She can say

anything. If I said it, forget it. Look, traditionally, it may have seemed like the man ran the house, but the woman was *always* king. Every night, when they went into the bedroom, the man would lay his head on his wife's lap and she'd stroke his hair like he was a little boy and tell him how things were going to be and he'd say, *Okay*. Plain and simple. Beautiful."

"What fucking world do you live in?" Emily said. "Feminism isn't about who's king of the house. It's about women and their contribution to the world."

"What's a greater contribution than having children?" Steve said. "Loving them, raising decent human beings who go out into the world and spread that love?"

Emily scoffed. "A woman has to have children?"

"A man can't," Steve said.

"Idiot, I mean, what if she doesn't want them? What if she can't have them?"

"I'm talking about the ones who choose to marry and have children," Steve said. "That that's their responsibility, not a career. Today everyone has this idea they're supposed to be great. A husband and children just ain't good enough anymore."

"You realize what you sound like?" Emily's cheeks were red. She balled her fists, looked to the women for help.

"Look," Steve said, attempting to explain. "It's a matter of immaturity."

"Immaturity!" Emily was on the edge of her seat.

"Let me finish! The problem today is that people don't commit. If you're gonna marry and have children, you have to be mature enough to understand what that means."

"What does it mean?" Emily was baited.

"Sacrifice. If you go into it half-assed, thinking about yourself, everything is the husband's or the kid's fault. You're not only gonna be unhappy, you're gonna traumatize your kids. But that's what feminism has done. There's this idea that every woman can have it all—a family, a career—and some can. But most don't have the bandwidth for all of it. And those who rebel and go for a career instead of a family, my sister's a perfect example, end up alone with regrets."

"Horseshit," Emily hissed. "Narrowminded—"

"Enough! No politics!" Luce yelled. Emily flipped Steve the bird. A tense silence passed.

Luce reached for Megan's silver-plated cigarette case to read the inscription on its back. "The world is violent and... mer...mercurial?" She looked to Megan, who nodded. "It will have its way with you. We live in a perpetually burning building, and what we must save from it, all the time, is love. TW?" Luce shrugged. "Who's that?"

"Tennessee Williams," Megan said.

"Aww... That's fucking beautiful," Luce said.

"Yeah," Steve said, "to my point—"

"Does she die?" Emily interrupted. "Your character. From the cancer?"

"It's an open ending," Megan said. "But eventually it gets you, right?"

"Right," Emily said.

"Are you married?" Luce asked.

"Will be. Come spring." She held up her ring finger to show a simple, gold band. "He comes to town next week. I'm so excited."

Emily touched my wrist. "Could you help me, love?" She ejected from her chair and started toward Luce's back door.

❧

THE SECOND KISS WAS CHAOTIC. My feet barely hit the wood floor of the studio before Emily was on me. We bounced off the walls like pinballs and somehow wound up in the kitchen, where we careened into the refrigerator with a thud. She pushed me back, threw herself onto the counter, and wrapped her legs around my waist. Without breaking the kiss, I hoisted her from the countertop, carried her back into the studio toward Luce's bed and, despite trying to ease us down, we crashed to the mattress. She was frantic, rocking our bodies until she gained the momentum to roll us and mount me. She looked rabid, was whispering and giggling like a fiend as we kissed. I couldn't quite make what she was saying, then realized I wasn't meant to; she was talking to herself. For some reason, I was transported to the dream with the orgy women—not the fright, but the arousal. She leaned up, whipped her head toward the darkened hallway, then came down again and bit my lip and breathed into my mouth, "The loo." Clasping my wrist, she dragged me off the bed and down the hall to the bathroom.

The click of my belt, the pop of the button flies, then her warm mouth. The sensations—I hadn't been touched in months—were nearly unbearable. I pulled her to her feet, clamped her with my hands, front and back. She sighed, shivered, and her bony fingers snatched my forearms. "No need," she said, and plopped herself on the sink, opened her legs, and leered up at me. I moved toward her, a bit hastily, and met the cold porcelain, headfirst—literally. The blunt trauma sent me stumbling back with a yowl. She chuckled. "You're ridiculous." I reassessed the abnormally high sink basin and made another attempt by coming up on tiptoes, but I was barely able to hit the mark. If only I had longer toes. Her teeth clenched my earlobe. She whispered, "Let's go to mine."

It is unfair to give an account of what I witnessed when I stepped back into the studio. Not only was I buzzing from my bathroom stint with Emily, I'd been drinking all afternoon and may have smoked one of her joints. Steve was interrogating Luce in the corner by the computer desk. "What am I, an asshole?" he charged in a harsh whisper. That's when Luce saw me. Relief washed her face. She jerked her arm from his grip, said, "You're being stupid." Then Steve saw me; in his eyes, rage and desperation mingled. Luce hurried toward me, interlocked our arms at the elbows, and walked me back out into the garden.

"What was that?"

Strained emotion prevented her from speaking. She waved off my question and quickly composed herself. I assumed it had to do with what Steve had told me about him and Luce. Perhaps in her absence, he'd been simmering, waiting for the moment he'd get her alone, but when that time had come, she'd rejected his advances.

Then Emily stepped out into the floodlight. "What's up Steve's ass? He just stormed out." She looked around the garden, then to Luce. "Where did your movie star friend go?"

"Her fiancé called," Luce said.

Emily made a face as if to disparage Megan. "All proper, that one."

"Don't hate," Luce said.

23

———

Emily and I drove north on Beachwood Canyon into the foothills. At Luce's, the suddenness of Emily's pounce had taken me by surprise, left no room to think; now I was anticipating my performance and the inherent dangers of becoming involved.

We parked outside her building at the curb between two massive Moreton Bay fig trees. She stepped out and paused, entranced. "Look at their roots," she said. "Sensual, right?" In the play of electric light and shadows, their thick, whitish-gray roots looked like the gnarled limbs of buried humans.

We entered the frosted glass doors of the high, slotted wood fence that closed behind us and sealed the courtyard from the outside noise. The aroma of rosemary filled my nostrils as I observed the prothyrum's Zen rock garden: artfully placed stones, like those from a riverside, positioned on a wide, gravel bed aglow with the soft light of LED lamps. Now I saw them, the rows of neatly trimmed rose-mary bushes supplying the ideal fragrance for what was within the perimeters they hemmed. "Come on." She waited by an exterior staircase, which snaked up the cedar façade to the balcony entrances of the apartments. After seven flights, under the yellowish glow of fixtures meant to look like gas lamps, we reached her landing. The elevation provided a favorable view of the nearby Hollywood sign jutting from the darkened hillside.

She opened a waist-high gate, and we crossed onto a white, synthetic-fur carpet that covered the length and width of her balcony. The outdoor furniture was all wood, rustic. With the breeze came tinkling music from a row of metal chimes—suns, moons, stars—dangling from the pale arm of another Moreton Bay fig that closed off her balcony, hid it like a secret.

At the doorway, the fragrant memories of incense seeping from every fabric of the long, wide living room greeted me. She hit a switch and the dim light of hanging lamps, two with paper lampshades and a third, a tapestry with fringes, whetted the sheens of satin pillows—purples, whites, blues, and black—and created atmosphere in the space.

Between a canopied chaise longue and the coal-black mouth of the brick wall's fireplace, presumably where a coffee table would be, sat a huge, somewhat rounded chunk of greyish-beige stone encircled by an arrangement of satin cushions. I touched the stone and to my surprise, it was solid rock, not a composite. It must've exceeded a thousand pounds.

The walls were bare, save for one painting on a swath of raw duck canvas that nearly stretched the length of the sheet-rocked wall. The painting's Frazetta-esque image was a mirage: a half-formed figure etched in black with undefined features boiled out of a smoky burst of gray tones in a movement akin to exertion. The nuanced grays made it appear the figure was emerging out of another dimension, an effect created by the painter's use of the unprimed, unpainted sections of canvas. The figure's arms were outstretched, hands open as if making an offering of the two blackbirds that flew toward a swirling portal in the upper right corner of the painting—also an effect created by the use of the raw canvas.

A vertiginous sensation seized me as I recalled how, in my dream that first night I met Emily, she had the little black finch cupped in her hands and threw it to the sky just as the figure did in the painting. I was sifting through this as she approached with two tumblers, scotches neat, and offered one. I searched her for any sign that she might know what I was thinking, that she might somehow be aware of my dream, but she turned to her sound dock and queued music. I wanted to explain this brush with the sublime, a feeling that was not quite déjà vu, but as I tried to capture the fleeting sensation, the impulse withered.

In our discussions, we'd breached the nature and function of dreams, what she believed them to be. She claimed that while we are asleep, the subconscious mind seeks to balance our energetic centers by sorting what the conscious mind, the ego, rejects in waking life. The egoic structures are too rigid to allow parts of reality that threaten it; nonetheless, those realities exist and need assimilation. During sleep, the egoic controls loosen, and while dreaming, the higher self, the force within the subconscious, communicates in the archetypal language of images and symbols embedded in the collective unconscious, those tailormade to the individual that represent the rejected realities needing assimilation. Conversely, when there are no dreams, the energy centers are freely flowing. We can all interpret our dreams, but whether we receive the message depends on our understanding of what is being communicated. To this end, her dream instruction session ended with these words: "It's an old practice to not rise too quickly into daylight. To stay a while in the darkness."

The Rolling Stones' "Loving Cup" was playing. We were seated on the cushions before the huge stone, atop which were her tools: a disemboweled satchel of marijuana, a metal grinder, and a pack of rice rolling papers. "Better on the lungs," she said, then coughed as she finessed the stubborn corner of the thin, transparent paper to seal her third joint. To cover my anxiousness, I exaggerated my interest in the stone, ran my hand along its side. "How did you get it in here?"

"Magick," she said with a wink.

Luce once said that Emily's family had old money, "English dukes or something." That's where I'd gotten the idea of her ancestors rubbing velvety or tweedy elbows with upper-class English society. Emily hadn't yet mentioned her family, nor had she explained the difference between the English and the British, an obvious distinction I'd never considered. The English were from England, while Brits were those included in the United Kingdom. She was English on her father's side while her mother came from a renowned clan of Scots. Only later, when Emily told me about her family, did she reveal something that bears telling. Her parents were on the frontlines of the Vietnam War rebellion, which became a detestation of all things traditional. They'd been swept up in the feverish quest for a true spiritual path that would usher in the much-needed revolution in consciousness. It was believed, in their social scene, that psychotropics were the answer, the bridge to enlightenment.

To this end, her parents journeyed to the rainforests of Peru and partook in ayahuasca ceremonies with a renowned shaman. They weren't yet married, nor were they aware that her mother was pregnant. The spirits told them during a ceremony. You see, Emily's initiation into the esoteric preceded her birth.

She sipped her scotch and lit the first of her creations. After a few hits, she offered it to me, but I declined in favor of my scotch. Her offer held steady. The tobacco made the hits smooth, effective. We finished the first in a sort of holy silence.

"Now we're ready," she said. She jumped to her feet and headed to the corner by the front door, to the wooden armoire with the triptych and a center shelf that held a statue and two candles at its base. From where I sat, the lack of light, I couldn't make the statue. She struck a match and lit the candles. One of the passions, St. Matthew's I believe, eased into the quiet following a Nick Cave ballad. With the classical music and candlelight, the weed smoke gathering at the high ceilings, that ridiculous stone positioned like an ancient altar, and the shimmer of satin mimicking stained glass, the loft assumed the atmosphere of a chapel.

She returned to her cushion. She was facing me, staring into my eyes; it wasn't an aimless stare, nor was it flirtatious. It was a study. I squirmed, looked away, but she moved with me to not allow a break in our eye contact. I felt invaded; heat sensations coursed the surface of my face. After what seemed like five minutes, an expression rounded her cheeks, one I misread as I went at her with gusto, just as she'd come at me in Luce's, but she craned her head back, shoved me away. "That's passed. I want us to do something. Stand up." Impatiently, she waved me to my feet, then grabbed her iPhone to change the music.

A steady drumbeat, like the sonic pulse of an AI heart, suddenly transformed the chapel into a techno lounge. "We dance," she said. "Not together, by ourselves. Create your own space and own it." The tempo accelerated as other beats rose to thicken the pulse. She danced, swayed, waving her arms above her head and the cigarette between her fingers sent halos of smoke toward the ceiling. In response to the look on my face, she laughed, whirled in a pirouette. "Like dervishes. Like fools. Like whatever you want."

My self-consciousness was so acute it felt as if I was in the center of a Roman coliseum, hounded by the eyes of thousands of spectators. "Dervishes don't smoke weed and drink Macallan 18," I said, but I knew I was trying to justify my paralysis.

"Silly them," she said. "It gets you there quicker." Puffing on a joint, eyes closed, she allowed the trance music to enter, mesmerize, and draw her like an invitation.

My feet tapped to the slow-building, portentous beats that had me craving the breakbeat that never came. It seemed some psychological test of endurance. For Emily it was wings. She unclipped the straps of her overalls and freed herself in movement.

Determined to annihilate my self-consciousness, I lit another joint and smoked the hell out of it. I closed my eyes as she had, and soon the music became something more, presented images that replaced the fearmongering monologue which kept me rigid. It all happened in seconds: depictions replicating the chaos of a midtown corner flashed and bustled in my mind until I saw myself, the passive, broken idea of myself, standing there trembling in the cold, shaking an empty beggar's cup. Not one passerby spared his change, not even a glance of sympathy. *Stop begging!* screamed a voice. Then, one of the demonic faces that interrupted my meditations in those weeks after the breakup with Nadia, pressed into my mind's eye. I was unafraid and suddenly understood the demon was not my adversary, it was my power. A surge of irreverence sent a deluge of warm liquid through my veins, annihilating my resistance. My head was now bobbing to the beat, my limbs swayed and I was moving as if by the will of some other agency. Half an hour into my mad dance, shadowy shapes seemed to move back and forth across the ceiling—shadows that were not ours. Fearless, I called, "Come, come!" And I didn't know who or what I beckoned. My eyes opened, scanned the pulsing room—Emily was watching me. Naked, in candle luminescence, her pale skin glowed like moonlight. She moved toward me.

We sank to the cushions beside the stone, our bodies wet and throbbing from the dance. I attempted to lead the way, but she stymied my approach. She wanted my undivided attention, forced me to look in her eyes as she caressed parts of my body not typically known to cause arousal, yet the intensity of arousal her touch elicited had me twitching. Now she kissed me; again came the strange mumbles, giggles, exhalations.

Trance music. Dancing shadows. The unrelenting penetration of those lavender eyes. I struggled through tense moments of clenching, straining to withhold. "Control it," she said. I shifted my gaze to the beauty mark above the corner of her mouth. She saw I was giving in, dug her nails into my chest. "Fuck!" I knocked her hands away, sprang upright, but she pressed her forehead to mine, eased me back to the cushions, smirking with appreciation for my aggression. The sting from her nails had rebooted my nervous system. I was now present, unencumbered by results. I closed my eyes, sank into the motion, our motion, that became one with the trance music. Mental pictures: me as a child, a crucifix, Nadia, a book with my name, as author, on the cover. Then I heard a strange wail and was suddenly somewhere remote and vast, watching a disfigured Julie Sable floating off into a starless sky.

I opened my eyes. Emily's forehead was pressed to mine. "See yourself as you want to be," she whispered. "See you in my eyes." The blackness of her pupils blurred and sudden freefalling sensations rippled my gut. "See it." She pressed her palms to the stone, pushed her weight down. "See it," she said. My eyelids flitted uncontrollably, closed.

I was bouncing from star to star in the silent, dreamlike emptiness of the heavens. *The state of rapture?* I thought. "Yes," she whispered behind the kiss that returned me to her arching body. "Yes." She shivered in waves, all the while staring intently at the sigil on her wrist.

WHEN I WOKE, Emily was still asleep, curled in a ball on the cushions beside the stone. I entered the hallway in search of the bathroom. There were three doors. One was in the center of the hall, the other two were at the end, directly opposite each other. The centered doorway was for the bathroom, but curiosity goaded me. I assumed one of the rooms at the end of the hall was her bedroom. If any room, the bedroom holds the spirit of the person. The door on the right was locked. I reached for the handle to the door on the left. "No, mate." Her voice cut through me like an icy wind. Sheepishly, I turned to find her standing at the far end of the hall, pointing to the bathroom door. Her eyes beamed suspicion.

Late into the afternoon, we were still unwashed and

lounging on the cushions around the stone. We weren't entwined, teasing like new lovers; between us was the distance friends keep. I felt relieved over my return to sex. I was able, and it seemed a success.

She'd picked a book from the shelf, *Les Fleurs du Mal*, and we took turns reading poems to each other. That's when it started. I'd closed my eyes to listen to her husky voice when flickering images began appearing. I couldn't tell if they were from my dream or what had taken place the night before. Regardless, a strong feeling of apprehension overcame me. I thought of the fool depicted on the tarot card, blissfully and unknowingly stepping off the precipice. I interrupted her poem reading. "What did we do last night?"

She looked me over very matter-of-factly. "Research." She said it plainly, no pun.

"Is that how it's done? By focusing on the sigil?" She dismissed me with a wave of her hand. "Sex magic? Is that it? Tell me."

She exhaled. "You'd go mad if I told you what I know." That was the second time she'd made that claim. How can she say such a thing and not know the person to whom she said it would bend his life to know what the hell she'd meant? Especially in the moment before she places him inside her. Despite my apprehension, or rather in spite, my shoulders were again pinned beneath her palms as she whispered in my ear, "See it." By evening I was exhausted. This wasn't *just sex,* that's for sure.

I suppose a brief insight into her lectures about sexual energy is due. The law of gender states that all of nature contains both masculine and feminine principles. These are the forces responsible for causation on the three planes of existence—the physical, mental, and spiritual. On the physical plane, gender manifests in the sexes as man and woman. On the mental, as the psychic energies of the conscious masculine and unconscious feminine. On the spiritual, as the father-mother principle of the omnipresent God, the Creator and guiding intelligence of one's reality. But on the spiritual plane, the masculine and feminine principles remain polarized unless they have been regenerated through the process of transmutation; only then can the holy union take place.

Emily's system used the orgasm as a potential method of transmutation, which is why she referred to it as the "supreme achiever." During the sexual act, physical arousal is secondary to the higher purpose of spiritual arousal, which, in the right hands, can wield the law of gender to manifest the conscious will. It's believed that the feminine unconscious communes with the Deity; the unconscious will controls the individual and is always stronger than its conscious masculine aspect. Therefore, sex is used as a method of transmutation because the physical arousal allows for the elevation and strengthening of the conscious will to pierce the unconscious and impregnate it with its desire. Once this union is achieved, the unconscious sets to manifesting the conscious will.

Meditating on the union of desires led to an understanding of the deepest meaning in the Androgyne Myth. The search for our other half, for wholeness, is always the veiled desire for regeneration, for overcoming the fallen state. It has nothing to do with another person.

LUCE WAS PACKING for her film shoot in New Mexico, and Emily was preparing one of her herbal tea concoctions in Luce's kitchen. Charged by a flash of inspiration, I was on the cherry red sofa jotting notes for a new book idea. Bursts of light came from the shifting images on the television screen. When I looked up, Julie Sable's eyes were staring back at me. I unmuted the television to hear the latest news. Apparently, Julie had undergone several complicated surgeries. She remained in an induced coma. Her fans were devastated. So was I. Something about the whole thing didn't sit right with me.

That night, Luce insisted the two of us go for a walk. We started out along Franklin then turned down Orange Grove. The stars were on display. The palm trees looked illustrated, inked in black against the indigo sky. I commented on the scent of night jasmine, but Luce seemed not to hear. We walked five or six blocks in silence before she spoke.

"I just wanted to make sure you know what you're doing." She glanced at me. "With Emily. Just be careful."

"You say that like there's more to it."

"Maybe there is," she said.

The following morning before Luce left, Emily had worked it out with her that we'd stay there while she was gone.

"Why do you want to stay here?" I didn't understand; we had our own apartments. She said she needed to be away from her place.

"What about mine?"

"I like it here," she said.

WE WERE LYING on Luce's bed beyond the reach of the candle's light. Her head was resting on her outstretched arm as we made a study of each other—one of her exercises, which she called "get the doing." Connect to something in your own heart and mind, come from that place, then meet eyes with your partner and respond to what exists in her— what was she doing? Ignoring you? Taunting you? Judging you? *What's the intention behind those eyes?* Trying to read hers was like trying to write in water. *Ah! She's creating the mystery. No, too simple.* The more I stared, I realized I was being kept outside when I wanted to be inside. A pain shot through my center: *She's Nadia all over again. Inaccessible.*

Her fingers flicked the wrinkles in the sheet, created a sound that somehow made me feel lonely, restless. Flick. Flick. A new thought followed: *A reflection of my inner state.* This staring into each other's eyes and all her vulnerability-forcing exercises? Suddenly, I saw myself again, a beggar on a midtown corner. Flick. Flick—

I clasped her bony fingers, squeezed. "Get the doing," I said as her lavender eyes narrowed. Instantly, she sprung on me, kissed and bit my lips, tried to wrestle me back, but I overtook her and pinned her to the bed. She looked shocked, wriggled as if to test the strength of my grip. She knew she was trapped. Her head lurched, her mouth opened, I craned back, and she bit the air. I flipped her onto her belly, she freed a hand to claw at me, but I caught her by the wrist, forced her arm to the mattress. Despite her defiance, I pried her wriggling legs open with my knees. "Do you see it?" I chided. Fatigued from the fight, she slackened, submitted. I forgot myself in the surge of aggression that followed, caused the whiplash movements of her head until she leered over her shoulder with fearful eyes; she understood I was in control. When I finished, I released her wrists and dropped down beside her. It happened quickly: in my peripheral, I caught the motion of her right arm as it came off the bed; the slap landed on my cheek and ear, left my skull ringing. She was now above me, face flushed, anger in her eyes, rearing back for another, but I grabbed her arms, and we wrestled until she burst into wild laughter. "Bravo! You're a man again!"

According to her, since my breakup and the disorientation that resulted from becoming aware of and frightened by the shadow aspects in my subconscious mind, I'd been repressing vital energies. "You blamed those forces for bringing about your suffering but disorientation only happens so that a higher state of consciousness might follow." My taking charge was the reassertion of my masculine energy, my will to action.

Soon after, we had another session, the session that changed everything. There was no power struggle. We were at last together in the experience. Amorous feelings overcame me; she seemed equally affected. I was falling in love with her, and it wasn't because of her beauty.

Emily's phone woke us. She glanced at the caller ID, then sprung up and hurried off into the kitchen to take the call. Morning light was on the pebbled glass. I could hear the birds in the courtyard. *Tom Seals?* I imagined Emily and the movie star reuniting, envisioned the demise of our thing. Breathing, careful, I slid my legs off the bed and let my feet touch the floor. That feeling—just breathe into it. Don't label it.

Minutes later, she filled the doorway looking bewildered, gnawing her bottom lip. "*Les Trois Six*? I have the part."

"Congratulations," I said with a measure of relief.

She shook her head, looked around confusedly. "Have to meet the director for lunch." She snapped to it, began collecting her things. "Have to go to mine. I need clothes. I'll call after."

"Aren't you coming back?"

"I'll call after lunch."

She started toward the kitchen, paused, looked back as though there was something she needed to say, gave a barely perceptible head shake, then hurried through the kitchen and out the front door.

BOOK 3

24

If one walks through life without a care in the world, he is either enlightened or epitomizing the adage *ignorance is bliss*. But if he overturns the stones bearing the mossy weight of tradition and indoctrination, he can't help but find smothered ground. He cannot say, *Oh, I've had enough. Let's roll these stones back and continue as we were.* There's no turning back. One cannot un-know what one knows, much less undo what is done. Stubborn as we are, we try anyhow, don't we? To remain fixed, unchanging, denying the flow of life and its one constant: impermanence.

Everyone knows what the eye sees is far from the whole of what constitutes life. I find it amazing how much of our lives, what we imagine our lives to be, doesn't exist. Can you touch your greatness? The value of your Rolex? The beliefs that make you blind? The reasons you do the things you do?

I once believed we were the arbiters of our choices, and as such, we prospered or failed. If only it were that simple.

~

Emily never called after her lunch with the director. She never returned to Luce's. For days, my calls and texts went unanswered. Her match-strike smile. That husky voice. Her hand-rolled cigarettes and instruction. Gone.

I felt it coming, so I walked out onto the balcony to breathe the air. *What's this feeling?* It was love and so much worse than that. I breathed and fought against the rising discomfort, but it was too powerful. I hurried inside before my neighbors could see me, threw myself to the sofa, and it came in overwhelming proportions, moved through every inch of my body. This predicament of being weighed down by pride and needs that weren't real, and to be aware of it, yet still feel helpless? My hands ran my face as the grief escaped. I saw it now, the wound from long ago, literally saw the child me in the state I, the adult me, was presently in; the child was alive inside the adult, frozen in that same grief, only he was experiencing it for the first time, and as I watched him struggle, this strange phenomenon seemed to erase the concept of linear time.

When we did finally speak, about a week and half later, I was too timid to ask where she'd disappeared to, too afraid to hear the truth, of how I might react. Regardless, she showed no sign of thinking an explanation was needed. Then rehearsals began, and she was busy either working with an acting or a dialect coach. If I did happen to get her on the phone, she sounded drained, preoccupied. *Was it Tom? The Danish director? Her co-star on the film?* Or was she sinking into her character, the destitute sugar-babe who finds herself helpless against her impulses? Was she doing research and lending herself to sordid acts to understand sex addiction? No. She'd said it herself, that one didn't have to live the experience. Imagination supplied all that was needed.

This sort of inner dialogue, the seeking answers, analyzing every action and word as if to find clues or the subtext in things that were said, was incessant. I couldn't make it stop. You see, despite all the work I'd done on myself, nothing had changed.

To make matters worse, my writing career, like a sleeping child, had been caught in the conflagration of Nadia and Emily. I hadn't written in months. When I tried to write, resistance with the consistency of cement filled my brain. Suddenly, my purpose in life seemed nonexistent. Every moment of the day held a choice, an agonizing decision over what to do with my time, when all I could do was fester in anxious confusion. While there were people out there in the world giving their lives to help others, to feed and shelter the less fortunate, give a voice to the voiceless, I was completely self-absorbed, contributing nothing of value to humanity.

THE DAY after Luce returned from her film shoot, she came to my apartment for dinner. My preoccupation made it hard to follow her tangential stories. In the lull, I finally asked, "Have you heard from her?"

She looked at me, seemed to suddenly feel my distress. "I warned you." It was an I-told-you-so, how she said it, the way she looked at me.

"Did anything ever happen between you and Halvor?" I asked. "During the play?"

"No," she said as if my question was absurd.

"What about Steve?"

She dropped her hands into her lap, sucked her cheeks,

squinted, then to my surprise, nodded. "Once. Years ago. Back in New York. I was drunk. It was a mistake." That signature sincerity of hers was missing. "Why you looking at me like that?"

"I'm surprised is all."

After that evening, Luce disappeared. I didn't know what to think.

THEN IT WAS all over the news. Three months and three days after her accident, while still in a coma, Julie Sable's heart had stopped. That she was unanimously adored by the public, hers was one of those shock-deaths that made everyone stop whatever it was they were doing when they heard the news, utter their regrets, then resume life as usual. I don't know why, but I cried.

"You should stay a little while in the dark." Into the labyrinth. Why was I shattered by the ugliness I'd discovered inside myself? Feel I had to atone for it? For nearly a year, I'd been going about in a state of abjection like a tolerated mouse in an estate kitchen. It didn't suit me, the Aries born of fire. My purpose had always hinged on my ability to transform. In the alchemical work, fire was the substance of purification, and metaphorically speaking, I'd been in the fire my entire life. Not being happy with myself, wanting to be the best, choosing a career as a writer, my relationships with women—were all distilling agents, the trials and errors necessary to reveal my authentic self.

Emily had insisted, "Even dying in one's nature is better than following that of another. Befriend the ghouls in your heart and receive the secret influence of the heavens." I remembered the night we'd danced in her apartment, how the face of the demon appeared in my mind's eye, that which I feared, yet it freed me. Of course, I feared the demonic; the Catholic indoctrination still held me, even though I imagined I'd abandoned it long ago. How does one embrace what one imagines as demonic? Again, Emily's words came to mind: "Kill the dark by feeding it to death. Not by starving it." The absurd aspects of duality were staring me down. I'd reached the point on the axis where opposites meet and become equal in truth, unfounded and proven all at once. How does one render the absurd as a mere intellectual wall?

My ire flared and conjured a sense of righteous indignation for the meekness into which I'd fallen. Forthwith, I created a space to conduct my secret work and claim my power. I began by designing a sigil that held the meaning of what I desired. I taped it to the wall in the east corner of my bedroom above a shelf on which I constructed my altar with candles and a bronze censer. Come night, despite the outcries of my Catholic fears, casting aside all the worries of selfish intent, I lit the candles, stoked the charcoal brick, and buried it with frankincense. There, before the flickering flames of my altar, I took the fool's tarot card in hand because it held Emily's energy and placed my attention on an image of her held in my mind. Enflamed by the powers of my shadow and a swelling faith in the new reality I was visualizing, I chanted the words she'd taught me, sending them into the unseen realm to tug her strings and bring her to me. And not only her. I was manifesting myself as a prolific writer, and there he appeared, the man I wanted to be, and at his strings, I tugged.

After two weeks of this daily ritual, Emily finally called. Rehearsals for *Les Trois Six* had been put on hold due to financing issues. "Come to mine, then?"

When I arrived at Emily's, Luce was there. Apparently, they'd been seeing each other this whole time. Emily's pallid face seemed longer, thinner, looked waxen next to Luce's healthful gleam. They hardly acknowledged my arrival; both were seated on the cushions around the stone, eyes glued to their cell screens. Was I wrong to feel that Emily owed me an explanation? Or was I meant to accommodate her sudden distancing, take it like the servile student I'd been? With vehemence, I fixed my eyes to the back of her head, called her with my mind, sent commands to test her susceptibility to my will. It was on the third attempt, *Look at me, look at me now*, that she turned a curious glance.

Later, Emily was off gathering her things for a stay at Luce's. She'd complained that her place had developed a "funk." It did; the air held a medicinal odor. I rolled a cigarette as Luce, eyes squinting, surveyed the strange rune-like symbols sketched in charcoal on the sides of the stone. She stood and walked to the armoire. Now in the daylight, I got a closer look at the triptych panels: paintings of melancholy landscape scenes rife with alchemical symbolism. The statue on the center shelf I couldn't make from across the room on the night we danced was a bronze cast of the Sabbatic Goat. I'd seen it depicted on the covers of heavy metal albums, specifically Venom's *Welcome to Hell*. In the eyes of a God-fearing child, Baphomet represented pagan worship and sorcery. But in the occult documentaries Emily showed me and the books she assigned, the idol took on new meaning. There on her shelf, Baphomet represented the Androgyne, the hieroglyph of arcane perfection, adept wielder of secrets. Candles stood like pillars on each side of the statue—the candles she lit to commence our dancing ritual. Arranged on a square piece of black silk were offerings: bundles of herbs, a bird's skull, two bronze cups each with a copper penny inside, two red and two white marbles, and an array of gemstones.

"Look," Luce said. At the back of the shelf was the postcard of Marilyn Monroe Luce had given her. Next to it was a lock of kinky black hair. "It's a shrine to Marilyn." Luce seemed to know it wasn't the case, but she preferred *that* idea. Laid at the cloven hoof of the Sabbatic Goat, as if to be trampled upon, was my St. Christopher medal. That's when it occurred: I was in over my head.

"Guys, look!" Emily yelled. She came from the hall wearing a long, blonde wig. "Hot or what?" The yellowish strands utterly altered her complexion, intensified the color of her eyes, made her a stranger but for the voice I knew so well. The sight of *this* Emily transported me to the morning Nadia became unrecognizable and delivered the same sickening shock.

"I like," Luce said, lifting strands of the blonde wig, holding them lengthwise to inspect their quality. "Wow. Feels real."

"Decided my character should be a proper blonde." Emily turned to the side as if to assume the character then looked back at us with fiendish eyes. "Research?"

Even after Emily put the wig on Luce, who modeled it in the mirror, and the familiar Emily stood before me, I couldn't recover the familiar. She saw I was jarred, kept me in her stare, raised her chin victoriously. The wig was a ruse. She'd intended to shake me. Then I received a silent command from her: *Always be on guard.* She winked and

smirked. I took it that her grandstanding was an admission that she'd used her talents to counterattack my secret work.

THEY HAD FALLEN asleep on Luce's bed. I was stretched on the cherry red sofa, seething, unable to deny what I felt; I wanted her more than ever. But look, there beside Luce, she soundly sleeps. I closed my eyes, took deep breaths…

I was in Staten Island wandering my family's old house. In the ten years since my parents sold it, nothing had changed. I walked to the end of the hallway; there were two opposing doors, right and left, and I realized I was now in Emily's hallway. Strange sounds came from inside the rooms. The handles of both doors were locked. I reached for the molding above the door to the right, ran my fingers across it, and discovered a key. Just as I inserted it into the lock, pangs of melancholia somehow transported me to the woods that surrounded my family's house. Nadia's friend Kim appeared, but I interacted with her as if she was Nadia; she held my hand, smiled contentedly as we strolled the dirt path deeper into the woods. Eventually, we came upon a film crew preparing to shoot. Carelessly arranged equipment cases and light stands, sandbags, and handcarts smothered the ivy patches along the path. The sight caused the same irritation as when I witnessed someone litter. Out of a commiserating group of technicians, the handsome director emerged and approached; he'd been expecting us.

"What are you shooting?" I asked, but, taken by Nadia's beauty, he ignored me—it was now Nadia, not Kim. He asked if she'd like to act in the scene they were about to shoot. She let go of my hand and appeared willing for anything.

"Hey, you're smothering the ivy," I said. "Your equipment." He waved me off, took Nadia by the elbow, and led her away. "Hey!" I shouted, but my voice was soundless. The director and Nadia disappeared. Enraged, I swiped the camera lenses and smashed them on the ground, toppled light stands and overturned sound carts. Wild-eyed, I turned to confront the crew. No one was there.

I walked on as though none of that had happened and soon arrived at the creek I fished as a boy. Gazing at its familiar bends, I attempted to light the cigarette in my mouth, but my lighter, a red Bic, fell from my hand. When I bent to retrieve it, it wasn't on the ground. Somehow, the lighter was on the opposite side of the creek. Just then, Navid, with a long beard and his head wrapped in a turban, came out of the brush. Smiling, waving, he gracefully scooped up my red Bic and showed it to me. I smiled, nodded, held out my hands for him to throw it to me, but he put it into the pocket of his silk vest and headed back into the brush. I hopped rocks to the other side of the creek and gave chase. When I caught him, he spun—his cobalt eyes beamed with ethereal light. Seeing that I was mesmerized, he enjoyed a fit of laughter, then opened his vest to reveal Bic lighters ranging all colors filling the many pockets of his deceivingly slim vest. He then buttoned the vest and walked on without returning my lighter. I demanded he hand it over. He ignored me. When I grabbed his shoulder, the pupils of his eyes expanded, eclipsed all color. He moved at me, thrusting an index finger, but I struck first, and we went to the ground locked in battle. Somehow, he escaped. I caught up with him again at the threshold of the woods. This time, when he turned to confront me, he had the face of a leopard. He crouched, lurched at me, and I felt his teeth sink into my side. I managed to restrain him in a headlock, squeeze with all my might until I heard a definitive pop. His teeth released my side, and all at once, he went limp. I let go, and his body, already stricken by rigor mortis, collapsed to the ground.

Panic set in. I took off running through the dark woods that seemed to be thickening by the second. The idea of being caught and jailed was a lion snapping at my heels, impossible to outrun. I swatted my way through encroaching branches that stabbed at my head and feet. Pulsating trees, swirling vines, and swelling thickets merged into an inseparable mass that consumed everything in my wake. All sound was muted, as it happens underwater, and the vacuum-like mass of nature arched above me, a serpent about to strike. *Wake up!*

I was back on the cherry red sofa, my inner ears thick with the sounds from the nightmare. I swung my feet to the floor, sat up, breathed. *It was only a dream.* But there were still sounds, whimpers, breathy moans that drew my eyes to Luce's bed. The sheet looked pregnant with a shifting mass. I waited for the voice to call, *Wake up.* But I was awake.

The floorboards creaked as I moved toward across them. Luce's arms were thrown back behind her head, her eyes rolling in rapture. Now she saw me, had no reaction, neither apprehension nor shame. I reached for the corner of the sheet, tore it back. Between Luce's thighs, Emily's translucent forehead appeared a half-moon turned sideways. Her eyes fixed to mine like a lioness guarding her kill. I hovered above them in a whirlwind, sickened by what I now understood, sickened by an unbound desire to join; it wasn't arousal but a desperate attempt to be included. Luce's hand clenched my thigh. Her willingness to cross that line, to snip the threadbare tether, met no resistance. Emily's tangy mouth arrived and it was two sharing mine.

LYING in the ravine between Emily's and Luce's backs gave me the impression I was dust blowing through a valley.

Thin veils of golden light streaming through the top of the curtains caught Emily when she sat up in the bed. She shuddered from a chill then found me sitting on the cherry red sofa. Wrapped in the bed sheet, she crossed the creaky floor and deposited herself lengthwise on my lap. Her breath smelled of what I was regretting. She searched my eyes, frowned in mock sadness, then caressed my cheek as though mollifying a pouty child.

Luce rolled over, squinted at us, giggled. Emily sprung from my lap, leaped onto the bed, and pulled the sheet over their heads. Whispers and cackles ensued. There I was hoping for something, an acknowledgment that we had crossed a line, sacrificed something of vital importance. *Where does this go?*

A knock came at the front door. Luce's head of messy hair popped up from beneath the sheet. "Oh, no..." She scurried out of the bed. "Get dressed, guys, hurry. Told Steve I would go to the Grove with him this morning." She dressed in her discarded clothes and ran out of the studio into the kitchen.

Emily yelled after her, "Tell him to fuck off!"

Steve? His comment about our Big Sur trip, the insinuation of a *ménage à trois*; had he ordained it by speaking it? Or had Emily, in branding us her *research*? Emily hadn't moved from the bed. She was looking over her belly, poking it here and there, running it with her hand as if to smooth it down.

Luce came back whispering, "I didn't answer." Just then, her cell started vibrating. She exhaled and turned it face down.

"He'd shit," Emily said. They met eyes, then burst with villainous laughter.

Luce went into the kitchen to call Steve. Emily snarled at me. "Quiet, aren't you?" My acidic stare was melting her to the bone. "You taking the piss?" She slid off the bed and went into the bathroom.

I was thinking of Navid, the magician with his tricks. In my nightmare, he surely represented this whole pathetic journey; what began as mere curiosity because of Nadia and her books and led to a reassessment of my spirituality, then developed into a need to find spiritual sustenance and regain a semblance of normalcy. The very same need which prompted my blind trust in Emily and her practice. But the nightmare? I killed Navid, then nature attacked. *What did it mean?*

Emily exploded from the bathroom in a frenzy. She'd forgotten her satchel of marijuana at her apartment. She said she felt nauseous and needed it, asked me to ride with her to go get it. "Please." She fidgeted as I stared. I saw her now, a trickster like Navid. I remember what she said once. "We make people into what we want them to be. It's an act of violence. Especially when the cunts take the piss out of us by revealing something in themselves we failed to see." And they always do, only we don't fail to see it, we fail to accept it.

To this day what remains of her is a composite of impressions: Emily in the orange-hued diffusion of Luce's paper lampshade. She pauses, a hand-rolled cigarette between her fingers, tilts her head—there she is, the posh Brit, feigning serious contemplation. She'd mastered this effect, mirage of sophistication, but it was nothing other than a defense when caught off guard, a device to regain the spirit of her image. Framed by the stark flanks of her punky, black bob, which contrasts her slender, pale face, she resembles the Pre-Raphaelite muse Sophie Gray. Could that tiny beauty mark above the right crease of her smirk be the brand of sensuality? Lined lashes part just enough for the orange light to electrify what seems mischief and cunning in her lavender eyes. A cliché description of a woman's eyes perhaps, but the longer her stare lingers, I suspect she doesn't only know nature's secrets, but mine.

"Come with," she pleaded. I felt nudged by my shadow aspects; the drive would be a perfect opportunity to confront her.

I smiled, said, "Let's go."

The city of angels was warm and bright. Emily, pale in the daylight, anxious, bubbling, drove Luce's Jeep toward the foothills. The night before, she'd turned the eyes of a lioness on me, a cruel animalistic indifference. I had to restrain my desire to crush her translucent, bony fingers clenching the gear shift. She broke the silence. "It wasn't the first time, you know? Me and Luce." She let that settle. "Started before you and me."

I was deceived, but surprised? It was on display the night I met Emily in Luce's studio; they were shoulder to shoulder at the dinner table. The first time I'd heard mention of Emily was when Luce referred to her as, "my girl crush." Driving home after Leslie's that night, I'd asked Luce if she'd ever been with a woman, and she waved my question off as though it was utter ridiculousness. She lied to me. And Emily's transparency ceremony meant to divulge our deepest secrets—both withheld *that* secret. Months on end sharing our most intimate thoughts, now our bodies, and I still had no idea who they were.

I followed her into the rock garden then up the staircase,

and stood in the doorway while she searched for her satchel of marijuana, swiftly turning out her hiding places, coming up empty and increasingly agitated. My eyes wandered the icons, the ridiculous stone, the forced décor of her confusion. At a loss, she leaned her elbows atop the stone. "Where the fuck..." She suddenly tensed, looked up; perspiration glistened on her forehead. She drew several deep breaths as if to thwart nausea, then jumped to her feet and ran into the hallway. The bathroom door slammed. Sounds of dry heaving followed.

I approached the bathroom door, listened to her vomit. At the end of the long hallway were the two doors that had figured into my nightmare the night before. As if premeditated, I seized the opportunity, tiptoed to the end of the hall, and reached above the door to the right and ran my fingers across the molding... Voila! A key with a slot head just as I had dreamed. The feeling was disorienting, to have a dream so accurately presage waking life, but there wasn't time to consider this. I inserted the key into the door on the left and stepped into a dark room. My hand searched the wall, found the light switch.

I stood in a narrow, rectangular room, walls to ceiling painted white. Even the glossy varnish on the wood floor was white. Thick, white curtains completely covered the windows. Centered in the floor was an encircled pentagram constructed from pieced-together tears of blue electrical tape. Planetary symbols of the same blue tape, like those from my birth chart, were placed around the pentagram. There was an altar adorned with a mess of candles; a bronze censer containing charred knots of some pungent root; a forged copper dagger with a gem-studded hilt; dried herbs, flowers, and scattered crystals. Resting on the altar was a laminated card with a symbol resembling the sigil on her wrist, the symbol of that which she invoked. There was no mistaking the white room was an oratory for ceremonial magick.

I shut off the light and backed out of the room. The bathroom door was still closed. I unlocked the door to the right, entered, hit the light switch. Walls to ceiling were painted black. A thin, black carpet covered the entire floor. Long, black velvet curtains covered the windows. Centered on the floor and painted on the carpet in red brushstrokes was an inverted pentagram. There was an altar with a laminated card bearing a symbol nearly buried in red and black candle wax. On the upper deck of the altar, a statue presided, right hand raised toward heaven, left lowered toward the earth; the white onyx beast eyes of Baphomet stared back at me. There seemed life in them. Beneath the statue, a silver dish held a withered photograph; the ink was discolored in places from the once hot candlewax piled in red and black stalagmites on its surface. The photograph, what appeared to be a page from a tabloid, was of a bikini-clad Julie Sable emerging from the ocean. The beast's white eyes seemed to mock me. I couldn't possibly describe the feeling.

The toilet flushed as I passed the bathroom door. I hit the balcony, ran down the stairs, through the Zen rock garden, and burst from the front gate like an escapee.

25

J ulie was dead and Emily now had her part in *Les Trois Six*.

I recalled the day of Julie's accident, that morning standing on the bluff in Big Sur, staring down at the beach with the circle of stones. *Remnants of a bonfire?* When I'd asked her where she'd gone that night, she said, "To present my case." *Could this be?*

I'm still in Big Sur, on the edge of the bluff, miffed by how she'd used me to demonstrate the power of suggestion by having me listen to the wind and suggesting it sounded like autumn so that I imagined autumn landscapes without suspecting I'd been manipulated. It now seemed like a testing of my suggestibility rather than a well-intentioned instruction. All of it did. After the dancing ritual in her apartment, she used me in her sex magick, disoriented me while she worked, eyes fixed to the sigil on her wrist. Christ, when my eyes were closed, I saw the image of a disfigured Julie Sable floating into a starless sky. No wonder I felt apprehensive the following morning, sensed she'd violated my trust. Fool. Fool.

Let me be clear. Earlier, when I'd stated lifeforms surround us, I felt it was too soon to elaborate in that direction. So here it is. When alone in my apartment I'd felt things, felt poked, watched at times, unsettled by what I'd sensed in the air around me, and standing there in the black oratory, staring into the beast's white eyes, it seemed it was those eyes that had been watching.

During our stint at Luce's while she was away shooting her film, Emily mentioned the elemental spirits for a second time. "Spirits?" I asked. "Do you believe they're energies? Or do you think they're actual spirits, embodying a shape, a form?"

Her head tilted back, which drew the light sources to her advantage, made her appear maniacal yet sophisticated. "That chair?" She pointed to Luce's desk chair. "Does it exist or not? To me, it does."

"So there *are* spirits involved?" I asked.

She nodded. "Why do you smirk?"

"I don't want to be messing with spirits."

"Remember your nightmares? They mess with you. You're only discovering that we control them. Dominion over *all*. That is the law."

Those faces I'd seen in my mind's eye, those vivid demonic faces taunting me, gnashing their teeth. "Literally? Like evil demons?"

"Calling something evil is nothing but immaturity. An undeveloped understanding of our nature. Just as anything *good* stems from the aspects of our nature that have grown. The dissolution of duality is the crux of the mysteries. That's what the rituals are for. The perfection of nature.

"There's only one rule. If the secrets are used for selfish intent, it's black magick being practiced. Say, for instance, you fell in love with a woman and had the noblest intentions towards her—to love her and make her your happy wife—and you began working with the symbols and the words to invoke the help of spirits to win her, it's black magick you're practicing."

"Wait," I said. "You say these things shouldn't be used for selfish purposes, but even the motivation to lose the self is selfish. It comes out of desire." I'd caught her off guard, stumped her. "Such willfulness couldn't be separated from selfishness," I said. "So all magic is really black magic."

She looked annoyed. "Well, there has to be some desire to get to the point of desirelessness."

And magic with a k? Magic, as in the belief in one's ability to manipulate natural and supernatural beings and forces through ceremonies and rituals, seems to have originated in the near East, but magic-k arose from the occultism of Western traditions, specifically the system designed by Aleister Crowley. What I can say is that the reliable ancient texts on the subject were not written by superstitious people with a limited understanding of modern scientific principles, attributing the ways of nature, like lightning storms and earthquakes, to deities. Pythagoras, Socrates, Plotinus, Iamblichus, Swedenborg, and the list goes on, were the greatest thinkers of their times, especially regarding the active laws underpinning man's relation to the material and spiritual realms. Pythagoras practiced divination and made sacrificial offerings. Socrates freely spoke about the visits and conversations he'd had with his daemon oracle. Plotinus founded a school based on the practice of theurgy, which later influenced Iamblichus, who streamlined theurgical techniques for invocation and magical rituals. And Swedenborg, while performing breathing exercises that created an altered state of consciousness, received the higher knowledge from spirits, parties of them, who claimed to be from Venus and Mars and other planets in the solar system. Even Napoleon had his little red man, the "ghost" he bargained with that others had claimed to have seen.

And the demons of my Catholic religion? Esoteric Christian texts make mention of the Unseen, the progenitors of vice, the principalities not of this world. They made no bones about calling them demons. They'd categorized a hierarchy with divisions and distinctions so the cloistered monks could be prepared and know which demon was attacking them based on the vice being triggered. The attacks might come as such: the surreptitious demon presents images in the mind of the unsuspecting monk to persuade thought, image after image to fuel desire until unbound desire goads the will to action. Then the gates are flung open, other demons storm in to persuade the vices they serve and together they drag the tethered soul into ruin. The average man, who believes his penchants are his own, is helpless because he doesn't even know he is under attack. *The true enemies don't fight you. They slither into your mind.*

If Emily's ceremonies invoked demons, then her oratories, the black room specifically, were used for practicing black magick and selfish gains. Even if I was projecting my own ideas onto what I now believed to be true about Emily and what the black room meant to me, the fact is, she preyed on my vulnerability, and not only mine, but Julie Sable's.

I know, I know—psychology has done away with these explanations. For scheiße und giggles, enter the wisdom of the ancients. Let the idea in. Listen to your mind for ten minutes. You hear the voices, don't you? The ones that pull you to strife, fuel your anger and sense of righteousness.

The ones that tell you what you deserve and justify your lies and infidelities when they serve the outcomes you desire. What do you think these voices are? Just negative thoughts? Aspects of your psyche? And the thoughts you attach to? Don't they torment you and run you ragged, to where all your mistakes pile at the dead end of some unruly passion or selfish pursuit? If survival and preservation are the goals of life, and happiness is what we all seek, why would our minds turn on us? Do zebras run to the crocodiles? Groundhogs to the foxes?

WEEKS PASSED without a word from Emily or Luce. I'd disappeared without explanation and neither cared for one. I had to know. I Googled *Les Trois Six*. There it was. Due to Julie Sable's accident, the independent studio behind *Les Trois Six* had put the film in turnaround, which meant the studio was writing off the development costs for a film they no longer intended to make. The Danish director had moved on and was currently directing a romantic comedy with two A-listers. This could only mean that Emily lied about getting the part, meeting the director for lunch, and the weeks of rehearsals. Oh, the rabbit hole. Do you see the trap? This compulsion to draw significance out of everything?

A LAYER of dust covered the hood of Luce's Jeep. The shades in the kitchen windows were drawn. I pressed my ear to the glass panel. Nothing.

I walked around back to the courtyard. The curtains in

the rear windows of the studio were drawn. Attuned to the trickling of the koi pond's waterfall, beneath the grapefruit and avocado trees, I realized I was standing where Emily had stood the night I met her and she performed the vernal equinox ceremony. How I wished I could regain that first impression of her.

Across the way, the door of a garden apartment opened. A tall, blond man and a woman with red hair exited and started in the opposite direction. Megan and her soon-to-be husband. They held hands, and she playfully kicked at the ground as they went along. At that moment, I was stricken by how different our realities were and how theirs seemed pure.

The curtains in the studio windows parted. Behind the glass stood Luce in rumpled, mismatched clothes, that head of kinky hair pushed here, flattened there. The back door was open. I knocked and entered. Her unmade bed appeared sullen in the soft-lit corner. Dishes with unfinished food were piled on the coffee table. Discarded clothes were strewn on the furniture, and on the walls were many elongated aureoles of flickering light from the steady flames of votive candles lining the mantel and shelves.

She was hunched on the cherry red sofa. My jaw was tight. "Where's Emily?" She shook her head. "Where is she?"

She shrugged. "Said she was leaving to shoot the film."

"There was no film." I believed she knew the truth, yet she looked up at me with such surprise, as if she were the victim, not me. "There was no film," I said.

"What do you mean?"

I was reluctant to trust her, but the sincerity in her confusion prompted me to say again, softer this time, "There was no film. No rehearsals. It was all a lie."

She shivered from a chill, hugged herself. I moved closer.

"Julie Sable?" She glanced up at me.

"What do you think?" I asked.

"What do you mean?" It occurred to me that she hadn't seen the black and white rooms, that only I knew the score. Her face contorted. Yes, she was sincere and I was pulling the rug out from beneath her. Her eyes drifted from my stare as if to allow her to think; she seemed to make sense of something. Oncoming emotion bloated her face.

"I have to tell you," she said, sliding to the edge of the sofa. She was now struggling with the words. "She asked me to come with her. She didn't say for what." At once, her hands shot up to cover her mouth.

"What? Tell me."

"It was a clinic." She wanted to be sure I understood what she'd meant. Now she pulled the rug out from beneath me. "I swear I didn't know," she said, bursting into tears.

My skin was gooseflesh. The intentions behind my secret work to secure Emily, when I'd ignored the warnings, freed my shadow aspects, and chanted? I'd envisioned her as my wife, pregnant with my child. "It was mine?" I stammered.

Her nod was hesitant. "But...I think she wanted it to happen."

At first, I didn't understand. Why would Emily want to get pregnant only to have an abortion? It wasn't Luce's anguish, the severity underpinning the look on her face that brought me within range; it was what I knew about Emily.

I glanced to the opposite end of the sofa and saw her there in the orange lamplight, an index finger raised in warning: "There's no cheating the law. You must always give to get. It's best to make an offering and hope it suffices."

She'd given me the fool's tarot card and described the Catholic mass as a ritual sacrifice.

"She was here, after," Luce said. "Recovering. Middle of the night, she woke up screaming, blood all over her legs, the sheets. She was burning up. I wanted to call an ambulance, but she got crazy. She ran out. I went after her, I couldn't find her. I call, she don't answer. But I swear to God, after she'd left, I don't know. There was something here. I don't know what, but." Right then, I noticed all the candles burning around the apartment—dollar store votive candles with depictions of saints and prayers printed on the glass.

She reached for the prescription bottle on the coffee table, wrenched the cap off, popped two Xanax, then spread out on the sofa and covered her face with a pillow. Soon after, she was asleep. I sat for a long while until it seemed there was only one thing to do.

MY FOOT WAS heavy on the pedal as I swerved around the clueless drivers or the texting morons crowding the West Hollywood streets. Only when I was parking on Beachwood before the two Moreton Bay figs did I realize I had no way of gaining entry into Emily's complex. If I rang the bell, she would deny me and the slotted wood fence was too high to scale. Besides, it was imperative I take her by surprise. The problem was solved when, moments later, a skinny hipster emerged from the gate. "Hold it," I charged.

I took the stairs two per stride to the soundtrack of tinkering chimes. As I crossed onto her balcony's white, furry rug, my steps went quiet. That the front door was wide open, it seemed ominous, as though I'd stumbled upon a fresh crime scene. The frame of the doorway showed a narrow view of the loft. I paused, listened. Only the soft, glass-shatter treble of the chimes. As I stepped over the threshold, a low, guttural roar awakened, then a loud thud against the back of the door, and it swung into me. I threw up my forearm to shield the blow, stop its momentum. Emily's maddened face swung round from behind the door —she looked possessed.

"Go away!" She pressed her weight against the door to push me out, but I fit my hip in the jamb so she couldn't close it.

"Was it mine?"

She screamed as the struggle with the door continued.

"Tell me!" Now I laid my shoulder into the door and suddenly it gave—I tumbled forward then the door quickly swung back, slammed into my head, and knocked me out onto the balcony. She'd used my force against me. A thunderclap sealed the door. The locks fastened. Just then a breeze moved through the chimes that awakened a sense of horror as I glanced around and felt the watching presence of something primal and dark.

I COULDN'T SLEEP that night. As I paced the living room, I caught a glimpse of myself in the mirror: sunken cheeks and the wide, flat stare of dead eyes. I could almost recognize Victor Cerrone circa Nadia, some resemblance in our features, but not in the eyes. I looked like the lone survivor of a war, the war between Pluto and Saturn. Death *was* certain.

I paced and smoked, trying to imagine the child that would've come from our *research*. Would it have had her husky voice and pale skin? Her lavender eyes? Even knowing what I did about her, the idea of her wanting to get pregnant only to sacrifice the baby seemed farfetched. *For a role in a movie?* I didn't want to believe she, or anyone, could do such a thing. And the look on her face, her eyes when she was slamming me with the door—like the possessed women from the orgy in my nightmare. Had her self-experiments backfired? Had the demon she invoked in her black oratory entered her and scrambled her mind?

What about your experiments? You ignored the warnings, too. Fearing my damnation, I picked up a Bible—I only had it because Hemingway said it was the best place to lift titles for novels, though most of the good ones had already been taken. I opened the cover and sifted the thin pages, but I had an idea where to start. *The New Testament. Yes.* I dove into St. Paul's letters to the Corinthians, and after a few pages, found myself amazed. *This was not the Bible I read as a child—wait. I'd never read it, not once in all those years of Catholic school.* I knew only what I'd heard in readings at mass.

I now saw Paul's letters as mystical treaties, lessons in truth; this conclusion was hinged on all the other spiritual books I'd read, even those Emily had assigned. I moved on to the gospels, and I was suddenly able to discern their deeper meanings, particularly in Christ's words. All the things Christ warned against, I reveled in for decades, and there I was, alone, purposeless, disconnected not only from the world but myself. I had reached the promise of iniquity. Death. Suffering. Hell.

WHEN HE ARRIVED at the other side in the region of the Gadarenes, two demon-possessed men coming from the tombs met him. They were so violent that no one could pass that way. 'What do you want with us, Son of God?' they shouted. 'Have you come here to torture us before the appointed time?' Some distance from them, a large herd of pigs was feeding. The demons begged Jesus, 'If you drive us out, send us into the herd of pigs.' He said to them, 'Go!' So they came out and went into the pigs, and the whole herd rushed down the steep bank into the lake and died in the water.

Matthew 8:28–32

I had returned to the reality where angels and demons exist.

A longing for purification overtook me. I ran into my bedroom, and in surrender, threw myself to my knees. Prayers came forth, earnest prayers that discarded, as if in one pious stroke, my former conceit and all the intellectualizing that spiraled me away from faith. I pleaded for forgiveness, for release from the dark forces that led me astray. I prayed and prayed, not the standard prayers, but words that flowed out so readily they seemed somehow rehearsed, as if I knew exactly what to say. There in that posture, peace suddenly settled my heart. *God's grace?* I bawled like a child until exhausted, then fell onto the bed.

I awoke the following morning in a calm state. Logic persuaded me that nothing I had tried to manifest had manifested. Yes, Emily and I were irresponsible; she got pregnant because we weren't using contraception. I'd made the same mistake with Nadia. But with Emily, I couldn't even be sure the baby was mine. She'd lied all along, was probably sleeping with Tom, and who knows who else.

There was nothing to gain by obsessing and trying to rationalize Emily's sick games. Nor would it serve to punish myself over her pregnancy. Regarding Julie Sable's death, if intentions determined the outcomes of things, I was not culpable. I had no bad intentions toward her.

Then it happened. The impulse to write returned. It was time to draw the lines, get it all out, and purge. What began as a journal detailing my strange journey segued into the memory of the transparency ceremony, when it was Emily's turn to share her deepest secrets. She was lying on the floor with the candles positioned at her five points, head, hands, and feet. Tears were streaming down her cheeks, her strained voice pitched like a child's. "My parents told me lies. Made me believe I was special. How could I be special? They sent me off to boarding school..." Suffering is the impetus. Sometimes the pain and the fear of pain is so over-whelming one seeks not the grace of surrender but the power to dominate, to control life rather than be subjected to its vicissitudes. But her confession shed light on her foray into the occult. It came out of disillusionment, as did mine. She was correct, we *were* bound by a sympathetic affinity: the need to end the chaos and restore order in our lives. We wanted control, believed it could be won.

Before I knew it, I was writing my first real novel, *Apophenia*. The story begins with a childhood trauma that marks the main character, then jumps forward to find her struggling through young adulthood, seemingly the victim of life's unfortunate circumstances. By chance, while in a bookstore, she comes across a grimoire of ceremonial magic and is taken by the idea that one can gain powers to assert her will on reality. Blinded by the desire to overcome her pain, she spends a year studying all the occult literature she can find and begins experimenting with rituals and invoca-tions. At first, she doesn't seem to produce results, but when she finally receives a sign that the rituals are effective, she wholly commits herself. Then she learns her meddling led to the unintentional death of a rival. Her conscience shows her how her obsession with controlling life instead of accepting life on its terms has set her against nature. Tormented by guilt and confusion, unable to distinguish reality from fantasy, and convinced that the voices in her head are those of the demons she'd invoked, she spirals into madness, places herself beneath an olive tree in Barnsdall Park and ends her life.

I was possessed, wrote like a madman, two hundred and twenty-seven pages. The characters, the story, the logic all worked. Over the next three months, I revised *Apophenia*, wrote two short stories, and began a feature screenplay. At night before bed, I read the Bible, my new practice. St. Paul was most appealing. He had also been in hell before he'd heard the voice. Redemption is possible. His words fortified me against the feeling I'd get when night fell, when it was quiet, and it seemed I was not alone.

And when I was never more alone, off in the story world, I'd be reminded. I remember one evening, while at my desk, how it snatched me. The dread of absolute loneliness, that I can never be truly known by another. I stood, walked to the open doorway, surveyed the hills. It was that landscape, that air somehow pressing me with its energy. I witnessed the blue dusk mingle with the electric light of the cigarette stand on the corner and the sibilant swishing of the breeze in the palms. *Sshhh...* It was magic. *Sshhh...* The sway of *listless-ness... Sshhh...* Soon, I was in a trance-like state, carried by a stream of images that seemed a correspondence between my heart and mind orchestrated by a deeper region of intelligence. Images that displayed a chronology of my life's pivotal events and how each had contributed to bringing me to that exact moment in time. My ordeals were suddenly laced with purpose. I could see the scope of the design, the connecting principle, how all that had transpired was necessary to break my patterns of inauthentic living and open my heart to true understanding. There *were* fingerprints on the grand scheme of my life.

I had to love Nadia as possessively, as passionately as I did because I was meant to lose all sense of self in the attachment. The stillness she caused in my mind on the night we met—what, in my arrogance I perceived as desire—was really this deeper region of intelligence communicating what it had known all along: Nadia was my path to death. The demise of a false identity.

Emily was right: "Awakening can only come to us through that area of life where we are most imbalanced. Where our thoughts and ideas have wrongly accumulated. Lose yourself to find yourself." It was no coincidence she appeared. I've said she took all that was gathered around me and placed it inside where it had always been. It seemed ironic: two completely self-involved women would inspire spiritual growth in this self-absorbed tyrant. It was all so clear now. Their shared purpose in my life was to reveal myself to me. It sounds incredibly narcissistic, I know, but that is what life does, reveal us, and it needs devices for such delicate operations.

Nadia buried me and Emily resurrected me. This shift in perspective made me see that I had no right to be angry with Nadia, Luce, or Emily. None of us were to blame; it wasn't like we had a choice. Our coming together and all that had taken place between us was God's will; my suffering was due to my rejection of God's will. Hadn't He given me all I wanted so that I could see what I wanted was not right for me?

"For while the mind of man looketh upon second causes

scattered, it may sometimes rest in them, and go no further; but when it beholdeth the chain of them...it must needs fly to providence and deity." I printed Francis Bacon's quote and hung it on the wall above my writing desk.

THEN CAME a phone call from a movie producer who wanted to adapt my play *Nigredo* for the big screen. "I run development for Jenna Winters' production company. She loves your play. It's a strong female lead. Hollywood needs strong, female-driven stories. Jenna wants to fast-track it." Before I could respond, she added, "If you're open to it." Jenna was the highest-paid actress in Hollywood, an A-lister. For her, the light was a steady green.

I wondered. *Nigredo* was not a well-known play. The brief attention it received was just that. No one had put it up since our run at the Cherry Lane. On the shelves of the Drama Bookstore, among thousands of ancient and modern classics, it was invisible, and based on the publishing royalties, obscure. How did Jenna Winters come across it?

A week later, I met Jenna at her house in the Pacific Palisades. She answered the door in yoga pants and a gray, chunky sweater. Her smile was genuine, handshake firm. The exterior view of what appeared a modest ranch house proved deceptive. The layers of the house descended several stories of the hill to a bottom level with a landscaped yard and a slate stone infinity pool.

We stood in the glass sun porch admiring the coastal views before settling on rattan chairs with white cushions. Midday sunlight made the green of her eyes magnificent, threw reddish highlights into her sandy hair. She was personable and confident, and the conversation came easily.

We smoked American Spirits, sipped coconut water, and every so often, she'd pick a piece of watermelon from the arrangement of cut fruits in a bamboo bowl on the glass table. Twice, business calls came in, I presumed from her agent, but she kept them brief and apologized each time she returned.

The whole afternoon passed without mention of the screenplay. We talked about our lives—we were the same age—our hobbies, our childhoods, and found common ground. At one point, as if obligated, she offered a candid account of her much-publicized marriage to a famous director. The whole affair had been chronicled, from the fairytale start to the bitter end. He'd been accused of sex with a minor, a fifteen-year-old girl, who starred in a film he directed. The young girl had consented to his advances, but she was, of course, underage and therefore, presumed not to know what was best for her. "Which was the case, wasn't it?" Jenna shrugged. "Not in any woman's best interest to be sleeping with a married man." But after that incident came to light, other allegations arose that blindsided Jenna. "Truth is, it wouldn't have lasted anyway. He wanted kids. I didn't."

Suddenly, it occurred: we *were* talking about the screenplay. This was how it's done. I'd know how to rewrite the character in *Nigredo* for Jenna by getting to know the nature of her disillusionment.

"What are you working on now?" she asked. "Besides *Nigredo*?" I hesitated. "It's okay if you don't want to talk about it. Know how this town is."

"No. It's fine." I felt compelled to tell her. "A novel about a girl mixed up in the occult."

"So, you write fiction also?"

"It's my first real novel."

"The others fakes?"

"You could say that."

She smirked and sipped her coconut water. "Do you have experience with the occult?" It seemed a loaded question.

"Why do you ask?"

"Well, the novel. The title of your play. My husband was fascinated with all that, maybe a little more than fascinated."

"The title came out of a conversation with a friend," I said. "Deep guy."

"Lots of that in this town," she said. She mimed one trying to exert mind control, touching a hand to her temple, wiggling the fingers of the other as if to draw something toward her, but she stayed on it too long, and the mime and the joke took on dark tones. All afternoon, she'd exhibited sophistication, spoke with distinction. True, I hardly knew her, but it seemed out of character.

"Isn't it freaky here?" she said. "Something in this place, man. The energy. You know what I mean?" I nodded. "Strange birds gravitate to the arts. To this business especially. How many writers and actors get all spiritual as if making themselves better people will warrant success." There was a glint in her eyes; she seemed to be looking straight to my heart. "Half the people who make it are fucked up. Psychopaths. It takes that sort of disconnect. That level of narcissism." She paused, trailed off somewhere. "How about Julie Sable," she said. "Crazy, right?" I nodded, but had that icy feeling inside.

"Did you know her?" I asked.

"I met her. I didn't know her." She was staring at me again.

"What made you think of her?" I asked.

She looked away, grew pensive. "She just came to mind."

"Out of curiosity, how did you come across *Nigredo*?"

"It's the most random story. This past June, I was in New York doing a play at the Brooklyn Academy of Music and I was staying at the Mercer Hotel. One night, the girl who worked there, the hostess, was sitting in the lobby crying. When I asked if she was all right, she got all nervous and started apologizing. She'd been so sweet to me, I felt horrible leaving her there. Wasn't quite ready for bed, so I invited her up to my room and we ended up smoking cigarettes by the window, drinking scotch until dawn. She told me her life story. Was married young. The husband was controlling, blah blah blah. Anyhow, at some point, we were talking about my work, and I said that I wanted to do more theater. Next day, as a thank you for lending an ear, she gave me two gifts. One was a little illustration of a fairy in a tree with these colorful like swirls and the other was your play."

I wondered if Jenna saw the blood rush out of my face as I was involuntarily transported back to Nadia's bedroom on that first night we met, laid out on her faux sheepskin and eyeing her framed illustrations; then to the Cherry Lane Theater with Nadia beside me wiping tears because the play had touched her.

Look how the chain grew taut, and connections I'd thought were severed supplied the integrity of the Unseen's beneficence. It's the height of arrogance to imagine our little minds can comprehend the ineffable. All at once I felt chastised and blessed.

The following morning, after praying the rosary, I decided to call Nadia to thank her for helping my career. It wasn't until the space between the fourth ring that the reality became hyper-real: we'd not spoken for so long, I had no idea what to expect, or how her voice might stir me. Then the call was answered. There was crackling as if her cell speaker was rubbing against clothing, then a brief silence.

"Hey, stranger." It was past noon in New York, yet she sounded as if she was still in bed.

"How are you?" My voice was weak.

"Oh, I don't know," she said. "How's LA?" Her voice had changed; it was scratchy, strident.

"Is what it is," I said. A long silence followed. *Tell her about Jenna, thank her for mentioning* Nigredo. "How's work?" I asked.

"Got fired."

"What happened?"

"Ran its course," she said. Those words and the silence that ensued? I felt it, knew something was coming. "I'm sick," she said. "I'm in a hospital."

"What's wrong?"

"Doctor sent me for blood tests. Hormones are all over the place. One minute I'm laughing, next I'm crying."

"What is it?"

"They don't know yet. But I'm here with the psychiatrists, so. Ha." Another long silence left me aching to hold her. I wanted to tuck the hair behind her ears, kiss her eyelids. "Please know I'm sorry for hurting you," she said. "I never meant to. I was terribly confused—"

"It's okay," I said, unable to bear her apology.

"Don't pretend," she said. "I hurt you and I'm sorry."

"Neither of us are to blame. For whatever reason, it was

all necessary." But in that moment, I felt spurned, defeated, robbed.

"Necessary? What do you mean?" She sounded angry. I inhaled to keep my voice even.

"Nothing, just..."

"What? You meet the girl of your dreams? She pregnant? What?"

"Oh, Nadia," was all I could muster.

Not long after that conversation, Halvor called. Kim had told him that Nadia lost the Hester Street apartment. After she'd been fired, she was unable to pay the rent. She'd been staying at Kim's, and one night, she swallowed a bottle of sleeping pills. Kim found her unconscious and called an ambulance. Nadia was revived, examined, diagnosed as bipolar, and admitted to the psych ward. "She didn't mention that," I said.

It wasn't shocking, just heartbreaking. The swings from high to low, the depressive spells, the manic bursts of joy and hope—it was there all along. Somehow the fragmented pieces of the turquoise ring in the white bowl now came to represent her, the same image that gave birth to *River Without End*. Wasn't it strange? Nadia met the same fate as the character she'd inspired.

MY ADAPTED screenplay for *Nigredo* went into production later that year. The buzz I received from the script got me a literary agent, a big literary agent, who was willing to read my first draft of *Apophenia*. She liked it and passed it off to the agency's publishing department. Of course, the editor I was now working with gave me many notes. She felt the novel fell between contemporary and literary fiction and needed to be one or the other. I took it all in stride; after all, it *was* business, and they intended to publish my novel.

That spring, I was here in this apartment, financially flush and doing rewrites. I had regained a sense of purpose and was back to what would be considered a normal life. Then the call came. It was on a Thursday in May around midnight when Emily's image, the one with that smirk, lit my cell screen. Last I saw her, she was ramming my head with her front door. That I felt strong again made me believe I was safe, so I gave in to my curiosity.

"Victor?" She sounded winded.

"Emily," I said. True to form, she skipped the pleas-antries and asked me to come 'fetch' her. No, *Hello, how are you?* She just got to it—fetch me.

"I have to see you. Will you then?"

Much confusion remained about what had taken place. What was real? What was imagined? Only she had the answers. Perhaps she would apologize. Acknowledge her cruel scheme and the rituals that had interfered with the lives of others. She might even confess the abortion. I assumed the trembling in her voice on the call was contrived. I'd witnessed her conjure sentimentality, even empathy in others when she wanted their favors. But hearing her voice again ignited the burn in my gut, envy for her brand of selfishness, made me realize that I hadn't digested it all, not sufficiently enough to envelop her in a compassion that would immunize her against my ego. At least Nadia's condition gave her a reprieve.

I shut my laptop, slipped on my boots, and set out for the long drive into that misty night to fetch her. The odd and inconvenient rendezvous point, a gas station on the Pacific Coast Highway just below Malibu, seemed all too appropriate for a reunion with Emily. What the hell was she doing out there? My hands were tense on the wheel. In my mind, I had her against the ropes, ducking accusations, blows she couldn't defend. Or was I underestimating her? How safe was I?

Approaching Malibu, the Pacific Coast Highway wound around netted cliffs. On the roadside in the pathetic haze of the gas station's fluorescence, my headlights found her, burned rings around her irises. She'd lost weight. The punky bob had grown out; her hair was shoulder-length, messy, sort of lopsided as though she was wearing a wig.

The door opened, and the sound of the Pacific came in on cold air. Shivering, she slid onto the seat and slammed the door. The light in the car died, and the engine's soft hum resumed. A pungent odor of cigarettes and moldy amber seeped from her black mohair sweater. The white plane of her forehead was oily and beneath her eyes were Saturn's own rings. Hollows under her cheekbones hinted at the shape of her skull. As though she knew what I was thinking, she shied away from my stare.

We drove the highway, the narrow stretch snaking toward Santa Monica, without a word. The thumb and fore-finger of her left hand worked against each other like pestles grinding secrets. I glanced out toward the ocean where impenetrable darkness blended the Pacific and a starless sky into a vast space of nothingness. Though I couldn't see the churning tides, sensing their ceaseless motion gave way to a feeling I knew too well; it's like a reckoning of sorts, a reminder that all the wishes of my heart and all my memo-ries are destined for obliteration. From one so attached to life, helplessly disposed in a materialist's perspective, this feeling of dread is the darkness no epiphany could brighten.

I remember how the faint electric lights of homes scat-tered on the hillsides served as hope, an anchor, something concrete. But I soon saw that my need to draw that ominous abyss above the Pacific to the hillside, find certainty in their distant point of convergence, was bound to an ephemeral hope, as each span of distance closed without fulfilling my need. I kept stubbornly fixing to points ahead until surrendering certainty became the only sane option.

As we came into Santa Monica and saw the white haze above the lighted pier, Emily swiveled in the seat to face me. Her lips parted, a breath escaped, and in her dry, husky voice, she said, "Thank you for coming." It seemed sincere. "I didn't think you would."

"Neither did I," I said, wanting to hurt her.

"You're right to be angry. But none of it is what you think."

I scoffed. "You can't imagine what I think." I had to know. "Was it mine?"

She raised her brows without disturbing her hollowed gaze, gave an audible sigh, and chain-smoked for the remaining forty-minute drive.

I exited the 101 at Gower, turned right onto Franklin Avenue, and when she realized I was driving to her apartment, she went upright in her seat. "Not mine. Yours. Please."

I glanced at her. "Tell me, was it mine?"

She looked pained, said, "Please. Let's get there first."

When we arrived, I went inside, poured two glasses of wine, lit a cigarette, finished it, and Emily still hadn't come in from the balcony. My need for answers and explanations, to speak the many things I had not said that needed saying seethed in me. I wanted to tell her that I'd finally discerned her purpose in my life, to instruct her now and tell her how she'd erred.

She stood at the porch railing smoking, gazing over the

darkened slope of olive trees in Barnsdall Park. She sensed me watching her, glanced back. "It was you, then. I knew it when I did your chart."

"What was me?"

"The one who renounces me."

"Come on with this shit already," I said, throwing my hands up.

She looked down and grasped the railing. "You want to scald me. But can it wait until morning? I don't think I can bear being hissed at right now."

Agitated, I pulled the sofa cushions and laid a sheet. She appeared in the doorway. "Take my bed," I said.

She shook her head. "Sleep with me."

And that's all she meant. Sleep. The remarkable thing, of all the times we shared a bed, this was the first she'd held me. I wanted none of it, but she clung to me. *Why did I give her a pass, allow her back into my apartment, my bed even?* The clammy skin of her thigh was heating my left leg. Her head felt like a safe deposited on my chest. She was utterly still, even in breathing. I was thinking of the white and black rooms, the abortion, Julie Sable. Every so often, the pleasant, distant whooshing of a passing car on the boulevard, that soft, hypnotic sound, permeated the womblike serenity of my dark bedroom. Visions came of places I'd never been, yet they seemed somehow familiar. Images so vivid I'd swear I'd been transported to those places and was experiencing them with the fullness of all my senses.

I wandered rolling hills, damp and glistening beneath fog. There was the odor of wet earth. Then, trotting next to me, was a piebald stallion whose name I knew to be Simon. I arrived at a stable, white with forest green trim and yellow-lighted lanterns that intensified the blue of a fast-approaching dusk; inside the stable, shadowed haylofts recalled salty kisses and self-conscious memories of teenage groping—but whose memories? Then I was walking a broad, gravel driveway toward a Tudor estate. I opened its red doors, entered on a sitting room with a fireplace and a black marble mantel lined with heirlooms. I wandered drafty hallways that smelled of rose oil and high-ceilinged rooms where large windowpanes angled gray light onto tapestry rugs and walls crowded with gothic landscape paintings. At last, I found myself in a girl's bedroom. There was a canopy bed with sheer white curtains and beside it, a chair with pink tufted cushions on which sat a doll in a school uniform with black bangs and eyelids that blink. Tied around the bedpost was a red ribbon which I pulled loose and wrapped around my hand. A sense of comfort, something like hope containing all possibilities, rinsed me.

Emily's hand fell onto my chest—my neck hair bristled. I was back in my bed, confused yet calm as if I'd woken from a dream, but I was sure I hadn't fallen asleep. She rolled off me, abandoning the warmth she'd cultivated on my left side to the chill in the air, which rapidly spread throughout my body.

Come morning, my leg moved beneath the sheets into what felt like wetness. At first, I thought the sheets were cold, but no. I drew back the covers to find a darkened patch like a Rorschach blot where she'd slept. She'd wet the bed. I hadn't felt her slip away. I grew still, listened, heard only the sound of emptiness.

She was gone. On the bureau, scribbled across the back of a receipt, were these words: *I misused it.* That's all? She thought that would suffice? Again, I felt duped, but as I sat to ponder her words, I realized they contained what it was I'd wanted. *I misused it* wasn't only an apology; it was an admission that her practices had produced negative results and that she understood her responsibility. *But what about the baby? Was it mine?*

Then I recalled the visions I'd received lying next to her —fields bathed in fog, Simon posturing, and that red ribbon? At one point during our beach outing to Malibu, when Leslie did my tarot reading, we witnessed two boys hounding their parents to buy them kites from an elderly Mexican man peddling cheap kid's toys. The working-class parents were sprawled on their blanket as if it was the first time in a month they'd stopped moving. The boys made a racket before the parents addressed them, but not before a ballet of tears and shushing gestures entertained us. Emily, chin perched on her knees, quietly watched. Then, finally, the boys got their way. Their father seemed delighted to buy them the kites as if resuming peace was his victory.

"Sure," I said, "He gets to go back to relaxing."

"It's batshit," Emily said, throwing her hand up in protest. "Teach them to use their imaginations. I had a little eight-inch strip of red ribbon I saved from a birthday gift. I'd tie it into everyone's hair just to see what they'd become—it transformed them. Imagine? Just an ordinary thing with such power."

The visions I received lying beside her, very specific, meaningful visions like the reels of my own memories, were transferred from her mind. As fantastical as it sounds, all this talk of magick and demons and so on and so forth, she *could* do things. I only wonder if she'd consciously done it or if her mechanism had been so widely dispersed that she no longer had control. Because, according to the warnings, that is what happens.

∽

Come autumn, *Nigredo* hit the theaters. The reviews were fair at best, but Jenna Winters was praised for her performance. She sent gifts; we planned a dinner. Then, on December 3rd, I learned *Apophenia* would be published come spring. I wondered. The life, the version of me I'd envisioned in my meditations, *had* manifested—the outer part anyhow. The inner? Though I'd returned to God, prayed daily, the nightmares persisted. One was particularly perplexing in its meaning, but more so because of when it happened. December 17th.

I roamed the wet, West Village streets that weren't the actual West Village streets, and it wasn't a typical night, but hauntingly stylized versions like depictions found in German Expressionist films. Paced by dread, the feeling that something unearthly was pursuing me, I hurried along when I noticed a waterlogged copy of *Apophenia* on the porch of a brownstone. As I reached for it, Emily appeared at my side. Her head was unnaturally cocked and her wet hair smelled of the sea. She took my wrists, drew me closer, and whispered, "The living water is a lover of night." Suddenly, she was gone, but her icy touch lingered on my wrists, became unendurable pain that seemed connected to the sudden silence that now engulfed the city. As the air itself seemed to thicken and pulse with an invisible force, a gentle voice whispered, *Wake up.*

My eyes opened, but the sense of dread lingered as I glanced around. My bedroom seemed somehow changed. The air smelled damp, held faint trace of amber.

That morning, I took my coffee onto the balcony. I couldn't escape the strangeness of the dream and what I'd sensed in the room when I awoke. There was no commotion down below in Barnsdall Park, but yellow police tape was still stretched across the park entrance, and on the hill, another length of tape sequestered a group of olive trees. The day before as I gazed on the scene, my brief assessment concluded with the theory that a homeless person had over-dosed, something like that. The point is whatever happened had nothing to do with me. There was the emotional distance as when we hear of a tragedy in a place where we don't know anyone and therefore remain aloof.

My phone rang. Luce. It'd been seven months since we'd spoken. Perhaps she'd heard of my good fortune and wanted to congratulate me. In that spirit, I answered.

"Vic. God. I can't believe it."

"What?" That she was distraught only registered in the silence that passed.

"Emily," she said.

"What did she do now?"

"Vic, she's gone. They found her yesterday. In the park by your apartment."

At once, my vision shrunk back from the hills, shot inside me, enclosed me in a narrow corridor. I couldn't speak, could barely breathe. Luce confirmed what I already knew. Emily cut her wrists and bled out beneath the olive tree, there in the park amongst the addicts and the mentally ill.

In *Apophenia* I'd written her as wearied and resolved, trudging up the slope toward the olive tree, making nature the altar for her sacrifice. Delusion crafts her as Dionysius, the androgyne, god of chaos, preparing to transcend the constraints of Apollonian order. Dionysius was the perfect archetype for Emily; she taught the use of the wine, the weed, and the dancing ritual to liberate us from the prison of reason and indulge the ecstatic irrational, chauffeur to the mysteries.

Emily killed herself. I kept repeating it, went headlong into the fray. Was it because she couldn't comprehend life any longer? I remembered the words scribbled on the receipt: *I misused it.* Did voices from the shadows convince her of her responsibility, only in a more absolute sense, and goad her into giving her life to protect the integrity of her soul? "Sacrifice is death for life." She'd said it herself.

No. That's how it is in your book. Atonement was beneath her. She'd also said, "Suffering is the pain of understanding. It's necessary for the perfection of your nature." Her suicide wasn't an attempt to save her soul. Life is a quest for perseverance and could never ennoble her suicide as did my imagination.

Emily killed herself. She'd needed help, I knew that much from the last time I saw her, yet my pride kept me from reaching out.

I wept.

A TROUBLING NOTION WAS FORMING. *Was I somehow responsible?* Nadia and Emily met the same fates as the characters they'd inspired. It couldn't have been unconscious associations on their part: Nadia never read *River Without End* and Emily never read *Apophenia*. What led Emily to that olive tree—the exact location where the character she inspired meets her fate? Maybe under a different tree, but still. We'd never visited Barnsdall. I wish she'd read the book and put herself beneath the olive tree to make her sacrifice the exemplum of life imitating art, the art for which she perished. She'd have made me a visionary.

When we debated whether art imitates life or life imitates art, in the end, the whole thing would come down to Emily declaring, "Art must contain some search for meaning, attempt to explain the purpose of existence, some spiritual truth beyond logic." In writing my novel, I was searching for meaning, a conclusion that fit this wild narrative. There was no other way to end my book. It seemed fitting that she should be devoured by her own creation. But, if intentions shape the outcome of all things, the more I searched my heart, I couldn't deny that I wanted to hurt her, not kill her, just wound her with my book, as impossible as that might have been. But I *was* writing her as I attacked the keyboard, seeing her face and eyes, not some fictional character. I suppose it was the same for *River Without End* and Nadia. Had I, in my chaotic creative process, rippled the frequencies of the subatomic sea and sent suggestions, which they unconsciously received? Under the same principles that rendered the chant effective or made one's possessions retainers of their energy? I was aware of the phenomenon of entanglement and how its discovery threatened to derail the underlying principles of quantum mechanics. Surely, other mysterious laws exist that defy the logic of the scientific world. When people come together as intensely as we had, would it be erroneous to believe that we'd maintained some residual energetic connection?

What Emily said in my nightmare, *The living water is a lover of night,* I took as an allusion to the process of holy regeneration, death in flesh for life in spirit. There was a point when I'd believed Emily had returned to the mysterious waters of space where her spirit, freed from the chains of a body-ego, became the goddess of a constellation. Christ, I was half-expecting her to appear in my apartment at any moment.

However, all this time later, "reality" has settled upon this story. Rational explanations, the facts belying these outrageous behaviors and happenings, have emerged to contradict my perceptions and draw their own lines.

LESLIE HAD GONE to London for the service, where Emily's mother told her that Emily had been battling ovarian cancer for two years. Initial treatments were successful, but the cancer had come back. She underwent additional rounds of chemo and immunotherapy, but they failed. She then turned to a center in Mexico for experimental treatments, which at first showed signs of progress, but in the end, failed.

"Maybe she knew she couldn't have a child," Luce said. "That's why she...you know, wanted to get pregnant."

"But the suicide?" I asked.

"She was going to die anyway," Luce said. "That's why." She sounded relieved by this theory.

It was a peculiar feeling. Proofs for Emily's terminal cancer were suddenly abundant. Her disappearing acts could be viewed as secret rendezvous for treatments that she hid from us. She did look pale and drawn when she'd resurface, especially the last time I saw her. She'd even wet the bed. Incontinence *is* a symptom. The nausea and vomiting. Her blonde wig. The copious marijuana smoking and the diet of fresh juices, salads, and herbal tea concoctions. I've mentioned how she sometimes seemed burdened, withholding, inaccessible. The night we kissed on the rock formation in Big Sur, she said, "Oh, I love it here. I don't want to leave," and I thought she'd meant she didn't want to leave Big Sur.

If cancer was the puzzle, the pieces fit. Even her obsession with her science and pushing the boundaries—I suppose all that could support the cancer theory as well. Performing rituals, daring to control her reality and make it more than the given one? How could I pretend to know how a secret such as terminal cancer eats the mind? Could I blame her for living fiercely, sounding the depths of her flesh, while at the same time seeking union with the regenerative force, the portal to the mystical laws permeating all life? She wanted to be healed. The rituals were said to perfect nature. And look: knowing she was nearing the inevitable at such a young age, she didn't even seek our pity.

Other facts that had recently come to light also needed to be considered. Julie Sable didn't die from an accidental fall by a poolside, but from an aneurysm that burst in her brain. When the coroner's report was made public, it showed that she had an excessive localized enlargement of a blood vessel deep in her brain. Upon standing from a reclined position by the poolside, the sudden rush of blood to her brain caused the weakened vessel to rupture. It took three surgeries to stop the hemorrhaging, but she never recovered consciousness. Eventually, she'd developed sepsis and her heart finally gave out. Black magick didn't kill Julie, hidden health issues did.

And the troubling notion about real-life people meeting the same fate as the characters they'd inspired? The phenomenon of writing things that come to pass is not uncommon. Every man has a sense of the people he is intimate with, senses their courage and potentials, which hint at their trajectories. Call it seeing to the heart of a person, or maybe there's something to the idea of precognition. It happens to everyone at some point; they receive news about someone they know, which doesn't shock them because the outcome seemed inevitable. It's only shocking because it happens exactly as they imagined it might.

Apophenia and Emily bleeding out beneath the olive tree? I remember it so clearly, that misty night in Malibu, how, appearing in my headlights, she looked like one might imagine her ghost would look. Seated next to me, she appeared humbled, abjectly so, like a child torn between wonder and fear. And on my porch, as she finished her last cigarette of the night, gazing out over the olive trees in Barnsdall Park, she said, "I don't think I can bear being hissed at right now." Perhaps she was imagining what she'd do. Either way, her demeanor had unsettled me, created an impression that must've found its way into my book, right? Even in bed, how she clung to me, transferred her homesick longings into my mind, showed me her world before she was shipped off to boarding school, and her heart was ruined by need. She left the message scribbled on the back of the receipt, *I misused it.* The whole damned thing was ominous.

The only hangnail? I'd written the ending long before that night.

EMILY IS THE HANGNAIL. The facts? The what, when, how, and where—the dimensions of each are too vast. Trying to figure her suicide is a Sisyphean task. Luce's call, the sense of relief in her voice after having been supplied with the "reasonable explanations" for why Emily had the abortion and killed herself, provides a prosaic ending of sorts to this story. But Luce doesn't know what I know. Besides, the "reasonable explanations" don't necessarily contradict my experiences, nor does the science behind Julie Sable's death. They do what facts do, render things materially.

You see, no one knows if Emily's ceremonies had caused

Julie's aneurysm in the first place, then for it to burst. If all is mind, and our reality is determined by what we think and believe, and the combination of desiring and thinking *can* alter the outside world, who can say? Was it possible that she'd developed the ability to project some superconscious thought-form and by the hidden laws of her science direct the Unseen to do her bidding? The whole premise of ceremonial magick hinges on the integration of the conscious and subconscious for the very purpose of altering reality, but are there summonable entities? I contend there are other forms of intelligence, energies we haven't yet discovered; nevertheless, it's impossible to say if what Emily invoked in her ceremonies was innate to her own consciousness or outside of it, as in a dweller on the unseen planes of existence. I mean, in a world helplessly aligned to the study of matter and steeped in the values of materialism, how does one navigate the paradoxical nature of this stuff? It undermines one's sense of reality.

No one will ever know if Emily's suicide was a noble offering in some system of belief that was beyond our understanding or if it was the result of her being overwhelmed by the energies she'd emboldened. I know how the energies I fed, Lust to name one, had disoriented me and distorted my "reality." I admit my incomprehension but deny coincidence. My life would be in contradiction if I were to claim anything other than everything happened exactly as it was meant to happen. Emily's fate is no exception.

Remember my Chinese horoscope from the day she branded us as research? *A foreigner will enrich you.* Just with her, it's that whole contradiction one finds in the sex-addicted guru or the alcoholic monk, how the mentor dies in imperfections so the student's attachment to perfection can be released. *Eat shit. We're all human.* Ideals create martyrs.

The passage of time has allowed me to really *see* her, and as much as I'm reluctant to admit it, she does deserve to be exonerated. In the state I was in when she came along, I was unable to see her for who she was. Her understanding of humanity, of emotions, and the workings of the mind, was far greater than mine. Her spiritual work had truly liberated her from the anchoring values and morals that hold the material world to order, all the codes and labels of one like me. You see, she'd gone out into the wilderness, courageously ran toward the frontier, do or die; I'd gone out, got frightened, and ran back to the fold. Perhaps her greatest virtue was her courage and to this point, her suicide could then be viewed as an attribute of that same courage, her way of controlling the outcome of her illness; rather than be killed by it, she would destroy the illness by destroying its host. Emily's courage was great. And I suppose, if my perception of the external world is only a representation of my inner world, the confluence of heart and mind would tell me that Emily was destined to be *my* sacrifice. A victim of my mediocrity. My fear. Of all that was superior and therefore what reflected truths about a reality I was unable to accept. Me, the recalcitrant, the apostate who judged her because I couldn't overcome my own limited belief system. Therein lies the measure of my responsibility.

Would it surprise you to know that I am now celibate? There was no disease, not of the flesh, no erectile dysfunction. Not an additional heartbreak that further disenchanted me. I'm not closed off, not afraid of vulnerability, and I won't feign humbleness for anyone's sake and say that women don't find me attractive. Celibacy is my choice. An attempt to achieve the wholeness I'd always sought without the distortions of sexual affections and all the other things of this world that lead one astray. In honor of the deepest meaning in the Androgyne Myth, with hopes of knowing the sanctifying union in this life, celibacy is my free-will offering. *That* I can control.

And all this I've told because it gnaws at me, what Gabriele said: "A dwarf on a mountain is still a dwarf." Not a day passes when I don't feel her. In the night, out of the corner of my eye, when I catch a shadow shift, I no longer question the chill, the raised arm hair. Or when, in some public place, I'm sprung from preoccupation by a father calling "Emily!" to a wandering child, and he moves swiftly to rescue her from a minor catastrophe, and a second later, I overhear the conversation of a couple seated at the table next to me saying something like, "Nothing is what it seems." I stiffen, look around.

The revelation that joins all that is seen to what's unseen awaits perception. Some are called to the table; the rest are characters in the fictions of their minds, unwittingly creating the stories of their lives, despite believing that they alone are the cause and effect. Only a foolish writer believes a period ends the thought.

I know that her visiting my dream the night of her suicide was to show me that I'm still stuck in the illusion, to prove something or other, that I'm still resisting truth. *How is that success you desperately wanted, Vic? All it's cracked up to be?*

Albeit success is now the patina of my illusion. Commercial fiction pays well. Apparently, mediocrity is praised nowadays, as *Apophenia* is a bestseller. Currently, I'm writing the screenplay for *Apophenia* the movie. I wonder who will play her. They say the A-listers are vying. A bidding war brews, yet her husky voice refrains, "Careful what you wish for."

Alas, I am no visionary. I'm a calcified penitent. This flesh is like stone, but there is life in stone, a dream of movement. And I still can't say. Have I hypostatized this whole story? I've told it the way I experienced it. When a writer is commissioned to write a true story, the truth of that story, the facts, are only relevant as they pertain to the artistic rendering of the story. There isn't room for every fact or detail, only those that give it meaning.

It's now dawn. From the thinning darkness comes the second day of the feast of Saturnalia. There is an ending in that, yes? Or is it an eternal becoming? The boulevard is quiet. First light arcs above Barnsdall, and the olive trees cast thin shadows that stretch like bony fingers on the slope. Soon, I'll leave this one-bedroom in the low-income building for my writer's home, the one I've always envisioned. But for now, I sit on my balcony in the cool, blue air, and listen to the birds in the branches above the Scorpio's altar sing of the mystery.

NOTES

Chapter 21

1. Edward Bulwer Lytton, *Zanoni (Philidelphia: J.B. Lippincott, 1862), 41*

www.ingramcontent.com/pod-product-compliance
Lightning Source LLC
Chambersburg PA
CBHW070651010826
48975CB00013B/467